Monopolove

Monopolove

A Love & Games Romance

Mia Heintzelman

Monopolove

Tule Publishing First Printing, April 2023

The Tule Publishing, Inc.

First Publication by Tule Publishing 2023

Cover design by Dot Covers

ISBN: 978-1-958686-88-1

CHAPTER ONE

HARPER

INCLUDED IN THE BOX

THE INSTANT MY sister, Rox, sees me fumble down the hallway, she perks up. "Happy New Year!" she announces at the top of her lungs. Then she doubles down. "We've got a lot to tackle today—a lot that I need to um…to go over with you."

As I round the corner to the kitchen, I squint at the light bursting through the open blinds and grumble something indecipherable. Frankly, it's too early, and her voice is way too…ready and raring.

Which I'm decidedly *not.*

Her New Year's goals started at approximately one second after midnight. Goals, which, along with reading every self-help book about finding love, apparently include bookkeeping.

"Harp?"

"Hmm?" I mumble.

I haven't had my coffee yet. Thus, I don't have coordinated motor skills nor the brainpower to hit the ground running. Especially not for whatever resolution she's so eager to get a jump on.

Unlike my sister, I'm not a bright-eyed and bushy-tailed morning person. I'm more caffeine-deficient grump and socket-shocked hair until late afternoon. I'm also not big on making grand resolutions I probably won't see through anyway. Beyond upping the number of times I brush my teeth from two to three times daily and drinking more water, that's about as good as it gets.

"Harp—"

"Ah, ah, ah." I give her a small headshake, warning clear in my tone. I can almost taste the rich, hot liquid as I pull out the drawer below the Keurig where we keep the K-Cups and lift the box lid.

Instantly, my heart sinks at the empty box.

I ransack the entire drawer, tossing the empty box, stir sticks, and stray Monopoly dollars—the ones Rox likely hid when she was the banker last time we played. I feel like I've played a four-hour game only to land on my opponent's loaded property and discover I've already used the last of my stashed five-hundred-dollar bills. I'm bankrupt and ready to make all sorts of ill-advised bargains for even a few teensy sips.

No, no, no, no, no.

The room tilts on its axis. The sound that spills from my lips isn't quite a whimper as it is a whooshing battle cry from my bloodstream.

"Roxanne Sloane." I use her full name, enunciating every syllable. "Please tell me you didn't use the last K-Cup. Tell me you have a secret stash somewhere and we're not completely out of coffee."

Because she's my sister, Rox ignores my clamped-shut eyes and the finger I'm holding up, my other hand planted on my hip.

"You used the last one yesterday."

Did I? That's right. Shoot, I did.

Her sharp tone rips through my haze. "Now, seriously. We need to talk."

With an impatient lift of my chin, I meet her unblinking gaze.

"I'm listening."

She draws her perfectly arched eyebrows together, and that's when I register the tilt of her head. The seriousness in her oversteeped brown eyes is so much more. It's a mix of worry and...*sadness*?

There's a heaviness to her faraway stare before she wraps her hand around to knead the back of her neck.

I flit a glance over to the coffee table stacked with mail, papers, and books, where she was sitting earlier.

Color-coded spreadsheets...

Together with my sister and my best friend, Nadia, we own Love & Games, a one-of-a-kind ode to classic board games. I'm the creative tier. I merchandise, choose the inventory and product displays, and represent the brand in the community. Nadia is the glorified HR department. When it's more than just the three of us, she'll handle recruiting, interviewing, hiring, and training staff. For now, she oversees workplace safety, labor laws, and company culture policies (i.e., social media). Rox runs the business end. She pays the bills, balances the books, that kind of thing.

And she color-codes profit and loss statements to explain earnings trends to Nadia and me.

This is not a Ferrari or sexy stilettos. Red is not good.

"What's going on?" I suck in a lungful of air and hold it. "I thought we had an amazing December. It should have rounded out a stellar quarter, right? The year-end numbers can't be *that* bad..." I let the words die on my tongue when her eyes flood with tears. "Holy shit, Rox. What is it?"

She shakes her head, kneading the back of her neck again. "It wasn't enough."

"*What* wasn't enough?"

"I thought I could fix it..." Rox swallows and lifts her gaze to meet mine. Then she blurts out, "Our cash flow is steadily declining. Our sales just aren't enough to cover our expenses and the deficit. We might lose the shop."

Dang, I was supposed to look at the numbers.

I'm so confused. Rox Sloane is nothing if not the person with answers. She's a financial guru. If there's a way to make a way, she will grab a shovel and grind out an alternative path. She is hardcore. Business. Numbers. Profits and losses, she just gets it. The notion that Love & Games could fail blindsides me.

How did I not see this coming? I should've been paying attention to my sister at the very least.

Shit.

"Okay, wait." My legs feel weak, and suddenly I need to sit down. "You said *deficit*?" I shoot her a curious glance over my shoulder as I walk into the living room and plop down onto the couch.

"Remember when the storm zapped the electrical back in June, and we had to pay out of pocket to get back up and running until the insurance reimbursed us?" When I nod, she continues. "Well, they're not. Apparently, 'acts of God' aren't covered."

Shoot, the repairs were somewhere over fifteen thousand. On top of our existing expenses and debt…

Not good.

I'm still reeling, still questioning, backtracking the past year. I vaguely remember Rox moving money around to offset the expense. We don't exactly have a cushion in savings, and the tiny line of credit the bank gave us simply won't cut it.

My stomach rolls as I curl up on the couch, searching Rox's eyes, trying to make this all make sense.

"Did you talk to Don?" I ask, referring to our landlord for the building.

She blows out her cheeks then slowly releases a breath that feels like a bomb drop. "He's claiming that it falls under regular maintenance and repairs as a tenant." *Shit.* She shrugs. "I tried to reason with him but getting him to reimburse us is a freaking longshot."

My breath hitches in my throat. "So, you're using—"

"The cash in the business checking to pay for rent, inventory, loan and credit card payments," Rox says. "Also, to fund payroll."

"Oh, my goodness."

Heat swarms my face. I feel nauseous.

A toxic mix of fear and anger twists at my gut and wrings my heart. I've got to think of something to fix this. This is not our fault, but we can't fail.

I don't have a backup plan.

The thought of eventually losing everything we've worked for due to something completely out of our control shatters through me. Tears prick at the corners of my eyes as I flit a blurry glance between Rox and the spreadsheets.

How is this happening?

A tingling sensation sweeps up the back of my neck. "I'm going to figure something out," I say, unable to sit here and look at my sister, internalizing this "act of God."

She swallows. The pride that normally flows from her is gone. It's like I've plugged up the drain and now she's drowning in it. "I didn't want to tell you or Nadia until I was sure we needed to start thinking about other options."

The vein at my temple throbs.

"Right. I need to start thinking of ways to fix this."

My skin feels impossibly hot under my sister's gaze. "*We* need to start thinking of ways to fix this," she corrects me. "Maybe we…could ask Dad for the—"

"No! We didn't need his money to build this business. We're certainly not going to let him bail us out."

Annoyance flickers across her face. "I figured you'd say that. Anyway, my only other solution to make an immediate dent is to maybe go to the bank and get a home equity line of credit on my house."

The pounding of my heartbeat grows louder in my ears. "I'm not going to let you risk your home over something that wasn't your fault." I blow out my cheeks and drop my head into my hands, kneading small circles over my racing pulse. "I just need to think."

I need to get out of here.

After a few seconds, trying not to let my head explode, I get to my feet. I shuffle down the hallway to my bedroom to slip on flip-flops and throw on my red coat. When I get back to the living room, I rummage around for my keys and phone then stuff them in my pocket. I try unsuccessfully to ignore my sister's imploring gaze latched on to my every move.

"Where are you going?" There's desperation, worry blended in the grooves of her tone.

"Right now, I just need to get out of here for a bit. Clear my head." My hand won't turn the knob, though. So, I'm just standing here, immobile. Staring at the grainy wood and blurred light shining through the coated glass of the front door. "I'm running out for coffee. Want anything?"

Black. Decaf. A sprinkle of cinnamon.

I know it by heart like we know everything about each other. We're sisters. We're supposed to know the tiny details—we're supposed to be able to talk through anything...

"Don't shut down on me, Harp."

I can't even look at Rox, I'm so disappointed in... Who should I even be disappointed in? Maybe that's what's really eating at me. There's no one to blame. Yes, we should've planned for emergencies, but one random event shouldn't unilaterally screw up everything for us. This isn't a game. We can't just mortgage everything and pray we land on Chance to send us back to Go.

I tighten my grip on the handle, absorbing the hardness.

Rox stands and a rush of heat swarms over my skin again.

Before she moves, I twist the knob and leave, headed for the café around the corner. I've got a lot to tackle when I get back. But first, coffee.

CHAPTER TWO

DECLAN

COMES WITH INSTRUCTIONS

I CHECK MY messages once more to confirm the meeting time. Sure enough, the Realtor my best friend, Murph, referred to help me sell my late grandfather's bungalow was supposed to meet me here at Java Joy Coffeehouse—her choice—at noon.

It's almost one.

Who plans a business meeting on New Year's Day anyway?

I swirl the last of the coffee around in my cup, finishing it off. Just as I stand to go, my phone vibrates in my hand. One look at the screen, I feel my shoulders drag downward.

Thank God I have my earbuds.

"Happy New Year, Mom," I answer as I swivel on the hard, wooden barstool to glance past the line to the entrance.

Still no sign of the Realtor.

"Please tell me you went out with Murph last night for a good time." She starts in on me right away. "I hate to think of you, all the way out there in San Diego, cooped up in Pop's drafty old house by yourself. Thirty-five is still young.

Maybe you'll try again..." Mom trails off.

The end of that sentence has nothing to do with Pop's house. Forgive and forget echoes in her silence—maybe I'll try my hand at love again while I'm here for the next four to five weeks deciding whether to make this stay permanent.

"I'm fine." I hear the short, stilted tone to my voice and chew my bottom lip before starting again without the edge. "I caught the countdown on TV while I worked on the kitchen backsplash. The house is really shaping up." *Mostly. The jury's still out on the water stain the plumber discovered in Pop's bedroom on the shared wall with the bathroom.*

She sighs into the phone, and I sense where this is going.

"Listen, I know you'd love for me to hire someone to complete the renovations, so I can get back to Vegas, but I'm in no rush. My patients are in good hands, and I'm enjoying being at Pop's. It's not a sprawling mansion, but there are so many memories in that place, and it's got great bones."

"I know, honey. You used to love being there with Pop every summer. It's a money pit, though. It's going to take a lot more than a fresh coat of paint and new carpet. Just fix it up as best you can and list it quickly."

"I don't know. The house needs some fixing up, but San Diego is growing on me. I promise, if there's anything I can't handle, I'll hire someone. Otherwise, I'd rather take my time. To be honest," I add, "it's nice knowing I won't run into anyone here."

And see the pity on their faces.

"All right, I won't push. Did I tell you I was at Target the other day...?"

Seriously?

As if getting stood up by a Realtor on New Year's Day isn't bad enough. Mom goes on about redecorating her bedroom, her bunches of ideas to freshen up Pop's bungalow. I get it. The need to overhaul everything, start fresh. For me, these few weeks are a chance to reevaluate what I want in life. Consider Murph's offer to join his ear, nose, and throat practice and build a patient list in a new city... Fix up a home with my own two hands. I'm excited about the challenges.

Even if I am a little overwhelmed.

Isn't that what life is about? Finding something exciting to look forward to? Choices and chances? The odds don't always end up in my favor but I'm still playing the game. I don't have to make any final decisions now. When I'm finished with the renovations, I'll decide whether to stay or sell.

The line goes quiet, and I sense the missed question in Mom's silence.

"Yeah," I say, not sure what I'm agreeing to as I tap the phone to check my messages once more. Still nothing from the Realtor.

Then a notification drops from the top of the screen. It's from Anytime Restoration. *"I'm running about fifteen minutes behind, but I'll be there by two at the latest."*

All this focus on the Realtor running late, I nearly forgot I'd made an appointment with a restoration company to check out the water damage at Pop's.

"Well, all right. I just wanted to check in on you. I'll let you get back to whatever it is you're doing..." She hesitates, though.

"What is it, Mom?"

I tip back my cup, remembering I already finished my coffee.

She says nothing for a beat. Then, "I meant to tell you, Penelope asked about you the other day…"

My pulse slams in my neck. Bile rises in my throat until I'm choking on anger. It's the unmistakable hope I've tried over and again to bury, but it's like a recurring virus.

It keeps coming back.

"Why does she want to know how I'm doing?" I ask.

"For what it's worth, she looked remorseful." Mom is always about diplomacy, leaving an opening for reconciliation, another chance to mend fences. But there's nothing to fix.

I don't want to hear this. It's why I put an entire state between Penelope and me. Why I'm considering relocating permanently.

"She's with someone else. I've moved on." *I'm trying to.*

After Mom hangs up, I slide the phone back into my pocket. I grab my jacket and empty cup, scanning the room for the nearest trash can and spotting one near the community board to the right of the register.

As I stride over to toss my cup in the bin, a familiar face on the board comes into view: Mr. Moneybags, the Monopoly mascot. I blink a few times to make sure it's not just dry contacts blurring my vision. Every time I see the cartoon character, excitement flutters in my belly. Memories of Pop and me building imaginary empires by the fireplace reel across my mind as I reach up to drag my fingers over the curled edges of the thin paper. At the top of the flyer, there's a bold black headline.

20TH ANNUAL MONOPOLY TOURNAMENT—
SATURDAY, MARCH 30
See website for details.

I'm still reading the registration fine print, remembering how much Penelope hated "childish" board games, when a woman's raised voice at the register draws my attention.

She's obviously just rolled out of bed and is still in sleep clothes. She's wearing gray sweatpants and flip-flops but the cherry on top of the ensemble is the red trench coat.

Someone celebrated New Year's Eve hard.

"Oh, my goodness. You're kidding me, right? I promise, I *have* money," she pleads with the barista. She draws a breath, and slowly releases it. "I've got the Java Joy app."

Her hands tremble, and with every shake of her head, a messy bun of thick chestnut hair threatens to spill over.

"Have you tried turning it off and on or checking for updates?" the employee asks. Her attempt at helping is lost in her disengaged tone, though. She sighs, then darts her gaze behind the woman impatiently. "Customer service might be able to help."

I cringe as the woman's shoulders cock back like she might slingshot her phone at the young blonde behind the register. *I would.*

"Is there a way to look me up? Please, I have the app. I come here all the time." She cranes her neck to look behind the counter. "Is Lucy around? She knows me."

Guess Lucy was the lucky one who got the holiday off.

The woman jams her hands in her coat pockets. "I have

like twenty dollars on this thing, but I got a new phone, and the dang thing is acting all wonky. I don't have my wallet, but I just really need *coffee.*" She drags out the word like it's a matter of life or death.

The other patrons in line and seated around the shop look on. To me, it doesn't seem worth it to create a scene over a cup of coffee. Then again, everyone has their vices. Sometimes they make you do crazy things—like risking a misdemeanor over a mocha latte… Or relocating on a whim.

Don't do it, lady.

"I'm begging you. It probably sounds like an exaggeration, but I'm having the worst day—*year*—already." The woman pinches the bridge of her nose. "I just received some really horrible news…" she rambles, desperately looking around.

The bald man behind her taps his foot, demonstrating his growing impatience as he glares at her.

Then a tall woman with short black hair who I assume is the manager approaches. She looks like she's about had it with demanding customers today.

I should take off to meet the guy from the restoration company who's probably halfway to Pop's, but I'm strangely invested in how this plays out. I snatch the tournament flyer off the board, shove it in my pocket, inching closer to the register.

"I'm not looking for a handout." The woman darts her gaze between the barista and the manager before tossing a shaky smile over her shoulder again.

When she turns back bowing her head, her shoulders curl, and I feel bad for her.

"You can check," she says. "I have money on the app—"

"Ma'am, I don't want to have to—"

"Hi." I step beside the woman, projecting my voice. The manager's tight smile looks like it might snap. "I overheard what's going on with your phone. I'd like to help..."

I peek over at the woman and flash her a tentative smile.

Beneath the weary, hard-shelled exterior, I register the humiliation etched on her face—one that up close is not a bad face. Beautiful, smooth golden-brown skin, a small round nose, and impossibly wide 7Up bottle-green eyes flicker back at me. The funny thing is, if the circumstances were different, I'd ask for her number. Forget about the fact I'm leaving in a month and see what happens.

But she's at the end of her rope. I know what that's like. I just want to throw her a lifeline.

I jam my hand in my pocket, pulling out the flyer with my wallet.

"Monopoly?"

For a second, I'm thrown off by her strained voice.

My eyes snap to the woman's then down to the flyer. Mr. Moneybags grins up at us from my pocket. "Yeah. There's a tournament," I say, feeling my brows crease reflexively under the weight of her scrutinizing stare as I tuck the flyer back into my pocket.

"This should cover whatever she wants," I say sharply to the manager as I slide a ten on the counter, then turn back to the woman. "Pay it forward. Hope your day—year—gets better."

An awkward silence ensues between her and the employees as I walk away. She gets her large, hot, caramel macchiato without reaching the end of her frayed rope. And maybe a good deed will reset my shitty day, too.

When I get to the door, I pull the lapels of my jacket tight against the cold air and fish my keys out.

"Wait. Don't leave."

I turn to find the woman's free hand waving wildly as her walk accelerates into a run.

"Thanks, I really appreciate what you did back there."

"No problem," I say.

She whips her phone out and starts swiping, tapping her thumb around a few times before she flicks up her gaze. "I have money. It's just, this phone is new. What's your CashPal or your Payback?"

For a second, I have no clue what she's talking about because I'm staring. At those eyes. The rosy blush to her cheeks. She's beautiful.

She clears her throat and gives me a small smile.

Right. Something about repayment.

When I don't immediately respond, she nods more to herself than to me. "That's okay. What bank are you with?" She takes a deep breath, holding it while she swipes to another app. "I'll repay you through the xFer app, then," she suggests.

"Oh, no. I insist, you're good. Pay it forward to someone else." Pulling out my keys, I smile and pivot toward the door, thinking about this wild day staying its southern course—getting stood up, Mom working Penelope into the conversation, how meeting this woman felt *almost* serendipitous. "Unbelievable," I mutter under my breath.

"Unbelievable?" A wide-eyed expression twists into a full-on grimace as she misunderstands me.

"No, I just meant—"

But she cuts me off. "Look, I'm super grateful. Buying my coffee was sweet and sort of the only bright spot in this crap day, but if it's all the same to you, I'd like to pay you back."

I blow out a breath.

"What's the big deal?" I sigh. "It's just a few bucks. Can't you accept a good deed?"

She gives me a blank look then opens her mouth but says nothing. Slowly, her eyebrows squish together like she's having difficulty finding the right words.

"It was a nice gesture—*just a few bucks*—but I can't," she says. "Thanks again, really, but I don't like owing people."

I'm annoyed. Why can't she accept a small gesture of kindness without making a big deal? For a second, I take in her sweats, messy hair, and those bee-stung lips before searching her eyes.

But she narrows them disapprovingly as she watches me watch her.

"Look, I ran out for a sec, for a cup of *coffee*. Figured it'd be an in-and-out trip. So, whatever you think about me..." She shakes her head. "I'm no one's charity case. I don't need to be rescued by some insanely good-looking guy with a savior complex. So, just pick an app, please."

She jerks her phone between us again.

Despite the compliment, my body temperature rises. I finger my collar, feeling the tension in my clamped jaw as I open my mouth to say something... But then I stop short and take the phone.

I force a smile as I enter my email address into the notes screen she's opened for me. "I guess no good deed goes unpunished."

When I finish, I hand the phone back.

As she thanks me and ducks out the coffeehouse without a backward glance, I wait a couple minutes, warming my hands in my coat pockets. Familiar excitement flutters in my belly when my fingers glide over the cool, crumpled tournament flyer. At least this day isn't a total loss.

CHAPTER THREE

HARPER

OBJECT OF THE GAME

"UM... NICE OF you to think of others..." Rox says from the couch when I return. Her tone drips with sarcasm as she looks up from the pile of spreadsheets, books, and magazines in front of her on the coffee table and hikes up an eyebrow at me.

Right. Unscrew the business.

I drop my keys on the entry table then pivot to face her.

She clears her throat, glancing from the half-empty coffee cup in my hand back to me. "Harp?"

"Yes?"

Rox folds her arms across her chest. "Seriously?"

I'm already hyped up on the coffee I didn't get to savor since I basically guzzled it down on the walk back. I wince, just thinking about that guy at Java Joy. "Don't even get me started."

Pay it forward?

Not the day, guy.

I close my eyes. "Is there any chance this whole day will

start over if I go back to sleep now? Maybe I won't be mad about the insurance claim, my phone, and every mortifying minute of the last half hour I spent at Java Joy."

"So..." She drags the word out. "We still need to talk about everything but are you going to elaborate, or keep me guessing why you went to get *us* coffee and came back with only *one* cup?" Despite the fact I was on the verge of tears when I left and the tension is still lolling in the air, Rox pats the couch.

I let my head fall back on my shoulders with a sigh. All I wanted was a good cup of coffee, my bed, and trash TV today. But I guess damage control needs to be now.

"You should be mad at me, freaking out," I grumble.

"Yes, and I fully plan to release the kraken on you after you make the one-coffee mystery make sense."

"Long story short." I drag my guilt-leaden body over, plop down on the couch beside her, and grab the fluffy pink throw blanket. "New phone. Old app wouldn't let me in."

Rox tilts her head to me. "Hmm. And yet, you were still able to procure *one* coffee..."

Planting my face in the pillows, I hold out the cup with only a few lukewarm sips left in it. "I didn't want to press my luck, asking for two cups when I was already causing a scene. You can have it, though. It doesn't taste the same when a random smug guy pays for it." I come up for air, snuggling the blanket around my shoulders, squeezing my eyes shut.

I don't have to look at my little sister to know I'm getting the stare-down. She's a hound for answers. There isn't an ice cube's chance in hell she lets anything go until she gets an explanation that works for *her*.

"Fine. When the app didn't work, I explained the phone situation to the barista." Rox eyes me over her brow. "While I'm practically begging, here comes this guy, going on about *pay it forward* as he slaps a ten on the counter."

Rox studies my face for signs of a lie. Seemingly satisfied with my explanation, she switches gears.

"Was he hot?"

"In a roundabout, tall, dark, and broody sort of way." Just because his deep voice did all sorts of magical things to my insides doesn't mean I'm going to fall at his feet in gratitude.

"Oh, boy. Double whammy. Good-looking guy buys coffee. Goes directly to jail. Does not pass Go. Does not collect two hundred dollars," she announces in her Mr. Moneybags voice—strangely both nasally and full of bass—before she chuckles and shakes her head. "Did you at least thank Mr. Tall, Dark and Broody before you chewed his head off?"

A tingling sweeps up the back of my neck.

"I didn't chew his head off. I just told him I appreciated the gesture, but I couldn't accept it."

"Interesting…" Rox presses a finger to her lips.

In addition to being my younger sister for whom the stars happily align, Rox is also an unfiltered hard-ass who willingly doles out tough love.

She's technically my half-sister, but Dad didn't raise us like that. There're no halves and steps, there's just family or not—no technicalities allowed. He's right, but when it comes down to it, her mom made her who she is, a number-crunching bossy badass who knows exactly what she wants.

My mom is a flower child, so I'm feelings and signs. She's the brain and I'm the heart. *Or maybe I'm the gut…*

It doesn't matter. I have a sense about *good deeds* guys. A couple of dollars for coffee isn't the same as Dad throwing money at a problem, but still. It's the principle of the matter.

"So, you don't think you were at least a little on edge after leaving here all bent out of shape over the business? You don't think you might've taken it out on this poor, innocent, probably delectable-looking guy with an open wallet and a heart of gold?"

"You of all people should know I hate owing anyone, let alone some random guy with a hidden agenda."

"It's coffee, not sex for money, Harp. I seriously don't think he has a hidden agenda," Rox parrots.

I flick my eyes up at her, registering there might be some truth in what she's saying. Even though I'm still mildly annoyed, I feel bad for snapping at him.

"So, you think I'm overreacting?" I ask.

Rox shrugs. "I was going to say projecting…" She pushes out her lower lip, the corners of her mouth tugging downward. "Maybe misdirecting. But okay, we can go with overreacting."

We both laugh because it's embarrassing and so classically me.

The man probably thought I was a loon with my sweats and flip-flops, freaking out over ten bucks. *And oops.* In all my ranting, I called him insanely good-looking to his face.

True, but again, embarrassing.

At least I never have to see him again.

I shift my attention to Rox's stack on the coffee table.

About halfway down, the corner of a familiar—expensive—cream-colored envelope peeks out. Its fancy calligraphic script and swirly floral print make me dizzy.

Rox follows my line of vision and tugs the save-the-date free from the stack. Which means she's already gotten hers.

After a long beat, I relent with a sigh. "When is it?"

"Harp, I know you and Dad butt heads, but he's getting married—"

"Again." I've heard this argument too many times. Two marriages were too many. Four is just like, *figure out what you want already, and stop dicking around.* At some point in this man's life, he's going to have to stop hopping from family to family, destroying lives in the process.

"He's not getting any younger, Harp. I know you're still mad at him…" Rox hits me with her soothing, careful tone. It isn't pitying, but I know what's coming. "But he's our dad. We need to be there for him."

"I know."

"Maybe you can take a date." Rox perks up. "It's in June. It'll be perfect weather. By the looks of this save-the-date, the venue is probably going to be even more froufrou than the last one."

She tilts her head forward, grinning triumphantly as if expensive food and delicious buttercream cake can overwrite a lifetime of having a man try on and discard families without the courtesy of dusting us off occasionally. *Is it so hard to pick up the phone?*

I tug the blanket tighter around me.

As mad as I am at Dad, though, he's getting on in years. I can't keep that kind of regret hanging over my head. My mind wars with memories of Dad and me playing Chutes and Ladders and Candyland. As I got older and Rox became a part of our family, it was Life, Clue, then Trivial Pursuit, her favorite. But Dad and I, we always had Monopoly.

Rox and me, our childhood was built on these games. We were imagineering Love & Games long before we opened the store. Losing it wouldn't just cast a dark shadow over those memories. Somehow, it'd be like losing Dad all over again.

I'm not letting this happen.

"I'll think about it," I say mostly to appease Rox, but also, Dad's wedding is all the way in June. Now, we've got bigger worries to think about.

"That's all I'm asking," Rox says.

Zeroing in on the papers wedged in the middle of her stack, I jolt upright on the couch, and tug the spreadsheets free.

"It's kraken time," I say, ready to rip off the Band-Aid. In an oversimplified nutshell, we need to stop the bleeding. "Obviously, with everything that's happened this morning, I didn't come up with a ton of solutions, but I have some ideas. First, I'm making the executive decision to veto any talk of you taking out a home equity line of credit. We're already at risk of being jobless. I won't be responsible for you being homeless, too."

Rox slouches into the crease of the couch with a bellowing *harrumph*. "It was just an idea."

"Thank you for trying to single-handedly clean up this mess, but no thanks. Also, Dad's money is out, too," I say, knowing that's not going to be enough. "The easy thing would be to take Dad's money, save the business, and be done with this whole situation—buy us some time. It might be easier still to draw up a promissory note and treat it like a business loan."

She tilts her head, listening for the "but." The two obstacles I simply can't bring myself to ignore.

"What will we have learned if we take his money, then another storm blows the electricity or there's a flood? God forbid he's not around when it happens." My throat tightens even as I say it. We just talked about Dad getting older. "Then what? We fail later?"

Rox gives me a conceding nod. "Fine. Can we leave him as a worst-case scenario?"

"Okay, but the three of us get to decide when that is." I blow out a sigh when she agrees. "Now, if cash flow is the problem, cutting expenses is the first step. I volunteer to take a pay cut."

"I will t—"

"Nope, you and Nadi are good," I say, focusing my attention on the red columns on the sheet. "My next idea is to cease all inventory ordering. Temporarily move to an on-demand model. We sell what we have on hand. Period."

"Agreed," Rox says, doing especially well at letting me take the troubleshooting reins.

One down, one to go.

Bending to pull my phone from my back pocket, I find Nadi in my favorites, and call her on ViddyChat. By the time we bring her up to speed, she's got her beautifully contoured game face on, too.

Adrenaline rushes through me. I'm pumped.

We're on the cusp of some semblance of an action plan to save Love & Games.

"We need more exposure, though." Nadi traces her fingertip over the edges of her bottom teeth. She's got big blue eyes, short blonde hair, and a seventies retro vibe about her, so she looks like that old-school model Twiggy when her lashes fan out as her excitement grows. "Foot traffic. People coming into the store and getting lost in the nostalgia of board games. Or even your Hasbro Nation people," she says, raising her eyebrows. *To me. Rox would never claim the Monopoly fanatics.*

I snap my fingers.

"Shoot." The image of the Monopoly flyer in the coffee guy's pocket floats to the surface of my mind like a lifeline.

The annual tournament.

Of course. This business started with a game of Monopoly. It's only fitting if we're going to fight to keep its doors open, it should somehow include the classic game. It feels like a fork in the road. Turn left and we close. Or turn right and land on Anything Can Happen Avenue. Or Chance!

"What's your idea?" Rox asks.

I glance over at our Monopoly board piled with teensy green houses, red hotels, and rainbow-colored money. Rox's battleship is on Boardwalk, and my top hat is stuck in jail.

Rox follows my gaze.

For the next two hours, we recap how this happened, then continue brainstorming ideas to fix it. We decide to review our current insurance. Then we go over the last year and a half's worth of P&Ls, balance sheets, and income and cash flow statements. We have a few account receivables, but nothing substantial. Like I thought, revenue is up but so are our expenses and lease payments. We have fixed assets and inventory, but as established, our losses are growing monthly. Cutting expenses is only part of the solution.

"What if we sponsor the annual Monopoly tournament?" I suggest.

Tournament sponsorship won't solve our problems either but getting people in the door to register will increase foot traffic while we think of longer-term solutions. Coupled with more social media presence, my pay cut, a halt on purchasing, and no new debt, it should at least stop the bleeding.

Our situation *is grave*, but all isn't lost yet.

Straightening, I stretch my back and refocus on Nadi's face on the screen. "We get to decide *when* and *if* we close."

"Damn straight," she says.

I may not be the financial wizard with an MBA and a business mind like Rox, but I understand the economics of supply and demand. We need more reasons for people to discover all the amazing treasures at Love & Games. *Rediscover* family game night. I've got just the creative skill set. Plus, about twenty-five thousand reasons to do something about it.

Rox jots something in her notebook. "Put me in, coach," she quips.

We all laugh but this is the energy we're going to need. Stress will just be counterproductive.

"Okay." I blow out an exhausted breath. "I'll be the face playing in the tournament to represent the shop. Also, I'm going to work on ideas for store events to coincide with in-store practice sessions."

We've got a little less than three months, but I'm game.

Nadi's contagious yawn works its way around to me. I need more coffee, but it won't be from Java Joy.

The thought immediately reminds me of Mr. Pay It Forward. Of how shitty this day began. My neck tightens at the humiliation I felt at the coffeehouse. The guy didn't think twice. He just walked up to help me when no one else did.

If I'm being honest, the jeans did make his butt look cute, too.

As I swipe away from ViddyChat to my notes, I find his email address. I study the prefix for a few beats. DWilde. *D? Derrick or Daniel. Drake. Delicious…* With a heavy sigh, I copy and paste the email along with the amount into my xFer account. Plus ten percent to show him how sorry I am for dumping all my hang-ups on him. Then, I press Send.

CHAPTER FOUR

DECLAN

THE SETUP

AFTER I LEAVE the coffeehouse, the downward turn of my day continues. I make a stop around the corner at the hardware store to pick up more boxes and a bottle of water. Of course, when I'm in a rush, there's a long checkout line. So, this day dictates, I end up swerving through traffic trying to beat the restoration guy to Pop's house, then the car in front of me slams on the brakes and I drop the bottle, spilling water all over my lap.

By the time I reach the house, there's an impatient-looking, burly man with weather-beaten dark skin and a thick shaggy mustache waiting on the porch—staring at my wet crotch.

So much for paying it forward.

"Sorry I'm late," I say, shifting the boxes in front of me as I hurry up the path to unlock the door. "I got caught in traffic."

He enters behind me, so I feel the weight of his stare on my soggy ass. I'm sensing the reason I'm late isn't the explanation he wants.

"No problem, sir. Kindly show me where you saw the water damage," he says with a thick accent as I hold the door for him.

I weave past the couch in the living room, veering right through the dining room and down the hall, turning into the back bedroom on the left of the bathroom. Pop never considered knocking down walls for an open concept, so the bungalow still has its original compartmentalized layout.

The guy flashes me a polite smile when we enter the bedroom. "Excuse me, but the damage is not in the kitchen or the bathroom?"

"Uh, no. It's just here," I say, setting the boxes on the bed then moving Pop's recliner from the back corner to reveal a pretty sizable water stain with faint brown edges. "The bathroom is on the other side of this wall.

"I see..." He folds his arms across his chest and walks over to squat down for a closer look. Then he drags his fingers over the wall. "Unfortunately, this is quite common with these older homes. This stain looks like it's been here for a while and it's damp to the touch. See these tiny black dots? I'm fairly certain they're black mold spores, so I'm going to need to remove the drywall to determine the extent of the damage."

I zone out for a second.

It's hard to hear over the tiny violin playing the sad song of my dying budget. I had one rule: no opening walls. There's no telling what's on the other side that'll make me susceptible to plumbing, electric, and any number of budget-breaking holdups.

Deep breaths.

I expected this. I knew going in unplanned expenses go hand in hand with renovations. Especially with an older home. Pop passed two years ago. Other than paying the taxes, I've done nothing with the place. Even before that, my visits were few and far between. Penelope never appreciated the quaint feel of the bungalow.

"I'm sorry. Is it necessary to remove the drywall?"

"Yes." *Not even a stutter.*

"Oof, I'm not so sure I can do that myself." Paint, backsplashes, even the occasional under sink leak, I can handle. I've never ventured behind the wall. "Unless you can recommend a good YouTube video..." I give a nervous laugh.

He chuckles, then glances once more—as if involuntarily—at my wet jeans.

"Okay, then." I scratch my temple. "Fingers crossed, I guess."

Then he asks me to leave the room.

He goes out to his truck to change into his full white hazmat suit and respirator mask. When he returns, he's in Pop's room for less than twenty minutes before he finds me in the kitchen to give me the good and bad news. The good: the black mold is limited to the one shared wall, and he can remove it today. The bad: I have two hours to clear a room of stuff it took Pop sixty years to fill. Oh, and the house needs to be vacated for a week after the mold is removed to allow the wall to air out.

Awesome.

He maps out the process for me but all I hear is drywall, insulation, plumbing repair, new paint, *money, money,*

money, more money.

The guy spends a few minutes in Pop's bedroom and now he's all laughs. Deep, guttural belly laughs.

Damn.

The minute the guy leaves, I call in a favor from Murph, who agrees to not only let me crash at his place for a week, but he'll be here in fifteen minutes if I supply beer and pizza.

Two hours' work for seven days of listening to my best friend lobby all the reasons I should move to San Diego permanently and join his practice. Fair shake, I guess.

With a plan in place, I toe off my shoes and start peeling my way out of these jeans, when the sound of paper crinkling in my coat pocket snags my attention. I fish out the folded tournament flyer and set it on the bed.

Seven days I'll be at a standstill with the bungalow. If I don't find something to occupy my time, Murph will generously fill it with "take my best friend to work" days, sightseeing tours, and paddleboarding.

No thanks.

After I change into sweats, I move into the kitchen then affix the flyer to the fridge with Pop's favorite bright blue and yellow "Sunny San Diego" magnet I picked out the first summer I stayed with him. For a beat I stare at it. Fixing up this house. Monopoly. Our game and our summers together. They feel like I'm not only renewing Pop's memory but giving it a fresh shine.

A rhythmic series of knocks and slaps rips me from my thoughts as Murph makes beats on the front door.

"Dec! I'm here to rescue you," Murph calls from the porch.

"It's open. Come on back. I'm in the kitchen."

"You ready to do this?" he says, sounding pumped as he rounds the corner into the small kitchen. He's wearing an old San Diego Chargers T-shirt and sweats, but his product-whipped blond hair and golden boy good looks are still perfectly in place. "We've got this, easy."

A laugh sputters from my lips because he's yet to lay eyes on *the situation*, as I'm affectionately choosing to call it. My lips twitch as I say, "Come with me, my friend." Then I lead him back to the room.

Murph blows out an exhausted sigh as he takes in the bed, two nightstands, a dresser, an armoire, a sitting chair, and my grandmother's vanity—all wooden and heavy-looking. And that's just the furniture.

"Fuck."

Slapping a hand on his shoulder, I nod. "I know. It's the sheer amount of stuff. I don't think he's ever donated or thrown anything away. But, lucky us—"

"You're going to owe me big-time for this."

The first hour we spend removing the linens from the bed, clearing surfaces, swiping everything into boxes before we double-team the mattress and box spring. Murph tackles disassembling the bed as I take the drawers, one by one, stacking in them against the wall in the living room.

When the pizza arrives, we take a five-minute break.

"So, what happened with Alana?" Murph says over a mouthful.

"Who?"

He washes down his food with a long pull from his beer then barks out, "The Realtor I recommended."

"Oh, you mean the one who I was supposed to meet at noon in a coffeehouse she picked? The one who never called, texted, or bothered to show up?"

The crease between Murph's eyebrows tugs downward.

"That's not like her at all," he says, shoving his hand in his pocket to pull out his phone. He unlocks the screen then taps out a quick message, I'm assuming to Alana. "That worries me."

"You think something happened to her?" I ask, shame spiraling through me for thinking the worst.

His phone pings a few seconds later. Relief flurries through me his shoulders relax.

"Her husband is also an otolaryngologist over in North Park. I've known him for a good while. They got married a couple years back and they're expecting their first kid, so..." Murph must see the worry in my expression. "No, she's good. They had a scare earlier with false contractions, so they went to the emergency room. Braxton Hicks from dehydration, so we're clear. I'm sure she'll reach out to you later today, though."

"Oh, yeah. No worries," I rush to say. "I just hope she and the baby are doing okay." I rake my fingers through my hair, blowing out a breath. I'm relieved this woman isn't in any danger... But a weight settles on my heart. I'm jarred by the direction my mind goes.

Marriage.

Kids.

Penelope and I had been together since college then we got into the same medical school. We did our residencies at the same hospital. After so many years, we stayed together. I think I always knew it was more out of convenience and familiarity than love. With our insane schedules, it was easier than searching for someone new. I thought it went without saying, the plan was always to get married and have kids.

I guess, somewhere along the way, the plans changed when we changed.

Murph clears his throat to get my attention. When I look up, he jerks his beer bottle toward the fridge. "A Monopoly tournament?"

"Oh, yeah. I, uh, picked it up at the coffeehouse earlier." I scratch the back of my neck, and shrug. "Honestly, I grabbed it for nostalgia's sake, you know? Pop and I used to play all the time."

He tilts his head in interest. "I know how much your grandfather meant to you. Are you thinking about entering?"

A memory of Pop's concentration face flashes across my mind. The deep creases between his heavy gray brows. The scrunch of his nose. He used to gnaw on his bottom lip when he considered whether to buy a property just to block me. Then I'd egg him on to trick him out of it.

A smile tugs at the corner of my mouth, but I shove the memory aside.

"Now that I've got seven days to kill, I'm considering checking it out." I chuckle. "I had a minute to look at the tournament website while I was in line at that little hardware store on University."

"Anderson's Hardware?"

I nod. "That's the one."

"Next time you're down there, you should stop next door at Love & Games and say hi to Pumpkin. She owns the place with a couple of friends," he says. "It's a pretty cool place."

"Yeah?" I haven't seen Murph's younger sister, Nadia, in years. "I think I will."

"Maybe she'll know something about the tournament." Murph scratches his temple, his lips twitching. "To be honest, the entire idea of it sounds like nightmare fuel, but to each his own."

A laugh thunders from my chest.

"Give me a break. I'm just going to check it out. Besides, you're the one who wants me to really 'immerse myself' in this city..." I slap him on the shoulder then head back to Pop's room.

"You know we've got beautiful beaches and museums brimming with art and history. A whole baseball stadium." He laughs, trailing behind me. "*USS Midway* is sitting right there on the water if you need something to do with your time. Heck, we've even got a world-renowned zoo. Everybody loves Shaba the elephant. Make this make sense for me."

We fall into busy laughter as we each take a side, hefting and angling bulky, solid furniture through the narrow bedroom doorway. One at a time, we add them alongside the boxes and drawers lining the living room until we're down to a matted Persian rug, a rack of clothing, and a few tattered boxes from the small closet.

"You know what's funny, though?" I ask as we stand on opposite ends of the rug. "Penelope hated board games. Said they were childish. For people who aren't cultured." I huff out a laugh. "While I'm all for an excellent book or an art gallery, I just remember how much fun I had playing Monopoly with Pop. How close it brought us with that common bond, you know? I want to share that same joy when I eventually have kids."

Murph shoots me a deadpan expression.

"Relax." I curl the end of the frayed edge of the rug and start rolling toward him. "I haven't found a woman I want to have kids with yet. Truthfully, though, I hope whoever she is, loves classic board games and amusement parks just as much as a good book, movie, or gallery."

He clutches his hand to his heart as relief washes over him. "Scared me there for a sec."

Murph is my best friend, possible business partner, and fellow physician. But he's also a guy's guy. He's got my back, wants me to be happy, but I know he secretly wants us to hit our milestones together. Let our kids play tee-ball together or ballet. Live in the same neighborhood. I think that's why he was so gung-ho about me moving to San Diego. He'd file the paperwork for me to join his practice today if I give him the go-ahead.

I slip my phone out to check the time. The restoration crew should be here any minute. Just as I'm about to tuck it back in my pocket, the phone pings with a notification from the xFer app.

Harper Sloane paid DWilde

1m 🌎

Here's your $ back with interest. Pay it forward. Thanks again.

Harper Sloane.

"Uh... Care to share what that look is about?"

I blink up at Murph. "What look?"

"I believe that would be considered a sneer. The vein at your forehead looks like it might burst."

For a long moment, I close my eyes. Annoyance flares in my chest at the idea of reliving any of this story.

I'll just give him a *brief* rundown.

"At the coffee place where I found the tournament flyer, there was this woman whose store app wasn't working. The staff wasn't empathetic..." I shrug. "It's New Year's Day, I'd been stood up by the Realtor, thought I'd reset the day. Figured, hey, pay for her coffee. She can pay it forward, right?"

Murph nods, one hundred percent engaged—but also, waiting for the story behind my irritation.

"Wrong," I say. "Instead of thanking me, she insisted I give her my email address to repay me."

"Let me guess. She was hot, wasn't she?" Murph asks.

On paper, Murphy Theodore Sikes is an esteemed otolaryngologist with a specialty practice highly respected in his community. The son of a cardiologist and a senior editor at a publishing house, and protective older brother to his little sister, Nadia, aka Pumpkin. His fully renovated house looks like a model home.

Almost.

There's an international beer bottle shrine in his formal dining room courtesy of Murph, Murphy's alter ego. Murph is my college roommate and fraternity brother with the standing record for longest keg stand. At graduation, he mooned the entire audience. His only real relationship lasted six months. That was a decade ago. So, yeah. Probably the last person I should be candid with.

"I tell you she was ungrateful, and you're interested in what she looks like?" I recap for my own clarity.

Murph leans back against the wall, crossing his arms like he's got all day.

I flick my gaze skyward. On a heavy sigh, I say, "Thick wavy hair. Fit, petite, comes up to my chin. Nice breasts. Long legs." *Fiery green eyes. Golden-brown skin. Smelled like flowers and strawberries.* As he leans forward, I shake my head. "Late twenties, early thirties," I continue. "Black or biracial, with green eyes—"

"I love Black women with colored eyes," Murph adds.

I scrape my fingers through my hair thinking about Harper Sloane with her wild hair and those full lips.

"So, then what happened?" Murph asks.

I don't have the patience or the words, so I flip the screen to him.

Of course, I'm met with an outburst of loud, raucous laughter—probably at the *pay it forward* or the *with interest.* But then his expression smooths as he leans in closer, squinting.

"Holy shit. Harper is the coffee lady? That's Pumpkin's best friend I was telling you about."

"Your sister's best friend," I parrot.

He fixes his stare on me then clamps his hands on my shoulders. "As in, co-owner of Love & Games directly next door to Anderson Hardware."

The room spins like one of those carnival rides where the floor drops out from beneath your feet.

Murph takes a step back from the box he just finished taping to scratch his head. The smirk returns as the doorbell rings. "Uh-oh."

"Uh-oh, what?"

"We're out of boxes." Murph chuckles. "Don't hurt yourself rushing over to say hi to Pumpkin on your way to the hardware store."

I shoulder past him, shuffling down the hall to the front door.

"Look, I met Harper Sloane in a random coffeehouse. I tried to do a good thing. It backfired. And now she's paid me back. *With interest.*" I toss him an exhausted expression over my shoulder, slicing a line through the air with my hands. "Nothing else to it."

He opens his mouth to speak, but reconsiders, pressing his lips closed. The corners of his mouth twitch and he nods a few times.

Good.

I let the hazmat-suit-clad crew inside, directing them toward Pop's room in the back of the house.

There's a moment after they pass us during which I'm sure Murph is going to make a big deal about this. About the chances of meeting Harper Sloane at the coffeehouse, and now she owns the game store I'll be passing—sometimes multiple times—daily going back and forth from Anderson's.

He says nothing, though, which rattles me even more.

Honestly, I never expected to see her again, so how can she matter, one way or the other?

This time here in San Diego is about renovating Pop's house, seeing what this city has to offer. New place, new headspace. The order I get to create, putting my ducks in a row while rediscovering me without the past weighing me down.

Head is in charge, not the heart.

"Want another beer?" I ask.

"Nope." Murph stifles a laugh. "I'm actually going to head out. Send me a message when you're on the way to my house."

After I close the door behind him, I survey all the furniture and boxes from Pop's room filling the already full living room. The picture frames on every wall, the keepsakes on the tables, and bookshelves all need to be boxed up.

Guess I should add bubble wrap to the list, too.

CHAPTER FIVE
HARPER

TWO-PLAYER GAME

When the shop opens Thursday, I'm still hanging strings of pink and red hearts in the window next to our Official Monopoly Tournament Sponsor sign. Every time the bell above the door jingles, a giddy bubble rises in my chest. Another customer. Hopefully, another sale helping Love & Games stay open.

The store really is magical. It's our little wonderland. Oversized wall graphics brighten up the space. Monopoly tokens and animated characters all in classic game board motif add pops of red and pale green. It's small but organized with pine shelves heaped with game boxes and figurines, giving it a stay-and-play atmosphere. It's uptown refinement meets pastry shop glamour. Except with games instead of cupcakes. Sweeter, too, with the scent of popcorn and candy.

The entry bell chimes.

Cha-ching. Cha-ching. Cha-ching.

"Welcome in!" Nadi's cheery voice pulls my attention to

the back of the store. "All games are twenty-five percent off for our New Year, New Valentine Sale. Please see me or another store employee for Monopoly tournament registration," she says, just like we practiced.

Great customer service equals greater sales.

A man's deep bass replies with a "Thanks," and I feel my smile grow wider as he disappears between the display rounders.

We are so going to do this.

Then, a funny thing happens. The bell above the front door keeps jingling. For at least fifteen minutes straight. Warmth fills my chest. I could break out into dance as each person asks about the tournament.

Rox and Nadi answer questions, complete registrations, hand them coupons along with their tickets. We are fighting for what we built. Every time I see a person exit with a Love & Games bag, my spirits soar a little higher.

I'm just about done with the window display, ready to take the baton from my girls, when Skates, a guy I used to play Monopoly with back in my competitive days, ducks his head into the window.

He's got a baby face and the most serious skater vibes, so it only seemed appropriate for his Monopoly game marker to be the skates.

"Yeah, Tops. Is it true? You finally did it?" His voice bounces off the glass.

What did I finally do?

I get to my feet feeling his eyes roam over me, and I'm wishing I'd worn my hair in a bun as it spills over my shoulders. It's winter, but today felt like an occasion, so I curled it and put on a yellow spring dress and makeup. A decision Skates is clearly in favor of.

"Good morning to you, too, Skates. What's going on?"

He tears his gaze away from my dress and shrugs. "Everyone's been talking about you today."

"What are they saying?" On tiptoes, with the staple gun in hand, I survey the string of paper hearts I've hung between floor-to-ceiling columns of stacked board games.

"No one can believe you entered the tournament." He blows out an impressed breath. "Wheelbarrow himself is already taking bets. He says he'll take the money, but he wants the bragging rights more."

Walter "Walt" Wheelbarrow Huang of San Diego, champion of last year's annual city Monopoly tournament, and gloating enthusiast. He works next door at Anderson's Hardware, but I've known him since high school. Years ago, I beat him, and he's made it his personal life goal to land a rematch.

My smile slips. "Awesome."

Aside from brand exposure, access to attendee data, and discounted tickets, I knew Love & Games sponsoring the tournament meant I'd be expected to enter. Represent us in the games. But somehow, I forgot about Walt.

My mouth hardens as a mirthless laugh slips from my lips. "So, bets?"

To his credit, Skates doesn't seem like he's here to gloat or gossip.

"He told everyone it was probably just a resolution—you'd bow out before the actual tournament."

"Oh." I swallow then nod slowly, smoothing my hand

over the sides of my sundress.

Skates dips his head to glance at a notification on his phone.

That's when I look past his shoulder. My heartbeat pounds in my ears, and I might as well be underwater. I'm drowning. All the air vacuums from me. I'm light-headed as I spot him. DWilde. Mr. Pay It Forward.

He zips past the window, headed to the back.

I freeze, but I feel my fingers twitch. I physically cannot blink. My first thought is, *Hello, handsome. You've walked back into my life. A do-over is in order.*

But then I remember the last time he saw me I was unshowered, in sweats, and projecting my frustrations onto him. Over coffee. And he had the flyer… *Which was, thankfully, before Love & Games signed on to sponsor the tournament…*

Hmm.

Inwardly, I'm high-fiving myself for the extra fifteen minutes I spent on hair and makeup, though, as I stretch to look past Skates.

He clears his throat and I blink out of my trance. "Sorry. What did you say?" I ask.

"Are you canceling on the tournament?" Skates asks.

As soon as I open my mouth to speak, Mr. Pay It Forward turns around. And holy hotness, that crooked smile.

My stomach bottoms out.

As it seems, he's watching me, too.

"So, you are canceling," Skates says, mistaking my panicked silence for agreement.

"No. I'm not canceling." I meet Skates's grave expression. "I needed to confirm it was okay to participate since the store is a sponsor. I'm in." I hate how my voice goes soft and shaky.

I walk past him, taking wide strides toward the back where Nadia is at the register talking—correction, laughing—with DWilde. From where I am, coming up the aisle, I get an up close and personal view of Nadi as she presses one hand to her chest, slapping the other over her mouth. Then she leans forward, giggling.

So funny.

"Tops, it'd be awesome to see you play again." Skates is on my heels as I walk behind the counter, pretending I've got something to do by the register. "We all want you to take him down. You're probably the only one who can."

"She is," Nadi cosigns, already sensing who we're talking about. "I can't stand that Wheelbarrow guy."

As they compare hate notes about Walt, I quirk a closed-mouth smile over Skates's shoulder at DWilde. This time, I get an unobstructed view of him leaning casually against the wall. Naturally, his dark hair is tousled, his brown eyes sparkling as he drags his gaze, painstakingly slow, over me.

Spoiler alert: my radar at Java Joy was spot-on.

He is indeed insanely good-looking. He's tall. Easily over six feet. Probably late thirties. No wedding ring. Lean muscles, straight nose, full lips. He probably smells fantastic, too. And he's swapped last week's dingy jeans for a fresh pair of dark-washed ones and a pale blue button-down pushed up at the sleeves. His sun-kissed forearms are fully exposed. Almost like he knew I'd be salivating and ready to scrap our bad first impressions.

Then it hits me, and I feel like an idiot.

Duh. He's waiting for me. He probably hasn't noticed the payment in his xFer account.

"Excuse me, Skates." I tip up on my toes, leaning my weight on the counter. "Hey. Check the app. The money is there," I say, aiming for helpful store employee as opposed to giddy and hard up.

He releases a throaty chuckle that somehow manages to sound seductive as he averts his gaze to look at the autographed and framed dollar hanging on the wall from our first sale. "Yes. Thanks for the tip."

Oh... Did he just...? No.

Maybe it's just me again. He could totally be nice, and I'm twisting everything he says.

Just your standard overreaction.

Because I'm a professional, I plaster on my store greeter smile. "Great. Nadia can take you at the next register if you're here to enter the Monopoly tournament." My voice is toothache sweet. I even couple it with a soft, *not questioning your subtext at all* smile.

But then he levels me with a stare. "Actually...I dropped in to say hello to Nadia. Her older brother is my best friend."

Murph?

I jerk up an eyebrow at Nadi, who corroborates his story with a quick series of nods. "Declan. They went to medical school together," she informs me.

DWilde... Declan Wilde. He's certainly hot enough to be a Declan.

My chest tightens with embarrassment.

"Oh, sorry. I just assumed because you had the tournament flyer at Java Joy… I'll leave you to it, then," I say.

Declan Wilde gifts me with an encore of the lopsided grin. Everything about his easy posture, the way he stares unblinkingly at me says our little *pay it forward* incident is a gift that's going to keep giving.

It's fine. I'm the one who overreacted at Java Joy. He's due a turn.

He shoots me a considering glance like he's turning something over in his mind. "Now that you mention it…maybe you can help me with something."

"Sure," I say, greeter smile still intact. "Shoot."

"I still can't wrap my mind around why it was such a big deal for someone to buy you coffee. Why not just accept a kind gesture?" He trails off but his expression is giving me all the *make it make sense* vibes.

"Look, I truly appreciate what you did, and now I've repaid you, so…" I shrug, but he doesn't budge. "I know you are friends with Murph, but is this why you came here? Better question, why does it bother you so much that I couldn't accept your money?"

"Couldn't or wouldn't?" Declan taps a finger to his temple in a gesture that feels awfully patronizing.

Because my hands are restless, I turn and heft one of the boxes we pulled from the stock room onto the counter. I slice open the top and fold the sides back to start unpacking the board games.

"Is this a thing for you?" I squint over at him. "Hunting people down at their places of work for explanations."

In my periphery I catch his slow smile and the fluttery stare. He's doing the deep pondering expression again.

Again, I'm watching every move, so I'm caught when he jerks his head up to meet my gaze.

"You know, I wasn't sure until just now, but...I'd like to register for the tournament. I'm sure you'll be a worthy opponent."

My pulse skyrockets as I shoot him a *you can't be serious* stare.

Evidently pleased with himself, he pushes off the wall. The weight of his full attention lands on me, ruthlessly taunting me.

I can't believe I've been fawning over this guy with his stupid smile.

God, I want to say something badass like *we're full* or *you're ineligible*, but this isn't about me. We need as many entrants as we can get to participate and spread the word. We need as many entrants as possible to keep the doors open.

Unfortunately, that doesn't exclude insanely good-looking guys with fragile egos.

It's fine.

I'm fine.

Everything's fine!

The challenge bubbles up inside of me. *This guy is too much.* Yes, I dumped all my hang-ups on him at Java Joy. But does he seriously think he's going to walk in here and beat me at Monopoly?

No, sir.

I've got news for you, Declan Wilde in your dark jeans and rolled sleeves. You are no rival.

"You sure you remember how to play?" I hike up an eyebrow. *Oof, this man has balls showing up here challenging me.* "Believe it or not, this tournament is for *serious* players. Not some guy who found a random flyer in a coffee shop and nostalgically remembers family game nights."

Nadi leans in close to my ear. "That's wildly specific."

"They will eat you alive," I stress as I meet his stare, drilling my point home. "You'll be out in round one."

Declan cocks his head, studying my fidgety hand movements as I fumble to unpack more board games. Which only makes me more nervous. By the smirk on his face, he knows it.

The idea of torturing me during this tournament probably gives him all the warm and fuzzies.

Lord, my chest is tight, my stomach is all tied up in knots.

This is for the store, I remind myself.

"Guess we'll find out," he says, taking wide strides toward the counter. He's like two inches from my face. His clean, heady scent swirls around me as his expression beams, "Challenge accepted."

"Guess so," I say, digging deep for my greeter smile.

"I may not have a cool name like Tops or Skates," Declan says just low enough for me to hear, "but I think I'll take my chances."

My stomach clenches deliciously, traitorously.

The vein at his temple throbs as his lips tilt into a smile. "Since you're running this show, please sign me up."

We're at an impasse. First one blinks, loses.

His dark eyes narrow, his lips part slightly, tilting in that alluringly crooked grin.

Oh, I can fight dirty, too.

I bare my neck to him as I slowly trace my tongue slow over my lower lip. Digging deep into my flirt arsenal, I sink my teeth into my lip like a damn sexy goddess, and he gets an eyeful of bare skin and a breathy exhale.

He swallows. Hard, before—

"Oh, up front there's a table with forms to fill out," Skates interjects helpfully. "When you're done bring it back here to the counter and they'll ring you up. You're in luck, too, games are twenty-five percent off today."

Declan and I turn to face him.

Shit.

Also, thank you for mentioning the sale, Skates.

What a relief, though. I'm hot, my skin is on fire, and I'm certain my libido just shot off warning flares.

After Skates leaves, Declan makes quick work of filling out the registration form. We take turns glaring at each other as I take his money and go over the rules, events, and practice sessions beginning this Saturday. Some of which he'll miss since he's in town "temporarily." Whatever that means. He says he'll be back for the tournament in March, though.

For my personal enjoyment, I pick his brain while reviewing his form and scrutinizing every delectable detail on his Nevada driver's license. Declan Wilde is brown-eyed, black-haired, six foot three, and one hundred and eighty pounds of devastating male beauty.

It'll be torture but it's going to feel good to beat him.

CHAPTER SIX

HARPER

THE SHORT GAME

THIS IS WHAT Friday nights have come to. Flossing my teeth like a good semi-resolutionary, while a two-year-old vision board on the far wall taunts me.

"I'm working on it," I snap at the paper cutouts.

They're all there—giant Monopoly tokens, inspirational quotes, adorable beach bungalows. Then there's the man and woman lying in a tent staring up at a starry midnight blue sky. Of course, there's also a half-naked woman from a bodice-ripper romance book cover with her back arched simulating midorgasm. And what visual goal collage would be complete without a magazine cutout of a bunch of too-happy women huddled and smiling about razors or tampons?

It's the empty white spaces that make me wonder what's missing, though.

"Check the chicken!" Rox shouts from down the hall.

Sliding the floss from between my teeth, I yell back that the oven hasn't beeped yet, then go to toss the floss in my waste bin. When it clings to my fingers, I bend to shake my hand over the bin, and notice it isn't empty.

As I pluck out Dad's save-the-date, the empty white spaces claw their way to the front of my mind. I haven't RSVP'd yet.

THE HONOR OF YOUR PRESENCE
IS REQUESTED AT THE MARRIAGE OF

EVERLY CHEN

AND

HARRISON SLOANE III

SATURDAY, THE TWENTIETH OF JUNE
AT FIVE O'CLOCK IN THE AFTERNOON

HOTEL DEL CORONADO
1500 ORANGE AVE
CORONADO, CA

COCKTAILS, DINNER, AND DANCING TO FOLLOW
WWW.CHENSLOANEWED.COM

Two thoughts flood my mind. First, Rox is right. The ceremony or the reception—probably both—are going to be extra froufrou. So, *if* I'm going, I need a date plus a show-stopping dress. Second, as I read the name of my next stepmother, I wonder if Everly will be anything like the others—carefree like Mom, a born badass like Rox's mom, Vanessa, or wicked like Jade.

Down the hall, the bathroom door slams, then the smoke detector wails.

Dang it, the chicken.

When I rush into the kitchen, the charred chicken fumes on the stovetop. There's smoke everywhere.

Rox swats wildly at giant gray plumes billowing from the oven with a dish towel, fanning them toward the open window above the sink. Even in the face of actual fire, she's undeterred in her mission to talk, though.

"How long are you going to hide in your room?" she asks. "Before you deny it, don't."

"The thing is..." I grab a second towel, waving it in front of the smoke detector. "I'm not avoiding you, I'm just...I'm mortified that we're in a financial bind. So, I'm focused on saving the shop."

A cool breeze filters through the window, giving us a hand clearing the air, and the smoke detector cuts off.

Rox tosses her towel on the counter. She steps back to grab a bottle of wine and two glasses from the cupboard. "Grab the brownies," she instructs as she makes her way into the living room near the front window.

The chess table is set up with our two chairs and our ongoing Monopoly game. It takes us a few seconds to remember whose turn it was last.

Spotting my top hat in jail, Rox throws the dice and rolls doubles.

Two threes.

I couldn't get doubles if my life depended on it, which is why I've been in jail for months. It's stubborn refusal to cough up the fifty dollars to get out.

I'm starting to see a pattern.

Rox moves her battleship past Go. "Keep the two hundred dollars. I'll buy it." She moseys past Income Tax and lands on Reading Railroad, which she quickly snatches up to complete her set of all four railroads. With a bite of brownie, she pulls her knee to her chest and leans back against her chair.

At this angle, the low light of the lamp glints off her small, golden locket.

Dad gave us both one when we were little. We're his "Daddy's Girls." My throat tightens as I press my hand to my neck where mine used to be before I lost it.

"Harp, what I need you to know more than anything is we don't have to be ashamed or embarrassed. We're going to make mistakes, but we're in this together."

I pour us both a glass of moscato before I take a sip.

"I know and that's the part that's eating at me. This business is about the three of us building something bigger than ourselves. I don't want to lose it because we didn't have a large enough cushion to soften the blow from unforeseen electrical damages from a storm."

Rox shifts in her seat, waiting until I look up.

"Your need to *save* the business can't be more important *than* the business. We'll keep brainstorming, trying different strategies. I heard you talking to Nadia earlier. Maybe we do need to draw the family game night crowd. Get the nostalgia back into board games. I liked your Monopoly-themed scavenger hunt idea to get the community involved, too. Let's do all of it." Rox nods reassuringly. "The point is, we share the struggles *and* the wins, remember?"

I nod, hearing her out.

She's silent for a few minutes.

There's a mischievous gleam in her eyes when she asks, "Are we going to talk about what happened at the store with that guy?"

"Who?" *I know exactly who.*

Rox cocks her head. I practically hear the unspoken *seriously* in her expression. She was in the back at Love & Games, but I know her radar hearing has a way of kicking in at the first hint of drama.

"Look, the coffee situation was one thing, but that display you put on..." She stares at me over her brow as she mimics me. "*You sure you remember how to play? This tournament is for serious players...*"

"He was being an asshole," I reason.

"You do this, you know? Blow things out of proportion."

I dig my fingers into my hair and scratch my scalp. "Whatever."

She purses her lips. "Not every guy is after something. He was trying to register for the tournament that's going to help our business. Do you honestly think challenging him in front of other customers is the best way to increase registrations?"

Well, when you put it that way...

"Fine," I say.

"All I'm saying is, be nice." She cocks her head. "Just...when you feel the urge to verbally attack him, pay him a compliment instead. When the tournament is over, feel free to chop off his pretty little head."

I shoot her a questioning glance.

"Puh-*lease*. Don't act like you didn't notice how freaking hot he was with his butt-hugging jeans. Those bedroom eyes.

That casual lean."

And those sweeping eyelashes. Nope, didn't notice a thing.

"Calm down," I tell her, ignoring the heat swirling up my spine.

My pulse quickens as the memory of Declan Wilde gleefully pops back to the surface of my mind. *Not that he's been far from the forefront since he came into the shop.*

"Harp, I've been reading all those first impressions and body language books. You guys, going head-to-head across the counter... All that sexual tension... Whew!" She fans herself. "It was *H-O-T* hot."

I wave her off, laughing, quickly losing the battle against the warmth spreading through me.

Rox passes me a brownie then takes a sip from her glass. The natural flush to her cheeks deepens as she smiles. "We're not glazing over this subject. There was real chemistry. Trust me when I say Nadia and I were two seconds from swooning when he challenged you. That's the kind of guy you need."

And there it is, ladies and gentlemen.

I bite the inside of my cheek to keep from laughing. Rox can turn the teensiest interaction into a heaving-bosom, pining session.

"Why do you always have to make it about romance?" I groan.

"Because you've got your blinders up, so I have to look for both of us." She shrugs. "My point is, if he's going to be flaunting all that deliciousness around, see what he's about. Trust, all that heat was not for Nadia or me..."

"So, just forget about his arrogance?"

"The man challenged you at your own game, bought

your coffee, then refused to be repaid. Hardly offensive. What do you think chemistry is?" She drains her glass. Then props her elbows on the table, steepling her fingers under her chin. "Sad. He was so freaking hot."

As if I hadn't noticed. "He wasn't *that* cute..."

She flicks a bluff-calling glance over at me.

I sigh, resorting to dropping my attention to the Monopoly game board where it's safe. With a tip of my glass, I polish off the rest of my wine, then shell out the fifty dollars.

"Here, I'm getting out of jail."

Rox bursts out laughing, nearly knocking over her empty glass.

"Why can't you be as bold about men as you are about anything Monopoly-related? At some point, you're going to have to start giving people a chance. Not just your Monopoly boo." Her expression smooths as she casts her eyes down. "Sidenote. We don't have to take Dad's money. We do need to forgive him, though. We've got to celebrate life with him." *While he's still here...*

I chew the inside of my cheek so hard I taste copper. I miss him so much, but he's got to put in the effort, too.

"Forgive Mom...even evil Jade," she says, using our nickname for stepmom number three. Queen of No—sugar, boys, dating, television, anything remotely fun. "I'll bet they thought they were walking into happily-ever-after, too." She picks up the dice but doesn't roll. Then she gives me a pointed stare. "And talk to me. I'm your sister. I love you. Like you said, we built this business, we decide when and *if* it closes. We're the Sloane sisters."

Her little speech is so obnoxious and sweet. With her

hair up in a ponytail and no makeup, it's like no time has passed since we were kids playing board games under the kitchen table.

"I know."

The corners of her eyes crinkle and heat fills mine. "I'm not crying." I blink, sending tears spilling over. "There's something in my eyes."

We both laugh.

The game goes on for almost half an hour until we're out of wine and too bloated from brownies to sit upright. We end up tipsy on the couch only halfway watching our television show *Door-to-Door Dates* as we scroll through Pinterest. On the TV, Lucas and Angelica make out in a bubble cabin on the High Roller observation wheel in Las Vegas. Rox shows me her Dating, Trivial Pursuit, and Wedding Wear boards.

"See, this one?" She points to a flowy emerald-green dress. "Against your skin with some gold accessories, neutral sandals… Gorgeous."

I sink into the crease of the couch, letting my head rest on the cushion as Lucas, set against a neon-lit background, lowers himself onto one knee.

On my phone, I swipe to messages and thumb, *"Congratulations, Dad. I'll be there. Can't wait to meet Everly and eat buttercream cake."*

"Maybe you can make a Wedding Wear board for me…" I say, holding my phone out.

It feels like a hint that I need something other than Classic Board Games and Artisan Coffee in my life.

Rox twists to survey me, shock smoothing the lines of

her face knowing I'm going to Dad's wedding. In no time, she swipes and clicks, tagging dresses, earrings, sandals on my phone.

"The comedy show is coming up at Mike's Mic," Rox mutters. "Seems we need a little stress relief."

"Mm-hmm."

"Nadia said she can get tickets. Anthony Goode is hilarious."

Neither one of us speaks, but my heart stutters when Rox sets the phone on the cushion and intertwines our fingers. She lays her head on my shoulder. After a few seconds, I lower my head onto hers. We love each other. We are and will always be sisters.

"I'm happy we're fighting for the business," she says.

I squeeze her hand. "We've got this."

My mind drifts to the smiling tampon girls and the empty white spaces on my vision board. I'm so glad Rox is in my life. I don't want to miss any more important moments. Even it if means doing the electric slide at Dad's *fourth time's the charm* wedding. Or struggling to correct my business mistakes. Or being nice to a Monopoly rival.

CHAPTER SEVEN

DECLAN

TITLE DEED

SATURDAY, I STEP into Love & Games for the first Monopoly practice session and discover that beyond knowing the game rules and how to play, Harper Sloane is right. I'm not a serious player. Not by her definition.

There's a line from the door to the counter in the back. Every single person is wearing "gear." Hats, custom graphic tees, themed jackets. In one standout case, dark brown face paint to complete his wheelbarrow motif.

The store itself looks nothing like it did last week. The displays and games have been shoved aside. In their place, ten cardboard tables with game boards, waters, and small bowls of individually wrapped chocolates. The game pieces and money are from the fancy collector's editions.

That's not it.

Giant cardboard cutouts of Mr. Moneybags and life-size game pieces section the room to give each table privacy.

I scratch my head, feeling like a fish out of water.

Initially, this was supposed to be a fun way to reconnect

with my past, rediscover myself. Low-key entertainment to past the time. After I saw Pop's autographed dollar on the wall last time I was here, it felt like a sign. One more way to stay connected to him. Beating Harper Sloane at her own game would just be a fun bonus.

To say I'm out of my element is putting it lightly.

None of the practices or events are mandatory. I could've registered online. But I'll admit, after talking to Murph, I was curious about Harper Sloane. Figured I'd give her the benefit of the doubt she was having a bad day at Java Joy. But then she challenged me.

"Welcome! I see we have some old and new faces today."

I follow the voice on the microphone to the back of the store where Harper Sloane is staring directly at me. "Don't be shy. We won't bite." She laughs.

"Hey, man." I look to my right to find Skates wearing a blue shirt that says Skates. "Glad to see you made it."

I tip my chin to him but I'm here for Harper.

Soon, the group is corralled into a huddle as our hostess reviews announcements about upcoming practice sessions leading up to the tournament. Next, Nadia raises a red paddleboard signaling who to ask for help. Then, finally, we're released to find an open table.

It's mayhem as people dash and dive for seats at certain tables. I must've missed the memo on cliques. Everyone seems to know where they're going. Which, apparently, is away from the wheelbarrow guy.

His table is the only one with two open chairs.

"Let's all take our seats, please."

I look over to Harper, who's biting back a grin behind

the microphone. Undoubtedly, this guy is the Wheelbarrow Walt her friends want her to take down.

"Hey," he says.

He's got an unruly shock of inky black hair. Even sitting, he's tall with a lanky build. His voice is nasally, face expressionless. Last year's gold medal hangs around his neck.

"Okay if I sit here?" I ask.

He looks over to his right to another guy with tawny dark skin and thin-rimmed glasses. After they reach a silent agreement that I'm worthy of being in their presence, Wheelbarrow chucks his chin toward the seat across from him and next to Glasses.

"We're the Jailbirds. I'm Walter, or Wheelbarrow Walt, but you can call me Champ." He snickers. "This is Eugene. He goes by Whistleblower." He pushes the bag of game markers to the center of the board, hope lacing his tone as he asks, "You got a name?"

I grab the Scottie dog marker. "Declan."

They both sigh. I'm pretty sure I've shattered their hopes of hazing a third for the Jailbirds, but…my road to rediscovery doesn't include a stop in the fanatic zone. I've got one pit stop to beat Harper, then straight to the tournament.

The first ten minutes, I'm left to my own devices. The Jailbirds whisper and pass strategy notes. They buy a utility each—one of the first tips Pop warned me against. So, it doesn't surprise me that over the next few minutes, I quickly learn the players last year must have sucked if Walt took home the medal. Not only does he look like a tool with face paint and a matching T-shirt, but he hasn't stopped talking about his "A-game" since I sat down.

For all his gloating and bets, I expected him to make quick work of beating me. But he's got no skills. In minutes, I rack up a solid number of properties and money to set me up to destroy them.

Overall, it's a good time wiping the cardboard with Wheelbarrow's ego.

At noon sharp, though, Harper Sloane walks over to our table with a clipboard under her arm and tight smile firmly in place. She's dressed comfortably in black sneakers and leggings, and an oversized wine-colored sweater. Her chestnut hair falls in textured waves framing her glowing brown skin. I only lose my focus briefly before I remember why I'm here.

"Just a few serious players over here, ma'am." I try not to meet her moss-green gaze, but I'm only human.

Harper's eyebrows bounce with amusement. Her lips twitch as she bites back a smile. "Wasn't sure you were going to make it. Figured your Saturdays were probably booked, donating to the less fortunate." *I.e., paying it forward.*

At least her head is in the game.

"Wouldn't have missed this for the world," I say, leveling her with a stare. "I need all the practice I can get if I don't want to be out in *round one*," I quip, referring to her challenge.

"Welp, that's what we're here for." Her smile is so tight and polite I think a little part of her dies inside to be nice to me.

She flits her gaze to the Jailbirds—who, ironically, still need to roll doubles to get out—then back up to me. More specifically, my glasses.

If I was a lesser man, I might be bothered by her stare. Lucky for me, I've got my eyes on the prize.

Her shoulders angle toward me, and whether she knows it or not, she leans in. Instinctively, I lean back. Heat swarms over my skin with her so close. She's standing right in front of me. But I'm not backing down.

Harper blinks first. "Well, let me know if you need anything. Our *staff* is here to help." *Noted. The staff, not her.*

"Will do."

This woman may be gorgeous, but she's as friendly as chicken pox the way she crawls beneath my skin and settles there. I'm antsy and itchy just being around her. But thankfully, she doesn't leave.

Harper sits in the chair between Wheelbarrow and me.

"So, you're playing today?" I ask.

"Not that I need the practice." She opens her mouth—clearly to criticize me—but stops short. "I like the glasses, by the way."

The compliment throws me right off. My posture goes rigid, and my neck tenses as I study her in my periphery. I'm attracted to her. She's a beautiful woman. But I'm annoyed with myself more than anything for accepting her challenge. I know next to nothing about Harper Sloane, but I'm curious. I want to know who she is, what makes her tick, what makes her switch gears from antagonizing me to complimenting me in sixty-seconds flat.

This San Diego trip is about trying on this city for size, though. Nothing else.

"Thank you. It's important to give contacts a rest sometimes," I say.

In short order—because I need this game to start so I can beat her then go about my day—I reach for the plastic baggy of tokens for her just as she goes for it. Our hands graze one another, and I'm zapped with an electric current. It jump-starts every nerve ending in my body. Heat blazes over my skin. My sensory receptors are probably going crazy, sending emergency flares to my brain, but how do I process it when everything about it... It doesn't exactly suck like I imagined.

"Sorry," I mutter, quickly releasing the bag.

When I look up, though, I follow her line of vision as she studies the game board then stares at me. A smirk tugs at the corner of her mouth.

"What?"

"Really? You're the Scottie dog?" She scrunches her face. "I figured you for the car or the horse. Maybe the iron."

"Funny, if it was anyone else, I'd be vaguely offended. What surprises you about the Scottie dog? And why the iron?"

Her laugh is loud and boisterous. It festers inside me. I hate how easily she's able to trick me into wanting to laugh with her.

"My middle name is Scott," I say simply.

"Ah, the plot thickens..." Harper fidgets, quickly tucking her hands in her lap when she catches me staring.

"When I used to play with my granddad, it was always assumed I'd be the Scottie dog," I say. "*Tops*, oh, queen of Monopoly."

Walt harrumphs like *queen* and *Tops* in the same sentence are a mismatch.

Of course, Eugene cosigns for him. "More like the bottom of the barrel." He chuckles.

God, I don't like these guys.

Harper Sloane is irritating but nothing like these two knuckleheads. Plus, if Walt is taking bets Harper's going to lose, that's just foul.

I sit up taller to pin Eugene with a challenging stare. "Says the man who's been in jail for the last three rounds." It's a warning to them both, but the instant I say the words, I feel the weight of Harper's stare on me.

I'm sure the last thing she expected was for me to come to her defense. If I'm honest, it shocks the hell out of me, too. She barely tolerates my presence, challenged my Monopoly skills, so why am I coming to her defense?

"New game. Short game rules. Roll," I say, handing her the dice.

The Jailbirds give us a collective sigh. Walt shakes his head like we've somehow shamed the honor of the game and Mr. Moneybags himself.

Like almost every game I've played with new people, we start off by arguing about the rules for Free Parking.

"According to the official rules," Eugene states, pulling out his own laminated copy of the rules.

The Jailbirds are dead set on nothing happening when a player lands on it, but Harper and I both agree on "House Rules" whereby all collected fines are placed in the middle of the board to be claimed by whoever lands on the space. Otherwise, where's the fun in that?

"Nadia?" Harper leans back, balancing on the hind legs of her chair. "How do we handle Free Parking at Love & Games?"

"House Rules," she calls back.

"Okay, then. Since Love & Games is my house..." Harper rolls the dice, the Jailbirds concede, then we start the play.

When my turn comes around again, I land on St. Charles Place. I quickly pay and stow the property card, but my mind is still retracing the last few minutes. I'm not sure how to play Harper Sloane's game. One day, she won't let me buy her coffee. The next, she tries to dissuade me from entering the tournament. Now... What the heck was that? Was that banter between us? We're banding together against a common enemy now?

Murph's words taunt me.

Complicated woman issues. Just your type.

The game is over in less than two hours. One look at the board, at the trio of red houses on *four* color-groups. My Scottie dog on Income Tax. The wheelbarrow on Boardwalk. Eugene's cannon in the slammer again. The winner is clear. Harper and I both have stacks of cash, but she's also got railroads, properties, hotels, houses, plus a self-satisfied glint in her eye because she's the richest player. Which means I'm rustier than I thought, and she wins.

I was this close.

"Congratulations." I force a smile, but I already want a rematch.

CHAPTER EIGHT

HARPER

CHANCE

BRIGHT AND EARLY Wednesday morning, Rox, Nadi, and I meet at Love & Games before opening. Rox is instituting the first of what will be weekly emergency meetings—or as needed, so she says. Which in Rox terms means whenever she comes up with another possible solution on a whim.

Thankfully, this is just until we're back in the black.

"Let's get started," Rox says.

Nadi and I drag our sleep-leaden bodies behind the register where my sister has laid out collated and stapled packets for us.

Sigh.

Just a quick fan through of the first couple pages, and already the strength of my coffee is being tested. I can tell the stale stuff from the break room isn't going to cut it for long. Based on the sheer frequency I'm predicting of these meetings and my self-inflicted pay cut, I won't be able to afford the professional stuff.

I make a mental note to sneak over to Anderson's to pick up the bulk box of K-Cups before we open.

"So, as you can see, I've got a recap of the first practice session plus preliminary numbers around tournament registrations." Rox's voice brims with excitement as she springs herself up onto the back counter behind the register to face us. She drove today, so it was traffic with a side of pop music and motivational podcasts the entire drive. *The entire drive.*

Now, more color-coded spreadsheets.

Like, I want to fix things more than anyone, but I'm hands-on. I need action, something tangible to put my mind to. Direction. Apply for the loan or the grant. Plan a sale and advertise it. Win the tournament. Input the price changes into the system. Even data entry I can do.

Talking just puts me to sleep.

Not even replaying the look on Declan Wilde's stupid adorable face behind those full-rimmed glasses when he lost the other day helps. *And lately, it's been fueling lots of...stress relief and self-care.* I don't have time to examine all the other bodily reactions it jump-started. I've got work to do, and thankfully, I don't have to see him again until Saturday.

I tune back in for Rox's good news.

"We're on an upward trend in registrations, and we're seeing a small boost in sales, so yay!" She bounces with infectious glee. Her morning glow is practically blinding, the way she lives for numbers, lists, solutions. It's what she does. Once her mind wraps around the problem, she dives into fix-it mode.

But I still feel like I need to pull my weight to solve this problem. At the very least, contribute viable suggestions and options to get us back on track. Yes, we share our wins and struggles, but *we* need to get us out of this bind.

"I have a few connections at the Chamber of Commerce," I interject during a lull in the conversation. They both stop and stare at me, waiting for the rest. "I put some feelers out to see what I could come up with. A friend mentioned crowd-funding." I dart my gaze between Rox and Nadi, who look dumbstruck that I've been doing anything other than sitting back and waiting for my sister to come up with the answer to our problem. *Wow. Tell me I've been riding my sister's coattails without telling me I've been riding my sister's coattails.*

When did I stop actively participating in my own life?

To drill in the point, Nadi, who, up until now, has barely kept her eyes open, blinks a few times before she squares her body to me. "How is this different from accepting a gift or a loan from your dad? It's the same principle, and by your logic, it's not sustainable going forward."

I pull in a lungful of air, then nod, acknowledging her point.

"Listen, I don't know that much about the inner workings of starting a crowd-sourced account or the tax implications for the funds. I imagine they'll be considered business income. But we're already applying for grants, loans for small business owners, women business owners." I tick off the possible solutions on my fingers. "We don't have the luxury of leaving any stone unturned. And this isn't a long-term solution, but I figure, coupled with the tournament, the expense cuts, our social media push, it's maximum exposure."

Nadi tilts her head to either side, considering.

"And you're right, lots of people get help from family, but this would be us immersing ourselves in the trenches. It could be a great way to help the community feel personally connected, too. Invested in our success."

Rox's posture perks up. Cupping her elbow with one hand, she taps her lip with the other. "Technically, it's not getting help from someone if it's a *whole* crowd."

A melancholy laugh rumbles through me.

My heart squeezes.

"I've been thinking a lot lately about why we started this business in the first place. Why it matters that we keep it going." Nadi puts her arm around my shoulders, hugging me close. "Guys, it's a big deal for three women, one wine-cooler-fueled night, to come up with an idea—albeit over flaky brownies and a game of Monopoly—pool our savings, and end up with a viable livelihood. The community needs to see us succeed. *We* need to see ourselves succeed."

Rox hops down and joins the hug.

"Look at my big sister growing up right in front of our eyes," she coos.

So, we throw another proverbial spaghetti noodle at the wall.

Between the pending bank loan, two possible grants, the tournament, the purchasing freeze, our commitment to liquidate on-hand inventory, and now the BusinessFunder crowd-funding account—which I plan to have up and running by end of day—something's got to stick.

We've made a small breakthrough, and it feels good. I

won't tell Rox, but she might be onto something with these emergency meetings.

TEN MINUTES TO nine, I slip out the shop and into Anderson's. I barely get two feet into the hardware store before I'm greeted, thankfully, by my friend Kelly, who owns the place, and not Walt. She's suited up in the company mustard-yellow apron to go with her steel-toed shoes. She's all vibrant red hair, a light dusting of freckles on her nose, and rosy cheeks to go with a beaming white smile.

"Hey, girl. How's it going? Saw that y'all are official sponsors of the Monopoly tournament," she says, unloading paint cans from a box and stocking them on the wooden pallet shelves. "Fancy."

My face grows warm.

"You know how it goes. Got to keep our name out there," I say, dancing around the truth. She's a business owner, too, so I know she'll get the gravity of our situation, but it doesn't make it any less humiliating.

Besides, I'm not here to chitchat. I'm just running in for coffee.

"Can I help you find anything?" she asks when I linger, and I'm about to laugh because I know this place like the back of my hand. If we did dissolve the business, I could apply here and be up and running an hour later.

But then Kelly's attention shifts past my shoulder.

"Uh, hi again," a vaguely familiar bass-filled voice bellows behind me near the door. The image of the man it belongs to I'm starting to know too well. "I'd like to get some neutral-colored paint..." He trails off.

Kelly doesn't say anything right away, so I assume he recognizes me, too.

Slowly, casually, I turn around.

"Harper Sloane." Declan flashes me his white bright confident smile. *And good lord, confidence is certainly...not unattractive.* "We've got to stop meeting like this," he says.

In the back of my mind, I should be working out a fresh zinger for a response. Something snappy like "I'm inclined to agree" or "Maybe if you stop following me around." But his proximity leaves me feeling off-kilter. And a little breathless.

He's all scruffy again today. No jeans this time. He's wearing a threadbare green Community Chest tee with loose-fitting black sweatpants that...*mmm mm mm...* Yeah, let's just say they fail to conceal his manly assets.

Good Lord.

Suddenly and grossly, I feel like I've got an excessive amount of saliva, so I keep swallowing as I give him a shaky smile. Every nerve ending in my body stirs and tingles.

Then, I realize I've just been standing here silently ogling the man.

I toss him an easy "Hey," which only makes matters worse because he walks all the way into the store and plants himself next to me. Well, next to Kelly. *It's a small store.* But since I apparently don't remember how to work my motor skills and I refuse to breathe, now I'm light-headed.

"Oh, so you two know each other..." Kelly flits an imploring glance in my direction like she wants me to fill in the blanks about Declan Wilde. Sorry, Kel, my body is knee-deep in the process of shutting down from utter humiliation. *Why does he have to be so hot? Why can't he just be another mediocre-looking gamer with awkward social skills and clothes that sufficiently hide his body? Why?*

I make the mistake of letting my gaze drop to his lips. I'm memorizing their fullness and smooth pink texture when he shifts on his feet, breaking my focus.

As I glance up at his eyes, there's no mistaking the heat in his gaze. He's watching me, too.

His breaths quicken as he steps backward, pushing up his glasses.

Literally, the last thing I need is a man-distraction. I owe it to myself and the girls to stay focused on Love & Games. Period.

So, that's all there is to it.

"Hey, Kelly, I really need to get going," I say, training my eyes on her. Not to my side where Declan Wilde's clean woodsy scent is doing its best to lull me into submission. "We're opening pretty soon, so I'm going to run back and grab a box of coffee for the store." Because I know this won't be the last time I see him, I quirk a small smile and say "Nice seeing you" to Declan Wilde before I turn down the nearest aisle and run-walk toward the back.

On my way, I hear Kelly telling him where the paint swatches are located and to holler for her once he's picked a color.

When I get to the coffee section, I grab the red bulk box of K-Cups for home and a pricey caramel flavored canister for the breakroom. Then I consider for a second whether it would be rude to toss the money at Kelly and make a break for the exit, then quickly scrap the idea.

"Dang."

I tuck the box under my arm, peek around the corner, then creep down the main aisle. I'm almost to the register when—

"Hey, I know you said you were in a rush…" Declan's voice startles me. I let out a gasp, pressing my hand over my heart. "Sorry, I didn't mean to scare you," he says between chuckles.

"It's okay, I'm just…really focused." I laugh. "What's up?"

His dark eyes snap to mine as he searches my face. "Listen, maybe we both got a little too into the spirit of rivalry, being opponents, the game. Walt really got under my skin."

I laugh again, like I'm some giddy teenager. It's the only thing I remember how to do around him, apparently.

"Don't feel bad. He's literally the worst," I say.

"Anyway, I thought we made a pretty good team. Since I don't know anyone other than Murph and Nadia, and we keep running into each other, I was hoping we could…" He pauses. I'm left hanging, wondering what he could possibly want from me, and praying he's not going to say a date. His tone is soft but measured as he shrugs adorably. "We could be friends…?"

"Oh." I try not to sound too relieved, but the word comes out fully round on my lips.

This, I was not expecting.

Under the stark light, magnified by his glasses, there's something unsettlingly sad in the gold-flecked depths of his eyes.

He scratches his temple, smiling. "I know. Probably the last thing you thought you'd hear from me, huh?" A pink flush spreads over his neck and cheeks. "I'm actually considering moving here, joining Murph's practice. For now, I've got a few more weeks to renovate my late granddad's bungalow. So, I'll be around a lot between Monopoly practices and picking up materials here."

"I'm sorry about your grandfather."

He lowers his head and murmurs his thanks.

With no warning, a wave of curiosity washes over me. Why is he thinking about leaving Nevada? Did he leave anyone behind? Is this gentle, endearing version the real Declan? Why did he register for the tournament? *Why do I care?*

A man with a pencil behind his ear and an expression of deep concentration wedges past us in the aisle.

My entire body tenses, my pulse quickening.

It's about ten percent to do with everything Declan's just said and ninety to do with the fact he's moved within inches of me.

We're alone.

For the first time since we met. We've been surrounded by a dozen people at Java Joy and Love & Games, but today it's just us and this *inconvenient* attraction that came out of nowhere.

Fire sparks in his eyes when I look back at him. He traces his teeth over his lower lip. "Should be less awkward if you don't have to creep down hardware store aisles to avoid me."

Shit, he saw me.

Guilty, I squeeze my eyes closed, wringing my hands together. Because I can't look at him, I focus on the boring off-white paint swatch in his hand. It's probably got a pretentious name like Driftwood Sunset or Ecru Eggshell.

"Is that the color you're going with?" I wince playfully, not even subtle about the subject change.

Declan chuckles though his smile doesn't reach his eyes.

A pang of regret strikes my chest. I wish I could go back and just say, *Yes, I'll be your friend.* Would that have been so hard?

Apparently so.

Instead of making it right, I let my shame coil around me. Without him asking me to, I help him look through paint samples and ask questions about his renovations. Though he looks like he wants to brush me off, he tells me he's at a standstill due to black mold, so he's busying himself with tasks to get ready for when things pick back up.

After he selects a warm bisque color, aptly called Biscotti Beaches, he thanks me for my help then angles toward the register. But I linger, replaying this exchange in my head. I feel like I've gone too far with this half-hatched rivalry we started based on what seems like nothing more than a bad first impression. This tender, playful side of him doesn't mesh with who I thought he was. And yes, my plate is full now, but it couldn't hurt to have another friend.

"Will I see you at practice Saturday?" I flash him a hopeful glance.

Declan's expression is unreadable at best. Instead of answering my question, he holds my stare for a sec then says, "Have a good day."

A few seconds later, he's gone.

CHAPTER NINE

DECLAN

PLAY

I ONLY KNOCK once before Murph yells that the door is open. He's sitting on a massive gray sectional in jeans and a T-shirt with his bare feet propped on the wooden coffee table. His thumbs jab at a controller, gunfire blaring from his headset.

Damn, he's in full gamer mode.

I'm at a complete loss here. Half his attention isn't going to cut it.

"Hey," he tosses over his shoulder at me before turning his attention back to the screen. "Go, go, go! I've got your six."

"What are you playing, *Blue December* or *Final Tombs*?" I set a six-pack on the dining table and round the corner into the living room to check the screen.

Please don't be Blue December.

When I see the television, I'm officially screwed. There are no zombies. The screen shows a close-quarters battle in a dusty, dilapidated building. Murph's video game character is in head-to-toe fatigues in a war zone rocking his preferred loadout and getting to work. The cartridges pop all over the place as he holds them off for the other players on his ops team to make a run for it.

If I wasn't crashing here, I'd make a run for the door.

Blue December. The latest multiplayer special ops war saga video game with first-person shooter technology reworked for intense cooperative play for up to sixty-four players—who can all talk at once.

"Hurry up. Grab a controller and a headset." Murph nods to an extra pair by the game console on the massive black entertainment center.

"Actually, I was hoping—"

"Goddammit!" Murph scoffs at Mindbl0wer69, whose player just stands there while gunfire rains in their direction. "Can you guys make some noise over there?"

Because I know I'm not going to get anywhere while he's playing, I grab a beer, Red Vines, and the extra controller and headset. Plopping down on the couch, I jump in. Immediately, the four of us corner the insurgents, and Murph gets a double kill.

"Woo! That was perfect." He hoots and punches the air.

"Dang, man," MoveslikeJ4gger adds.

"Heck yeah. A ten-kill streak." On the screen, Murph's gamer tag, Tr4sht4lker, flashes next to his character as he does a side-shifting dance.

While we clear the area and the team heads toward a set of stairs in the back, I glance over at my friend and college roommate, wondering why he looks like he's been jackknifed by a truck. His usual fresh-faced frat boy swag and product-whipped blond hair look worn down today. His posture sags, and his eyes are a vacant overcast sky blue.

Then I remember that he had back-to-back surgeries on the docket earlier, and this is how he unloads.

"Are you fucking kidding me? A headshot?" His voice thunders as he pivots toward me on the couch.

Over the headset, another player guffaws. "You got domed."

I flit a glance back to the screen to see my finger must have slipped. I've killed my best friend. "Oh, shoot, man. My bad."

He groans an impatient snort, cursing under his breath.

It was an accident, but maybe it worked in my favor. Murph pulls off his headset and sets the controller on the cushion to his left. With a deep sigh, he scrubs a hand over his face and looks at me for the first time.

"I would ask how the packing is going at Pop's and how things have been going with the tournament, but you look like shit." He uncrosses his ankles and crosses them again with the right foot on top before he continues. "For damn sure you're playing like shit. I assume you just came back from Anderson's."

"Yeah. I stopped by after I left the house," I say.

Murph lifts his brows expectantly and winds his hand in circles, signaling for me to get on with it.

"The plumber is back tomorrow, so I got almost everything boxed up and stored in the garage. Once he's done, the crew comes back to add the insulation and put the walls back, and I can start painting."

Murph sighs. We both know I didn't come here to talk

about Pop's.

Okay, let's get this over with.

I remove my headset with a light tug. For a split second, I consider being completely honest with him and giving him the full details of my head and my…chest region. I can't stop thinking about Harper, about how I could hardly think straight at the hardware store. I was rock hard off a conversation about paint. *Jesus.* Every time she opened her mouth that sexy rasp in her voice sent heat surging through me. *Damn, she smelled fantastic.*

"Is this about the house, Harper, Penelope, your nerd tournament, or a Harper/tourney combo?" he asks, skipping ahead.

"Really, you know me better than that. Penelope is a nonfactor." My tone is drenched with indignation, but Murph knows me too well to humor me.

"Oh, yeah? So, this is about Harper, then?"

I groan because he's just annoying.

"Listen, Dec. At the end of the day, I'm happy you found a new woman to obsess over, but…" He twists his mouth to the side, and I'm eager to see where he'll go with this angle. "To play devil's advocate, are you saying you applied for a cross-state medical license and picked up and came here for fun? Nothing to do with Penelope dating that dude?"

My jaw tightens. "You're reaching, Murph."

"Am I, though? You were just dying to come immerse yourself in manual labor to fix up a house you've been avoiding for the past two years since Pop died?"

I fall back against the cushion debating what approach

I'm going to take to translate this into short, uncomplicated sentences for him. I let my legs fall further open and scoot into the divot.

"Seriously, I've been paying the taxes on Pop's place. It's just been sitting there—growing black mold, apparently. And I'm considering a permanent move, but you're right." I fold my arms across my chest. "It started out as needing space from Penelope, but she made her choice. I've moved on."

"And?"

"And you're not wrong about the *Harper/tourney combo* as you so eloquently put it."

"Yeah, okay..." His brows bounce as he swings his feet to the ground, grabs my beer, and angles the cap to the edge of the coffee table. With one slap, it flies off, and he tips his head back for a long pull.

How should I put this?

"Last week, she was at the top of my least favorite people list."

Murph leans forward with an eyebrow cocked. "And this week?"

Words lodge in my throat as I replay our conversations in my head, trying to pinpoint the moment when she dropped on my list. Why it bothered me so much when she walked away from me and the woman at the hardware store. But then, during the Monopoly game and again in the aisle, there was something about the way she watched me.

I rub my chin. "Um... She's not at the top."

Murph studies me a second before he stands and goes to the kitchen for another beer. I follow him, halfway expecting him to laugh this off and talk about my complicated woman issues. The look of serenity on his face seems like an exaggeration, though. There's a lightness to his expression.

"So, you like Harper?"

Settling on a barstool at the counter, I pinch the bridge of my nose. "That's *not* what I said."

He snickers. "That's what Nadia and Rox said. Looks like she's gotten under your skin."

Ignoring the flutter in my stomach, I hook my ankles around the legs of the stool and stretch back.

Okay, I'll bite.

"For the record—in case you need to run it back to the gossip mill—I do not *like* Harper Sloane. There's still a strong ambivalence, I just said that I don't despise her. There's a difference."

He staggers forward, laughing, spewing spittle all over the floor.

I shake my head, blinking away the heat rising behind my eyelids. "My purpose for coming to you, and what I *meant* about needing to talk about the 'Harper/tourney combo,' was to find out what her deal is."

Murph takes another pull from his beer then centers his smug stare on me. His lips still twitch as he speaks. "According to my sister, you two *act* like you're at each other's throats, but it's obvious you *really* want to rip off each other's clothes." The corner of his mouth kicks up. "Personally, I think they're right, and the only thing mutual is denial."

The urge to set Murph straight feels almost urgent.

"If that's the case, tell me why she couldn't leave Anderson's fast enough when I ran into her there?"

"Wow. You're seriously out of practice."

"The store clerk says, 'So you know each other.' It took Harper two seconds to walk away, dodging the question." Heat swarms over my neck. "I'd say that's pretty clear."

Murph polishes off the rest of his beer then sets the empty bottle on the counter with a thud. "Listen, I know it's been a while but try to pay attention. Those two seconds...they're the proof she's keeping her options open. This is like She's into You 101."

I huff out a sigh.

Why on earth do I keep this guy around? *Why?*

"Remember back in kindergarten when you'd hit a girl and it meant you liked her?" He doesn't even wait for me to nod. "Trust me. I know about these things. She totally wants to you. For some reason, she seems to be into your whole rugged handyman look."

Murph is wrong. He wasn't in the aisle when she ignored my request to be friends.

"This is a *good* thing," Murph reasons. "Some of the best sex I've ever had has been with women who *detest* me." *I'm sure there are many.* "The best part about it? No strings attached." His eyes widen as he squeezes my shoulders. This, apparently, is his holy grail.

"Got to hate strings." My mouth waters imagining all the tangy-sweet flavors of Harper's smooth skin. How I'd like to drag my tongue over her swollen lips, down her neck to her breasts, and—

"I'm telling you. The best sex ever." He draws out the last word, ignoring me.

Except, when I say nothing, Murph points his finger at

me. "You don't believe me."

Shamefully, I might. Or, rather, I'm hopeful.

"Uh…no," I say, intrigued to hear his answer, though.

He doesn't validate my question with a response. Instead, he gives me a slow nod. I sense the wheels in his head turning, considering a course of action to prove it to me.

"Whatever you're thinking, don't. I'll take your word for it."

Murph's eyes light up. "If you're so sure we're off base here, why not put your money where your mouth is?"

"What does that even mean?" I huff out a laugh.

His smile hardens. "It means, she's probably going to Mike's Mic with Nadia next weekend to see that comedian, Anthony Goode. My sister gave me two extra tickets, so clean yourself up, and let's go see how she reacts to you." Murph presses his palms against the air. "If there's nothing to it, I'll help with the renovations. But, if the electric, hate-fueled attraction is there, you come check out the clinic. Make your pros and cons list. Together, we figure out the logistics for you to put down some roots in San Diego."

"You're that confident?" I press a fist to my lips, listening for the catch. Murph doesn't make wagers he isn't sure he'll win.

He shrugs. "I want my best friend here. Oh, and Alana and the baby are doing well. She's available to stop by the house. Study long, study wrong…" Murph goads, jabbing a finger toward me as he shakes his head. An ear-to-ear grin covers his face before he passes me on the way back to the couch.

I follow him, sinking down near the armrest, still convinced Murph is wrong. Harper Sloane doesn't even want friendship.

"I think I'll take that wager," I say.

He nods.

"To be fair, I'm going to have a small advantage. Harper and I have two more Monopoly practices before the comedy show. One this Saturday, then another the morning before the show." I take off my glasses, using the hem of my shirt to clean the lenses. "Does that make you want to reconsider?"

"Not at all. If I'm right, it may work in my favor." He presses his fingers to his lips and squints. "Do you sit next to each other or play together during these practices, or is it more of a solitary situation?"

"Now that you mention it, we did sit and play with each other."

The double meaning occurs to me when I say the words. Given Murph's perverted mind, I instantly regret it.

"Well, at least it's Monopoly. You won't end up shooting your partner in the head."

We both laugh.

I slouch low into the couch and pick up the game controller. This Saturday, I guess I'll know for sure what Harper's deal is. I just need to keep my cool through these next two practices.

CHAPTER TEN

HARPER

ROLL THE DICE

ROX PULLS UP the spreadsheet on the monitor and steps back, letting Nadi and me review the progress we've made thus far. This week's good news: Our social media activity helped boost the BusinessFunder account. We're over three thousand in donations so far. The bad news: The last donation was almost a week ago.

"It's okay." I force a smile, but inwardly I'm freaking out. We can't afford to backslide. "We can't expect not to have *any* fluctuations."

It's not a lie. A lot of factors could've contributed. Weather, holiday spending recovery, tax season is around the corner.

Rox and Nadi nod along in silence surveying my expression. They know how much it means to me to give our best effort to the store.

They also know I'm prone to freak-outs.

"You going to be okay with this?" Rox asks, flitting a glance between me and the screen. It feels like she's really asking if I'm ready to call Dad yet.

I'm not. I don't know that I'll ever be.

My neck and jaw stiffen when she holds my gaze. Heat washes over my cheeks. I'm reaching, trying—unsuccessfully—to cover my rising panic level.

We've been working our butts off. After today, there're only two more practice sessions before the tournament, both grants have been denied, the loan is still pending, and we've barely made a dent in increasing our cash flow.

"Yeah, I'm good." Nothing about my tone is reassuring as I narrow my eyes to the top right corner of the monitor to check the time. My body tenses when I see it's already quarter after noon. *And no one is here.*

Frustration and anxiety mount in my chest.

Luckily, the small bell above the front door jingles.

Our attention snaps to the door as Walt shuffles through. He's wearing a black wheelbarrow shirt with his personal game board tucked under his arm. Without so much as a hello, he finds the same seat he sat in last weekend.

"Hey." Nadi turns back to us. "As far as I'm concerned, we're still on an ascending trend. I'm not worried."

"Me, either," Rox pipes up. "We've still got over a month before the tournament, and we've stopped the bleeding. Every sale is helping. I'm not giving up on the loan just yet."

As nervous as I am about slow growth, she's right. We're still in this. We deserve to feel good about what we've done so far, I think as pride courses through me.

Until the bell chimes again.

In walks the other half of the Jailbirds. Followed close behind by Declan in loose-fit jeans, a black Henley, and those damn NC-17-rated Lens World glasses. It's distracting.

Shouldn't his contacts be rested up by now?

I force a shaky smile, but he doesn't see it, so I roll my eyes to no one in particular.

Apparently, too hard though because my sisters in arms behind me hum conspiratorially.

"What was that about?" Rox asks.

Nadi folds her arms over her chest, cocking her head, more than interested in my answer.

"Nothing." I sigh. "I was thinking, I'm going to give it another fifteen minutes for stragglers, but that's it."

Their eyes dart over to the tables where there are three people. Walt, Eugene, and Declan. No one else needs practice or they've somehow got this tournament in the bag. The store is still empty. Which means I won't be sitting at a different table this week as planned.

So much for giving Declan his space.

"Don't make him wait too long." Rox traces her tongue over her lower lip, staring at Declan like she hasn't eaten in days, and he's a piping-hot order of McDonald's fries.

When I drag myself over to the table, I feel their eyes burning holes in my back.

The board is already set up. Our markers are at Go with my tiny top hat sandwiched between the Scottie dog and the wheelbarrow. The bank and cards are neatly organized in front of Eugene, and the three guys have their game faces on. After we roll to see who goes first, Walt starts the play.

Since it's just the four of us, we play the long game.

Walt and Eugene go for Marvin Gardens and Indiana Avenue respectively, which is just random given the goal is to rack up as many color-grouped properties and as much money as possible. But at least I snatch up the railroads and all three light blue properties.

Except, Declan buys New York Avenue, closing out his color-group, and immediately stacks them with three houses each.

"You sure you want to do that so soon?" Walt jerks up his thick, dark eyebrow, chuckling like it's an amateur move. Declan doesn't say a word.

The two of us are keeping it cool. Or we *were* keeping it cool.

The next trip around the board, Eugene lands on St. James Place, and Declan collects his payout without any fanfare, neatly stacking his rainbow money. Then Walt lands on Tennessee Avenue. And that's when I catch on to Declan's quiet attack.

By the time I land on New York Avenue, his stacked five-hundred-dollar bills are practically in front of me, almost overlapping my property cards. He's doing it on purpose to get a rise out of me—which I'm admittedly enjoying—but I keep sliding my stuff over an inch, resolved not to take the bait.

"Your turn, Scottie." My tone is upbeat with exaggerated friendliness as I slide the dice across the board.

He darts his eyes to me, but still refuses to speak.

Real mature.

His dog is on Park Place, and I'm praying he passes Go and lands on one of my light blue properties. It's a stretch, but by golly, he rolls a nine, and I bite back the urge to break out into cheers.

He smiles, then flippantly tosses the bills over to me in fives and tens.

I bite my tongue. There's no way I'm giving him the satisfaction of knowing he's getting to me.

Though, in an unexpected twist, the rest of us go back to landing on his property. Every time we do, the corner of Declan's mouth hikes up. I want to scoff because I'd seriously rather lose to Eugene than let Declan see me flustered.

And then it happens.

Walt goes bankrupt.

Last year's champ. Freaking penniless.

He blinks, looking down in wonderment at the space where he kept his cash and all his mortgaged properties turned over. I want to laugh about Walt's pregame goading and shit-talking, but I bite my tongue.

Is this the rematch I saw in Declan's eyes last practice? Payback for not accepting his friendship outright?

It's petty, on all fronts, but beating Walt is big. *Huge.*

Walter "Walt" Wheelbarrow Huang of San Diego, champion of last year's annual city Monopoly tournament, who took bets out on me, loses. *Even if it is a practice and not the actual tournament.* He takes a big fat *L.*

While his utter annihilation isn't by my own hands, pure joy bubbles up inside me.

As plotted, Declan bankrupts the entire table. *With Boardwalk and Park Place, no less.* I'm still too busy riding the tide about Walt to care, though. Until Declan stands and proceeds to scrape his searing-hot gaze over me.

"Good game," he says, but it's not like *Good game, guys, it was a lot of fun.* It feels more like *Good game, rematch successful.*

I don't know why I'm letting it get to me, but I'm hot.

"Done with the quiet game so soon?" I toss him a playful smile.

The weight of his stare lands hard and heavy on me. "Was there something you needed?"

I scratch my temple, amazed at how far he's taking this. "Nope. Just…never mind," I say, physically fighting the urge to throw out a snide comment. "If you need to go, go."

Walt and Eugene jolt to their feet, looking afraid to get caught in the crossfire.

"You two are the worst." Walt shakes his head, grabbing his jacket off the back of his chair before following Eugene to the exit.

Rox and Nadi have slipped out, too.

Again, Declan and I are alone.

"You're serious?" he asks.

I shoot him a wide-eyed *as a heart attack* expression daring him to lay it on me so we can finally have this out.

"Never mind?" He huffs out a mirthless laugh. "Are we finally flirting with having a real conversation?"

Nice word choice.

"Let's," I mutter with a jerk of my eyebrow.

"Where should we begin? The coffee shutdown." A smile spreads across his face. "Maybe the day I walked into this shop to *see* about registering for this tournament, and you couldn't get me out of here fast enough? That was fun."

I feel my defenses rising. "Is that how you remember it?"

"Let's not forget you thought I'd put this petty rivalry or whatever it is you have against me before being a decent human being. If that wasn't enough, then, in front of the woman at the hardware store..." Declan erases the distance between us. We're inches apart now. So close I can feel his breath swarm over my face and neck. It shuts me right up. "You walk away rather than acknowledge you know me. I'm just curious. How do you think that made me feel?"

My mouth is all the way open, my neck craned back to meet his intense gaze.

Before I can eke out the words, he answers his own question.

"Exactly. I'd say that covers the high points, Ms. Sloane," he hisses my name. "So, again, was there something else you needed, or are we going to keep playing these games?" Declan scrubs a hand over his face. "You know what? I think I *will* go."

But he doesn't move.

The rigid posture and hard lines surface, and I hate the idea of him clamming back up.

"I..." I can't catch my breath.

My chest heaves, and my heart nearly stops.

When you're so close you can hear the other person's shallow breaths and erratic heartbeat, one would think you'd give said person some space. A chance to take a step back and gather a couple coherent thoughts for a comeback. Not Declan Wilde, though. He's ruthless the way he holds my stare, daring me to refute his points. Daring me to blink.

My knees start to wobble, and every inch of my flesh tingles.

One second, he's bankrupting the table and checking rematch off his vendetta list. The next his mouth...is a whisper away.

I search his darkened eyes as they peer into me. The muscles at his jaw hard and tense. His chest rising and falling like he's on the precipice of...something. A point of no return.

"Oh, my God. I've caused you to malfunction..." He chuckles.

Then, I make my trademark, irrevocable mistake. I mean to drop my gaze, but it snags on his lips. And of course, there's the cocky lopsided smile.

Shit.

Because I need to do something with my hands, I swipe a misplaced Monopoly box off a rounder, beelining over to the display. I take my time straightening the boxes as I let air refill my lungs. I'm dizzy and electrified all at the same time. *What is happening?* I want to lunge for him and yell at him, but what for?

I flatten my hands on the table to hold myself upright with my back to him.

"You can go," I say after a beat.

It's been established that he isn't my real-life rival, but again, here's another new development. Another glimpse. A very distractingly sexy peek. And it's...it's definitively worth exploring.

When I can catch my breath.

At the muffled thud of his footsteps, I figure he should be satisfied. Smugly validated and clear to walk off into the sunset knowing he's beaten me at every game.

But the jingle of the bell doesn't come.

Instead, a pair of rigid, defined forearms cage me between the table and his hard chest. I jolt around so I'm sitting on the table.

"What are you doing?" Fire blazes through my veins. My flesh tingles. Every nerve ending in my body feels like it's tethered by a tiny string that tugs low and tight in my belly. He's impossibly close, and I'm hard-pressed to choose where to focus. His deliciously full lips, slightly parted and teasing me. Or his dark, penetrating brown eyes.

"Do you hate me, Harper?"

The lips.

Always.

My gaze is transfixed with their outline, the small movements, kissing together with every word. I can't look away.

Oh, my glorious God.

I feel my eyebrows draw together as I swallow. I want to tell him yes, firmly, with all the confidence I felt five minutes ago. But the lie won't pass my lips.

He levels his stare until we're eye to eye, lips nearly to lips. His expression is as tortured and screwed up as I feel inside.

"It's okay. The feeling's mutual," he says.

My emotions trudge the peak of this roller coaster we've been riding. I'm at the top, looking down just before I free-fall.

Declan brushes his lips over mine, and my middle melts. My heart does stop. Or my breathing. It's hard to tell which, it's so unexpected. So gentle and soft. Tentative sweeps and curious drags of his tongue like he's sampling his favorite flavor for the first time. He takes his time peppering more kisses as he searches my eyes.

He's waiting for me to protest. Push him away. But I'd have to be in my right mind to do that.

I seem to have lost it.

Or maybe Declan's taken it. He's stolen my breath and my voice. The ability to think straight. My entire body is on fire, sizzling with every touch, every sensation. I'm blindsided by a need so powerful I'm totaled on the spot.

Holy hell.

What's worse is I've forgotten how to move my lips. Yet, I'm desperate. To be closer, for him to deepen the kiss.

But, like a well-trained adversary, just when he has me where he wants me, he pulls away.

He traces his tongue over his lower lip. With his thumb, he swipes at the corners of his mouth, and the cocky grin tilts his lips.

"I guess I'll see you next Saturday. I'm, uh…I'm glad we had this talk."

And then he's gone.

In his wake, I'm speechless. Still kicking myself for not pushing him away before I got a taste. Now I'm craving him—which is like hating onions my whole life then tasting one as an adult and deciding my taste buds have grown up without my knowledge or consent. I don't care if it'll make me cry, or how cute its butt is in dark-washed jeans, I want the damn onion.

CHAPTER ELEVEN

HARPER

TAKE A RIDE ON THE READING

RIGHT AFTER THE first no-name comedian's jokes bomb, Nadi tosses me a wicked grin. "Girrrl…"

"Let me guess, Declan stopped by the store again?" I sip my cocktail. "I'm like a dating show savant. It's not even interesting when I can predict his next move before he even makes it."

Not that I saw that kiss coming…

Rox and Nadi both sigh conspiratorially.

"I'll give it to him, the kiss was…" *The only thing I've been able to think about since it happened a week ago. The reason I let Rox and Nadi run the third practice. Why my entire afternoon, I finalized the scavenger hunt with local business owners, so I wouldn't pathetically drool over him in front of the Jailbirds.*

I hold my palm up for my girls to take turns slapping it with high fives, while I suppress the heated memory of Declan's mouth moving against mine. His wet, hot tongue grazing my lips with precision. All I had to do was scoot back a couple more inches on the display table and pull him between my legs—

"All this competitive enemies and plotting stuff is so damn hot. I'm so dang jealous." Rox leans back in the booth fanning herself before she downs her cranberry vodka. "I'm going to need another drink."

"Shit. You and me both," Nadi says.

"Really, though? If he's going to throw flirting in as a tactic, he must know women do it better. All I had to do was ignore his little apology *email.*" I laugh even though I had to permanently delete it not to respond. "The man resorted to email. He was desperate. I bet he looked so defeated walking into Love & Games asking where I was today."

Nadi giggles. "You should have seen him. It was sad. When I leaned in, he really thought I was about to tell him where you were." She gasps for air, her hand pressed to her heart. "I'm like, *Friend, I'm going to need you to learn to read the room. Ask before you kiss next time or risk losing a limb, but your instincts may not have been too far off.*"

My stomach hardens. "You didn't."

"I did." Nadi nods until she senses it's sunk in.

"What did he say?" I cringe.

"He's all, *Are you saying what I think you're saying?* and I'm like, *If you think I'm saying go get a fresh haircut, spray on some cologne, and find something other than Monopoly to talk about, you might just get to take a ride on the Reading.*" Her eyes light up with amusement.

I want to curl up in a dark hole and hide.

"Right?" Rox is breathless as a snort-laugh slips out. "Like pick a card and take your chances already."

I shake my head, completely mortified. All I can do is laugh though because my friend is wild and unpredictable.

Cat's out of the bag, I guess.

The three of us burst into a fit of giggles. We laugh until we can't breathe. Or, until the man a few tables in front of us shushes us and gives us the evil eye. Evidently, a full-house comedy show isn't the best place to have a panel discussion on the error of Declan Wilde's strategies.

"Let's give him another hand and take a short break," the emcee says. "Refresh your drinks at the bar. Then come on back for Anthony Goode, ladies and gentlemen."

We join in the applause.

Other than the ripped vinyl seats snagging my new jeans and the first comedian's bombed jokes, I'm having a great time.

"Ooh, I can't wait for Anthony Goode to roast someone," I say, fully expecting the girls to agree, but their eyes are fixed just over my shoulder.

"Don't look now"—Rox sucks her teeth in annoyance—"X marks the spot."

My shoulders tense as I follow her line of vision.

Literally. My ex, Mark.

"Hi, there!" His jovial, corporate-climber voice booms over the din of the club.

"Hey." I drag the word out, but the landing is flat.

Mark shoves his hands into his khaki pants. "Happy New Year is in order, I guess."

"Yeah. How's it been so far?"

I lean out of the booth to hug him. He holds it a little too long for my comfort, but I'm not even mad. As I twist back against the seat, I notice Murph and my new favorite craving walking toward us.

Declan's gaze darts between Mark and me when they reach our table.

"Hey." It doesn't land flat. The word comes out on his familiar throaty baritone, hard and sharp.

It feels like we're in a tournament matched up by skill—Mark, Boring Beige, the sweet safety ex versus Declan, Scottie Dog, the brooding fantasy doctor. They stare each other down, ready to mortgage and bankrupt the heck out of each other.

Except Mark may be the secret five-hundred-dollar bill hidden under the board.

All is fair in…showing another man a little extra attention to make the one I want jealous.

"Mark, this is Declan. He's a participant in the Monopoly tournament this year." I rest my hand on Mark's forearm, downplaying the whole sexy doctor/rugged renovator bit.

Mark extends his hand, his shoulders drawn back, chin high. His stance says he's ready for the challenge.

Then Declan introduces himself. "Nice to meet you. Dr. Declan Wilde."

Uh-oh, using the title. Touched a nerve.

He shakes Mark's hand. Well, his whole arm in a show of strength.

Everything about Declan is tense, hard. His posture is rigid as he straightens in direct contrast with his clothes. He's in loose-fit jeans and a denim button-down rolled at the sleeves. Tonight, he's sans the sexy glasses but the new tapered fuck-boy haircut is purely orgasmic. All of which tells me two things: he's taking Nadia's advice, and he came to play.

I'm game.

The instant he releases Mark's hand, he turns his stony brown eyes and cocky half grin on me.

"Looks like you could use a refill." Declan wedges his wide strong frame between Mark and me to help me out of the booth. Then, in the most gangster move yet, he rests his hand on the small of my back before turning to Mark. "Nice meeting you, Matt."

Holy shit.

My mouth falls open as I angle myself in the direction of the bar, hating how much I love the way my skin sizzles beneath his touch.

When we reach the bar, I don't have time to analyze it like I'm dying to because Declan settles on the stool next to me.

"Uh-oh. First, you're hunting me down at the store, now here at the bar." I toss him an exaggerated look of disbelief. "Careful, someone might think you like me." I dip my fingers into my hair, suppressing the urge to look at him.

In his typical easy way, he leans back on the barstool, folds his arms, and crosses his legs at the ankles. "I sent you a message last weekend. Email, actually. It wasn't anything super important, but—"

"I saw it," I mutter evenly.

My ego bruises slightly when he doesn't confirm that he does like me. *That he's been thinking about the kiss, too, which why would he? He's leaving in a couple weeks.*

He's tight-lipped as a group of people pass by us.

Then the lines of his face harden. "I didn't see a response, so I assumed it went to your junk mail."

"No. I received it."

When I turn to face Declan, a self-satisfied smile curves his lips. "You like me." In classic *always sure of himself Declan Wilde* form, it isn't a question.

"Yeah, okay..." Heat burns my cheeks. I roll my eyes like he's way off base.

"At first, I thought, *What have I done wrong to this woman?*" He balances his weight on the barstool, bouncing back, his grin growing wider. "Then, when I kissed you, and you didn't kiss me back..." He trails off, but I can practically see his ego expanding.

There's a burst of laughter off to our right, so perfectly timed.

"Okay"—I hold up a palm—"you're reaching—"

"No, hear me out. Over the short time I've known you, not once have you shied away from giving me a piece of your mind." He tucks his lower lip between his teeth and nods like he's organizing his thoughts. "But you didn't push me away when I kissed you. No response to my email. Then, I show up tonight, and you throw that guy in my face but let me guide you to the bar."

He's not wrong.

The man is reading me like a book.

The day he kissed me in the shop, I'd held my breath and stared at his mouth like a dog in heat. Him calling me *Ms. Sloane* was as seductive as if he'd called me Mrs. Robinson. For goodness' sake, I should've expected him to snuff out the little white lie I've been telling myself. I'm not going to admit it to him though… Not yet. *Or at all?*

"Are you about done coaxing your oversized ego?" I've got to raise my voice for him to hear me over the chatter of the crowd.

It's the strangest thing. When he smiles, it's nice. Sexy even. But when he's intense and the veins at his temple throb, when the crease between his eyebrows deepens and the cords of his neck tighten… *Holy shit.* I can practically feel the flames sweeping off him, and it is hot.

Libido-detonating hot.

The heat curls down my spine as my mind reels back to Rox's comment a few minutes ago, and my stomach clenches. It's definitely the *competitive enemies and plotting* thing that makes arguing with Declan so hot.

Like, shut up and kiss me already.

"There she is." He releases a deep, throaty laugh as he watches me, and that fire rushes up from my neck to my cheeks. "I really appreciate how eager you are to die on this hill." He chuckles.

"Says the man who entered a Monopoly tournament to psych me out."

This time, a full-body laugh comes out, boisterous and alive. "Someone is afraid of a little competition, I see." He clutches his chest. "If I recall correctly, I won the game. Maybe you're just a sore loser."

I huff out a laugh.

"Maybe you don't know how to let loose and have fun. You're scared I'm going to beat you in the tournament."

A smile quirks his lips. The hard lines of his face soften. Something shifts in his tone as he averts his gaze. "Maybe you shouldn't have looked at me like that back at the store."

The low timbre of his voice sends a shiver over my skin that might as well be his fingers trailing my spine.

"Like what?" I risk stealing a glance at him.

The muted light contours his beautiful face in shadows. Heat and mischief blaze in his eyes. He licks his lips like it's a promise of pleasure, and I can already feel myself leaning in.

But then he answers me.

"Like you felt the same intense pull, drawing us together."

My head swims. I shrug even though I'm anything but indifferent when it comes to Declan. If anything, I feel too much—more than I'm comfortable admitting.

Declan reaches his hand out and chucks my chin up. The familiar heat burns in his eyes—a mix of lust and humility—and it catches me off guard. I suck in a breath, but he doesn't withdraw. Instead, he traces the curve of my cheek with the pad of his thumb.

Even though I shouldn't, I lean into his hand.

"What if I don't want to be your rival anymore?" His voice is gruff, just above a whisper.

The sound around us fades.

A war wages inside me between loving the warmth of his touch and loathing how completely it unsettles me. I need to do something. Say something. Tell him I don't want to be rivals either. But I can't get past the kiss, and I'm scared to start anything when there's a marked expiration date.

I need him to tell me this isn't just another game to win.

Declan slowly drops his hand, and while I hate how cold my skin feels in its absence, I manage to keep my knees from buckling.

I slide my hands into the back pockets of my jeans. I don't trust myself not to reach for him.

Around us, the music blares to life. The emcee is back on the mic, and the show is starting.

I couldn't care less.

Static cracks the air as someone taps the microphone. "This next guy is from Chicago. He's been working stand-up for over ten years. You might have seen him on *Wild Comedy* or *Knock Knock* on Flixshow. Please welcome..."

In a move I'm not nearly prepared for, Declan gently tugs me between his legs by the waistband of my jeans until our faces are inches apart. He slides his strong hand through my hooked arms at the small of my back, coaxing me closer still.

"I like you, Harper."

My heart somersaults in my chest. Hearing him say the words. Knowing I'm his choice. I'm weightless.

He's changed everything about the way I'm hardwired to respond. This moment is petrifying and perfect. Just like that, I shove down the heavy, hollow feeling in my stomach. All my reservations. Something inside me shifts. Snaps. This may not go anywhere beyond this fledgling moment, but I realize I want it to.

Not just another kiss. So much more, and I don't want to keep fighting it.

It's too hard.

Our eyes are locked, but neither of us speaks. We let the silence stretch between us, but he worriedly searches my face.

"You smell like—"

"Like what?" The words rush out on a desperate whisper. It's a strange unrelenting curiosity, almost defensive. I need to know how he sees me, hears me, feels me, *smells* me—

"I don't know if it's your shampoo or your body wash or a combination." His voice is low and tentative. "It's a sweet, torturing mix of strawberries and flowers."

My pulse quickens, and my breath stutters as he levels me with a hungry stare. I'm a tangled mess of throbbing, liquid anticipation and raging, hot hunger. He's on my skin, settling right below the surface. Desire hums through my blood in a slow burn of need.

Then, he leans in.

Our lips are a breath apart, and my heart lodges in my throat when the mic crackles, pulling me back to reality.

"Are you guys seeing this shit, too?" A collective rumble of laughter fills the room. *Anthony Goode.* "I'm up here trying to get a few fucking laughs. Meanwhile, look at this couple at the bar. They look like they want to go at it right here."

Declan and I stiffen.

Please let there be another couple at the bar who's caught Anthony Goode's attention.

"Don't think I won't stand here and watch. I mean, is this a fucking comedy show or a motel? They look horny as fuck. Don't they, y'all?"

More laughter.

I squeeze my eyes closed. "He's talking about us, isn't he?"

"Yep." Declan slowly removes his hand from my waist. A nervous chuckle shakes his shoulders. "And the entire club is watching us."

Awesome.

"Should we get out of here?" he asks.

Like only the master of comedy would know to do, Anthony Goode drives his punchline home as we pivot toward the exit for our walk of shame. "Oh, don't stop on our account. There's a Sleep Lodge down the street. Make sure you've got more than one condom, bro. Y'all might go a few rounds tonight."

The funny part is Anthony Goode isn't wrong.

CHAPTER TWELVE

DECLAN

ROLL AGAIN

HARPER AND I run out the club like we are being chased. The street is mostly empty aside from a serious-faced bouncer and a few stray pedestrians, but I'm not ready to stamp an expiration on this night.

"Did you see the looks on Rox's and Murph's faces?"

She digs around the bottom of her purse, giggling. "Right? We're standing there getting crucified, and they practically break out in cheers."

"Your friend, Mark, looked like he wanted to murder me."

Our laughter fades as she pulls out her phone and taps at the keys.

"I wanted to die on the spot," she says.

All I can concentrate on is the teensy Rideo rideshare app open on her screen. This thing with Harper was supposed to be about the tournament and answering Harper's challenge. I was supposed to be keeping it casual, making a friend while I worked on Pop's house, but...

"You're leaving?" I blurt out.

Her eyes flutter up to mine, and all the light is gone from them. The dark forest green is shrouded in thunderclouds of smoke and mirrors.

"I…" she starts then trails off like it just hits her what I'm asking. "Oh. I came with Nadia. I'm just going to have a Rideo pick me up. I didn't want to assume—"

"Actually, I was hoping you wouldn't mind hanging out a little longer to finish talking." *Pick up where we left off in the club.* "We don't have to go anywhere. Maybe walk down University?" I smile and look up. "The sky is clear tonight."

It's midnight blue, blanketed with bright stars and promise.

Harper's smile is tentative but warm. A light pink blush dusts her bronze cheeks, and I'm lost in the sexy way she pulls her bottom lip between her teeth. She drops her eyes back to her phone and cancels the ride.

"Okay." A soft smile spreads over her face.

We both turn toward the neon-lit shops, walking in easy silence.

As I squint down the street, I can almost pinpoint the dentist, the Thai restaurant, and the tattoo place I passed after leaving Java Joy the day we met.

"Any chance we can start over?"

Harper presses her lips together, considering what I'm asking. For both of us to let down our guards and get to know each other. As much as I know I'm going to hear it from Murph, I don't *just* want to hook up with Harper. I want to know her. I want to keep laughing and playing and fighting, and if she'll let me, make up with her.

"I'll start with something simple," I say, breaking the ice. "It's a new year. Any resolutions or goals? How's everything going so far?"

"How's everything going so far for you?"

My mood lifts. "Is there a reason why you're answering my question with a question?"

She gives me a quick glance, and I silently plead with her to humor me.

"Fine." She sighs. "Love & Games is doing pretty well. The community has come together to get the word out about the tournament, and Nadi is a freaking rock star with our social media. I'm hoping we'll have a big turnout for the scavenger hunt next Friday."

"And you, personally?"

She rolls her eyes good-naturedly, seeing right through my ploy to know more about her. "I'm...I'm okay. My dad is getting married for the *fourth* time this June, and I've agreed to go." She shrugs. "I have you to thank for this—after browsing through those color swatches with you, I'm also considering painting my bedroom a different color."

"I see."

Harper's face scrunches, and it's everything I can do not to laugh aloud.

"You see?"

"Yeah, I just... No far-off vacation or bungee jumping? No skydiving or plan to take over the world? I thought you might've made some fun resolutions or wanted to do something spontaneous."

Her mouth falls open, and before I can brace myself, she playfully jabs me in the shoulder. It's a grade-school *I'm going to fight you so I don't kiss you* thing, and I'm loving every second of it.

I like her like this. Just Harper. Playful, easy, open.

"Ouch. I thought we were past the crazy coffee lady thing." I rub my arm before she cranks her arm back for another shot while laughing uncontrollably.

"You—"

This time, I catch her fist. When she tries the other, I catch that one, too. I've got both of her delicate wrists in my right hand. I'm lost in the moonlit glow on her golden-brown skin. The slight pout of her full lips. The fire blazing in her forest-green eyes.

I feel so much, it takes me a few seconds to register all the laughter is gone, replaced by a heavy silence. I pull her close against me, binding her hands to my side, picking up where we left off in the club. When her lips part, though, I'm the weak one.

I'm the one all tied up in knots—a prisoner to her piercing gaze.

I don't just like Harper. I want to see where this could really go.

The realization settles on my chest with the weight of a freight train. *How can I want her so bad after such a short time?*

Harper's eyes are wide and searching as she watches me lower my mouth to hers. When our lips touch, my heart stops. Every insecurity I have latches on to my throat, squeezing, strangling the breath from me.

For the second time, I'm on the lonely end of a one-sided kiss.

My eyes are still closed when I release her hands and straighten my posture. I can't move. I'm paralyzed in the past. It's Penelope telling me she doesn't love me all over again. It's me failing to read the room. I don't know how to accept it or how to walk away with my chin up.

I swallow and take a deep breath, but then I feel slight pressure and open my eyes. Harper's hands are flat on my chest as she stretches up on her toes and comes within a centimeter of my lips. Her touch burns through all the layers of my clothes. My skin prickles with electricity. Heat surges through my veins as I scrutinize her face. I'm blindsided.

Every inch of me craves this woman.

"Just so you know, I need my hands free when I kiss." Her voice is a warm hug, reaching round and stilling my nerves. Affection and heat gather in her sparkly eyes as they flicker back to life. She's beaming and beautiful as she slides her hands over my stomach, bunching my shirt in her fists.

How many times have I noticed her hands, watched the flutter of her fingers, read their movement, wondered what it would feel like to have them set free on my skin? I should have known they needed to be free.

"Is that so?" I grip her hips, reveling in the trace of her touch.

Harper answers me by brushing her lush lips against mine. She works her hands over my nape before wildly scraping her fingers behind my ears and into my hair.

I answer with deep strokes of my tongue, pulling, tasting, savoring her moan.

The kiss is so much more than I imagined.

It's light and dark—no gray. Sun and moon. Incandescent bursts of fire as I explore this radiant and celestial being. We share sensual licks and sucks, sweet nips, and blazing-hot bites. Our hands roaming free. Everything about it is steeped with longing. Every stroke of our tongues is purposeful.

It's not the hot sex Murph talked about. But if this is what we've been working up to, it all feels worth it.

The low, sultry rumble of laughter that slips between our lips is pure magic. When she slowly pulls back, I'm speechless…breathless.

"So much better with my hands free, don't you think?" she asks as if I would ever be able to debate the amazing merits of her wandering hands under my clothes, skidding across my skin.

Gently, I tug her arms loose until her soft hands are in mine. One by one, I lift them to my mouth to kiss them, lingering a little too long.

"Do you know how much I think about your hands?"

As she drops her gaze to look at our intertwined fingers, I follow her line of vision. Against hers, mine are so much larger, cooler in hue. She has creative, expressive hands. I'm just lucky to be connected to her.

A flash of worry dilutes the joy on her face. "Is something wrong with them?" she asks.

"No. But they tell on you." I smile, unsure of how honest I want to be. "Sometimes, I think they know how you feel even before you do. When you're nervous or antsy, they're wild, flailing. You drum on walls and tables. When you're angry, they shake slightly with a small twitch like you're a second from balling them up at some unlucky person—maybe me."

This earns me a musical laugh. Then she looks up at me. "I don't know...I'm always unsure of what to do with them."

"Maybe you'll let me hold them."

Without hesitation, Harper weaves her left hand in my right one and tightens her grip.

For a few minutes, we walk in uncertain silence. I know I told Nadia I'd find something other than Monopoly to talk about, but when I see the way Harper lights up, I don't fight it when the conversation circles around to this game that brought us together.

She leans into my side in a fit of giggles over a Scottie dog joke.

"Touché, Tops," I say, rubbing it in.

"We all go by our token names. I still prefer the original ones, but there are a bunch from every edition. I'm the top hat, as you know. For me, it's about holding my head up high, which now that I say it, sounds even more geeky."

"What about Wheelbarrow Walt?"

"Ugh. Walter Huang." She closes her eyes and shakes her head. "I've known him since high school. He works at Anderson's Hardware. I beat him once years ago. Like completely obliterated his game. He's been volleying for a rematch ever since."

"Ah."

"He has a huge Hasbrothers following, too, but he's basically in twentieth grade right now. Seriously childish."

"Wait." I stop in my tracks. My smile too wide to contain. "Did you just say Hasbrothers?"

Her gaze darts to the ground then up to me, and she

swallows.

"It's too late now. You might as well tell me everything."

At least ten seconds go by while she seems to weigh the pros and cons of letting me into her world.

"There's an entire language. You have no idea." It's almost a whisper, but she doesn't even blink. "Hasbrothers. Hasbros. Hasbromance. Hasbrothels. Hasbrowns. Hasbribery. Hasbroke. Should I keep going?" She cringes.

I don't dare move, but I feel my lips quiver.

A quiet pause simmers between us before we burst with laughter. It's painfully clear I had no clue how hardcore Monopoly fans could be. It's one thing to grow up playing games with Pop, learning the ins and outs. Every year devoting two months of our lives to buying Happy Meals daily for the mini-Hasbro games.

"What did I just get myself into? I mean, are you part of a"—I bite the inside of my cheek not to laugh—"Hasbrothel?"

Any barrier wedged between us before tonight fades away. The lingo, the game, how deep into the Hasbro Nation Harper Sloane is, they're all a virtual wrecking ball knocking down our walls. We laugh.

A lot.

"Wait..." She holds up a finger and digs in her purse before whipping out a folded paper packet.

"What's this?"

Amusement lights her eyes as she shoves it toward me.

"TIPS FOR WINNING MONOPOLY," I read the title aloud, mind blown and feeling way out of my league.

"What?" Traces of a laugh seep into her tone.

My tongue is clamped between my lips as I nod. "So, you just carry this around with you at all times, just in case you need to take down some rogue Hasbrother who's gotten out of hand?"

Harper's laugh intoxicates me.

With a long inhale, my attention darts from the page to her wide-eyed gaze and sweet smile. I can't take my eyes off her...off those lush lips. "Dare I ask what the Sloane Twist is?"

The second the words leave my mouth, Harper squeezes her eyes shut. "Ugh...why did you have to see that?" She groans and peeks one open. "I may or may not have been obsessed with the movie *The Cutting Edge* when I was younger. There was this impossible figure skating move called the Pamchenko Twist."

"Not sure how figure skating relates but this is getting interesting."

"Shut up," she says, giggling.

I halfway expect her to reach out and swat me. She has a megawatt smile as she bites the tip of her finger. The gesture is sexy beyond belief.

"It's a strategy my dad and I came up with."

Heat swarms my neck and my cheeks, and I do my best to focus on the paper where it's safe. "Guaranteed win, huh?"

She cringes and nods. "You're laughing, but it's not easy. I shouldn't even be showing you this since you're technically still my opponent." *I must admit I love that small technicality.* "We both need to practice this if we want to beat Walt."

The *we* and *practice* run warm in my chest.

After a few seconds, I drum my fingers on my thigh.

"Okay. Well, since I don't have any surefire winning strategies named after me, let's do it. I'm in. Next practice, I want you to treat me as your protégé so we can pull off this takedown."

At the end of the block, Harper and I turn back toward the club where I'm parked.

She clears her throat like she's ready to get down to business. "So, two questions for you. First, why are you considering moving from Vegas to San Diego? Second"—Harper peeks up at me sheepishly—"how'd the painting go?"

For a second, I consider telling her about Penelope. But everything about this moment feels uncertain. Fragile, like we need to be careful with it.

No point in weighing us down so early on.

"To your first question, there are a lot of factors. Pop's house. A new challenge working with Murph and the ENT practice. Plus—and this is going to sound really cliché—I just needed a new adventure. New city. New people. New life, you know?"

She nods, and I'm grateful she doesn't ask me to elaborate on the old.

"I think about it sometimes, too," she says. "Just pick up and go one day, but then I remember this is where my family is. Where the business we built from our kitchen table is..." Harper trails off, and for a few minutes, it's nothing but the whistling breeze and the faint buzz of the city around us.

When she doesn't finish her thought, I pick up where I left off. "As far as painting... I've done nothing." I laugh. "After the mold situation, there's been a lot of waiting while the plumbing was fixed, new insulation, installing the new drywall. I'm ready to start tomorrow."

She blinks up at me, and her expression shifts.

Our stride is so slow we're nearly standing still.

"Okay, don't read into this but...want some help?" She flashes a small smile that reaches up to my heart and squeezes.

I'm reading directly between the lines.

"Will it be weird if I say yes?"

She shakes her head.

A surge of warmth courses through me and my heart skitters. "Listen, Harper. I know we're just getting to a place where you don't want to feed me to a pack of ravenous wolves..." A smile dances across her lips. "I'm enjoying tonight, but I want to spend time getting to know you."

"Me, too."

We're almost to the car, and I feel the tension building as we near the club.

Harper tucks a few flyaway strands behind her ear. She seems fidgety, like she's as unsure as I am navigating this new dynamic building between us. Are we friends? Enemies playing games? Is this truce just for tonight?

Whatever this is, the easiness, I can't ignore the fragile feeling of this lightness. I'm so scared one wrong word or move will jeopardize it. So, I squeeze her hand and slow to a stop. I lean in and kiss her forehead just as the sky breaks open.

The rain comes down in a warm drizzle, dotting her beautiful face, but she doesn't move.

"Declan..." The way she breathes my name, I feel it coursing, pulsing through my veins.

Then, she stretches up to me, and runs the pad of her thumb over my bottom lip. She clasps her hands behind my neck, kissing me. It's more desperate than the first kiss. It's hungry, urgent like she'd been holding back, and now I've given her a reason to let go.

Maybe she's good with casual, or she feels the ground moving beneath our feet, too.

Up until this moment, we've been in an endless loop of two steps forward, one step back, going nowhere. Finally, it feels like we're moving ahead. Whatever obstacles were in the way before, they're gone.

"Harper…" My heart pounds against my chest as I weave my hands along the curve of her waist and the kiss intensifies.

When she moans, a dam comes crashing down inside me.

We're right back where we were before we left the comedy club. The intense pull, drawing us together. I don't know how it happened, but every second I'm near this woman, the magnetic field around us grows stronger, pulls me in deeper.

After she breaks the kiss, the only thing I know is that I don't want this night to end.

CHAPTER THIRTEEN

HARPER

THE LONG GAME

"JUST WANT TO make sure you get in," Declan says from the driver's seat.

My night never ended outside the comedy club. Declan and I ducked aimless and carefree in and out of the rain talking about everything under the moon until it turned into the sun.

It's just before nine in the morning, but he'll be back to pick me up by ten.

After the hormone wake-up call of our electrifying see-you-later kiss, who needs sleep? My knees are shaky, and my skin is still tingling. The minutes can't windmill around fast enough.

"Spend the day with me."

He'd mouthed it into the kiss. The contours of his voice so raspy and gruff. Ragged with a desperate breathlessness I felt skimming the surface of my skin. As tired as I was, I didn't have that kind of strength to say no.

Good God, I've never wanted a man so bad.

And I know it feels fast. Like we're rushing in, jumping over vital steps in getting to know each other before we really get our footing. The momentum is scary and thrilling, but every layer of my defense is unraveling, and I'm hanging on by a thread. I want to feel these feelings without worrying about timing and the fact he might not choose to stay in San Diego.

All I want to do is let go.

I shuffle up the stairs and jam my hands into my purse, searching for my keys while he waits for me to get inside. The hum of his car running feels like a metronome ticking, my heart the weighted pendulum taking swings against my chest. I'm a wound-up spring because of a few kisses like a teenager.

"It's okay, you can go. I know they're in here somewhere," I call out nervously and prop the luggage-sized tote on my knee for better leverage, giving it a vigorous shake.

The sound of clinking pocket change and jingling keys zips through the air.

"I hear them." I flash him a reassuring smile, but he doesn't pull away.

Why didn't I find them before I got out of the car?

I drop my chin and peer into the junky depths of my bag. My finger pokes through a rip in the lining, but the curved, smooth, heart-shaped metal of my locket sends a chill down my spine, and I gasp.

I thought I'd lost it.

With both hands, I hold the leather edges and spill over onto my knees on the porch. I use my keys to widen the tear and free the locket, and my heart breathes a sigh of relief.

"Oh, Daddy," I whisper to myself.

I get lost in a memory of the night Daddy gave Rox and me the golden trinkets. It was his second wedding when he'd married Vanessa. I remember how beautiful I'd thought she was with her face-framing highlights and green-gold eyes against warm bronze skin. She'd stood there with Rox, a miniature version of her in a ruffled ball gown with sunny, loose brown curls and pinched-pink cheeks.

Her coppery brown eyes were unmistakably Daddy's.

All those years I'd wished for a sister to play with, and it turned out I had one all along. They'd just never told me about her.

I'd been standing behind a tall table with a pale yellow cloth twisted and tied around it with a cream bow. I watched him with his new wife and daughter. I couldn't understand how we'd switched places.

"Congratulations, Harrison. Vanessa. All the best to you," Mom had said, and my mouth about fell open.

As my parents hugged, I was still wrapping my mind around what it meant to Mom and me. How Dad got a do-over with a brand-new family. How disposable I'd felt. Like he'd gotten everything he needed from the old model, and now he was replacing us with a new wife and daughter who looked almost scarily like us.

"Don't be rude," Mom had said to me. "Come on over here and tell your father and Vanessa congratulations. Wish them well." She'd said it like she wasn't angry to be replaced, a charity case to throw money at.

I was lost in a storm of emotions—sadness, irrevocably wounded, tossed out, and replaced. How could she have wished them well when he was hers, too?

A knot forms in my belly remembering how Dad fished his hands into the breast pocket of his fancy tuxedo, pulled his hand free, then whipped it behind his back only to stretch out two tightly wound fists with his knuckles up.

He'd played this game of "which hand" with Rox, too.

Rox and I tapped the velvety firm backs of his hands at the same time. He turned his fists over and sprawled his fingers open to reveal two small golden lockets, for "Daddy's Girl." Or "Girls." It was plural now.

"You okay?"

The worried tone of Declan's voice snaps me back to the present, and I shake off the memory.

I fling my keys up in the air as I get to my feet. "Found them!"

Declan hesitates for a beat like he's weighing the truth in my answer, almost like he knows I'm not okay.

After a few seconds, the driver's side door swings open, and he rounds the hood in wide strides toward me.

I channel all my nerves into the heart-shaped metal in my hand and squeeze.

When Declan reaches me, he slides both hands up to my nape and into my hair. His breathing is shallow as he searches my eyes. But he doesn't say a word. The wounds are all over my face.

Before I can speak, he backs me against the front door, and his lips crash down on mine, biting and licking my wounds away.

The fact that he kisses first and asks questions later is every reason to let go with him.

"HOW WAS THE Sleep Lodge?"

I close the front door behind me and glance over at Rox on the couch. She's got a huge grin on her face.

"Good morning to you, too." I bite back my own guilty grin as I check my watch. I can spare five minutes to give Rox the fun-sized version of last night and still have forty minutes to shower and put on something to make his jaw drop.

I flash Rox a quick look. "I've got to get dressed, but…I think I can multitask…"

Rox is off the couch in a whirl of blankets as she trails me down the hall to my room. I'm already shimmying out of my jeans when she gets right to the dirt. "I saw you all pressed up against the door. Did you all…?" She lets the sordid details die on her tongue.

This is why I love her so much. Why no matter how much we butt heads or how we came to be family, I'll never regret my sister.

"Did I shave my legs?"

She knows good and well I only shave under two conditions: a hot date or I'm wearing a dress.

"Ugh, so then what? You held hands and talked?" She scoffs as if it's the worst thing two people could get into.

"And got kissed so well it was almost as *good* as sex. Ran in the rain…talked and laughed…" I tick off the amazing events of last night, then pause for effect while she eats out of the palm of my hands. "Got felt all the way up."

Rox squeals and claps. She's a sucker for romance.

"So, you're saying you got a little taste of the good stuff? When are you seeing him again?"

I nod and glance at my watch as I slip it from my wrist and hop into the shower. "Thirty-seven minutes, to be precise. Will you grab me a new razor under the sink?"

The squeak of the cabinet door opening is followed by rustling noises before the shower curtain is yanked open with a whoosh of cold air. Rox has the razor in her right hand, but her left arm is draped over her stomach, and her eyebrows are practically in her hairline.

"Excuse me? Are we planning on letting fine ass Dr. Declan Wilde finally get a little taste after the hard time you gave him?"

Because she's called me on my shit and I don't have the time nor a good enough zinger to come back at her with, I flick soap suds in her face and snatch the razor from her hand.

"Oh, so that's a yes. Are we letting him slide into your—hopefully—sexy, pink lace panties, you little Sleep Lodge hussy?" She laughs.

I pull the curtain closed then peek my head out. "We are not letting him slide anywhere. I am, though…hopefully."

Rox snaps her fingers for emphasis.

"Okay. Well, I'm just glad you're making decisions and being proactive about it. All that Monopoly rivalry is paying off." Her tone is laced with pride. "What's the plan?"

There's silence for a minute because I can't talk while I shave.

"Breakfast then check out his grandfather's house. Next week, I'm going to help him paint—and maybe decorate. I'll probably work in a little Monopoly before I ravish him," I say as I rinse off.

"See. Priorities. Sex should always come before food, and definitely before a freaking board game."

We both laugh because she's right, but what would I look like screwing him in the car then trying to muster up the energy to eat, shop, and play when I'm already working on negative sleep hours?

It doesn't sound that bad.

After I towel off and head to my room, Rox helps me pick out a cute purple jumpsuit and a perfume she "guarantees" will make him horny. Judging by the tent in his jeans this morning, he needs no help at all.

"In all seriousness, though, what's the plan? Knowing you, you'll find a way to overthink it. Your nerves will get in the way, and let's face it, your flirting isn't exactly up to *Door-to-Door Dates* status," she says, referencing our favorite reality dating show.

I hadn't given it much thought. I figured we'd eat and get comfortable, and whenever he kissed me, I'd escalate things somehow—maybe whisper something sexy in his ear.

Shit. "You're right. What do I do?"

She chews the inside of her cheek and darts her eyes from me to my closet before a light bulb seems to flash. "On second thought, scratch the jumpsuit." She slices her hand into the hangers and pushes a section back until she gets to my summer dresses. "This pink one. Ooh, and men are suckers for the sweet, girly look. With your legs and some light makeup—"

"That one makes my butt look big."

"Exactly. If he's smart, he likes curves, too. With that pink lace bra and panty set, he will not be able to resist you." Rox winks as if this is the *coup de grâce* to diminish his willpower. But then she pauses from her masterminding for a sec. "Unless you want to go commando. It's cold, but fewer barriers. I'm just saying..."

"I think I'll stick with underwear, thanks."

"Okay, I was just trying to help you reach your goal."

By the time I'm dressed and "glowing" with all the highlighting bronzer magic she's dusted on me, it's nine fifty. My worries about starting something with him when he might be leaving resurface, and my nerves are shot.

Evidently, it shows.

"Can you please not ruin this for us?" Rox murmurs. "Sex is supposed to be fun, Harp."

"I really like him, but I'm so out of practice, and what if I can't do casual? He's not even sure he's staying in San Diego. What if he leaves? What if you're right and this is just the *competitive enemies* thing?"

Rox shoots me a sidelong glance and waves me off.

"Stop overthinking everything." She slices the air with her hand. "Casual or not, you deserve mindblowing, fireworks sex for a change without second-guessing it." *Fair point.* "As far as him leaving, you said he hasn't decided either way, so...that's that. And I hope you don't believe anything about competitive enemies. If nothing else, this man has proven he's a worthy adversary up for the challenge."

"Maybe I'm just nervous and scared the magic will be gone when he gets here."

"Magic? What do you want, beach sex with sand in all the wrong places or some crazy cardio position that leaves you with burning thighs and leg cramps the first time out? Don't make it complicated. Let it happen however it happens."

Another good point.

I giggle at this scenario.

Then, worry boomerangs back to me.

"Lord have mercy, woman." Rox takes one look at my face and sighs. "You're opening up, and what this guy brings out in you is..."

The way she trails off, she doesn't have to finish the sentence. I know it's excitement. It's fun. A happiness I haven't felt since...I can't remember when. Declan makes me want to roll the dice.

I smile. "I'm having so much fun."

"Yes. Play and be carefree for a change." She throws up hands up victoriously. "When you see him, I want you to kiss him. Let him make your knees weak. When the time is right, take him in your hands. Lick his neck and behind his ears. Rub your hands over every muscly tendon on his body. Then, when you can't take it anymore, let go."

Well, shit.

"Right. Okay. Got it." I'm pumped, and I feel like a hairless, leggy sex vixen on a mission to claim the best orgasm ever.

CHAPTER FOURTEEN

DECLAN

ADVANCE TO GO

AMUSEMENT AND HEAT dance in Harper's eyes as she leans in and gives me soft kisses on my lips. She lingers, deepening, tasting me like we've done this a thousand times before. Her hands are wild and wandering, and I'm seconds from my semi going fully hard.

"I could be wrong, but...I think someone missed me," I tease.

There's a closeness between us that wasn't there twenty-four hours ago. The kind that comes from watching the dusk dance into daylight across the soft, warm honey curves of a beautiful woman's face. The kind worth losing sleep for.

She nods slowly, pulling her lower lip between her teeth, and it's almost my undoing.

Her hair hangs loose over her bare shoulders, framing her beautifully boned face. She's wearing a blush-pink dress in the same shade as her light makeup, giving me teasing glimpses of her dizzying curves and radiant brown skin.

It's been an hour since I last saw her and already fire licks through me like it's been a lifetime. It might as well be for the way her body presses against mine. I bunch fistfuls of fabric in my hands, tugging her closer still. I'm electrified by her sweet floral scent. Lost in her minty taste, and we're still in the doorframe.

"Hey," she whispers, blinking up at me from beneath sweeping eyelashes as she takes a step back.

We might never leave her house.

"Hi." My eyes dart to the couch again then to her thighs. I'm consumed with thoughts of rubbing my hands down the smooth length of them. "Nice dress."

"You won't be going anywhere if you two don't get out of here now," Rox says as she enters the living room.

I straighten as she leans on the back of the couch.

"Oh, hey," I say. "Nice seeing you again."

She quirks an impatient smile, then tells me to hurry and get her sister out of here before she has a chance to come up with more questions, doubts, and random inner thoughts. So, we say our good-byes, and I glide my hand over the small of Harper's back and follow her out the door.

An hour later, we've grabbed food and end up in Pop's tiny living room. I spent the week moving everything except the couch and the TV to the garage, so it looks bare.

"Blank canvas," I say, fanning my arms out and spinning.

Harper walks around, trailing her fingertips over the walls and the fireplace tucked in the corner. Then she turns to me. "I have a house that looks almost exactly like this on my vision board." She looks directly at me, but I sense she's lost in her thoughts. "The blueprints are practically ingrained in my mind. I'm surprised your granddad didn't knock down any walls or change the crown molding. God, and these wood floors... It looks like everything is original."

Warmth fills my inside watching her light up talking about her dreams.

"I know where I'll put the lamps, rugs, paintings... I've got it all planned out in my head. Eventually, it's going to happen, too." A shaky laugh spills from her as she follows me into the kitchen, where I start plating the omelets we grabbed while we were out. "Sorry, I'm rambling."

"No, I love hearing about it," I say. "Maybe you'll help me decorate this place because honestly, beyond painting, I'm clueless with the design stuff."

I pull out the utensil drawer, grab two forks, and set one on her plate before I slide it across the counter.

"Oh, my goodness. I'd love to." She's beaming and beautiful as she walks over and plants her elbows on the tiled edge of the countertop.

"Sorry, no chairs or barstools." I shrug. "I packed up everything and stored it in the garage while I paint and replace all the fixtures. I've been uh..." I watch, mesmerized by her every move as she straightens, takes her fork in hand, slices the edge through the cheesy omelet, and lifts it to her mouth. "I've been eating in front of the TV..." I suck in a lungful of air.

The corner of Harper's mouth tugs upward and she stops chewing, her eyes finding mine. They're a vibrant green, dancing with gold flecks.

"Are you just going to watch me eat or...?"

"Can you just do that one more time?" I swallow, struggling not to round the island, glide the thin strap of her pink dress over the slope of her shoulder, and fill my eyes and my hands with her soft curves. "Please."

Then she does.

Slowly, she dips her fork into the omelet, peeking up at me as she turns it in circles. Then she lifts it to her mouth, and I feel myself harden.

Jesus Christ.

"You're so beautiful." The words are featherlight and filled with the fiery hunger zipping through me.

A warm pink blush grows on her cheeks as she thanks me.

I can't think straight. It's been so long since I've been with a woman and felt such an overwhelming need to be close to her. Not just physically, but emotionally. Since I let myself get lost in the tiny movements of her delicate hands, her scent, her laugh. The light in her eyes when we're doing nothing more than standing together in the same room.

But I'm not foolish enough to believe Harper and I can move at such a fast pace, that sex wouldn't send us into overdrive, and we end up crashing.

With Penelope, we operated on expectation and familiarity. We'd be sitting right next to each other and mentally be in different places. Sex was just part of our routine. With Harper, I already know I could be a million miles away or a state away, and she'd still be with me. I'd think about her hands in mine, on my chest, weaving through my hair.

"You're bad," she says over a mouthful, pointing her fork at me. "I'm over here innocently eating food, trying to be respectful of your grandfather's lovely home, and your mind is—"

"Made up," I say, shoveling a forkful of cheesy egg in my mouth. Then I duck into the hallway headed for the living room with a beautiful, curious woman on my heels.

She flashes me a megawatt smile as I walk over by the fireplace, retrieve Pop's Monopoly game box from underneath the couch, and settle on the floor.

"Oh, sir, you are not ready, but challenge accepted," she says, already toeing off her shoes.

We play in comfortable silence for a short while. Somewhere in between moves, we slip out of opponent roles and into mentor/protégé. She teaches me how to quickly snatch up the railroads and avoid the utilities. We focus on completing the C-Gs, or color-groups, on the first two sides of the board, stacking them with three houses, the "sweet spot," at the beginning of the game.

Then we get into her own etiquette rules.

I'd never thought there was much to Monopoly, but Harper patiently eases me into it.

"No one likes it when you just make up rules out of nowhere." She shakes her head like the idea alone irks her. Along with this gem, she warns against the easy mistakes—stealing from the bank, taking too long on turns, deliberately miscounting moves to avoid or ensure landing on a space and getting into arguments about who gets to be which token or the banker. "It's like, we all have our favorites, but it's stupid to get worked up over something that has no bearing over who wins."

"What about buying a property I know someone else wants?"

She shrugs. "Lots of players argue about that, but I'm of the winning mindset. If grabbing your property ensures I win, isn't that the entire goal of the game? We're all trying to bankrupt each other."

I nod my agreement, enjoying how passionate she is about the game.

"And that's another thing..." She straightens her property cards in front of her. "Don't be one of those people who gets all cocky when you win. Ugh, it's just so... Just think about Wheelbarrow."

We both laugh as she rolls the dice and takes her turn, continuing the game in the same unweighted easiness. I work *Sloane Twist* into every corner of our conversation while she blocks me from completing color-groups. We share meaningful glances as we trade properties. Our hands spark as we reach to move our tokens and pass the dice, but we're mostly quiet.

She bumps my shoulder and tosses me a questioning stare.

"This was the spot where I used to play with my grandfather." An easy smile dances on her lips at my wistful tone. "Pop, David 'The Shoe' Wilde. We played so many hours I lost track."

"He sounds amazing, Declan. Do you have a picture?"

My mind wades through memories of Pop and me taunting and teasing each other as I fish out my phone from my pocket. "He'd always win, but it was never about winning or losing. It was always about the fun we had playing the game, you know?"

When I glance over at Harper, she squints at me.

"Are you a secret Hasbrother? A Hasdoctor? This is a safe space. You can tell me."

I chuckle, shaking my head as I take my turn. This simple comfort, talking about my past with Harper without it weighing us down. It warms my heart. We're not Tops and the Scottie dog competing. We're Harper and Declan, enjoying each other's company on a real level.

I finally find an old photo of Pop and me in our matching Community Chest T-shirts. When I turn the screen to Harper she gasps.

"Holy... Oh, my freaking goodness. Pop is Poppa Dave?"

"I know." A laugh rumbles through me. "I saw the autographed dollar at Love & Games, but I didn't know if you'd remember him."

"Remember him? This is so wild. He was our first customer. The funniest, sweetest guy. We *loved* him so much." Tears spring to her eyes as she covers her mouth with her hand. "We thought maybe he moved."

I nod a few times.

"After I saw it on the wall, it made me feel a bit closer to him, you know? Like we might've stood in the same spot." *Like a sign.*

A heavy silence stretches between us during which it feels like neither of us knows what to say next.

"We've been going nonstop since last night. You look tired." Harper's tone is tentative, her voice tender. "I can call a Rideo..."

I shake my head.

"No, I was thinking this is nice. The game. The quiet.

Us."

She drops her gaze back to the board. "Is it weird to you, too, how we just flipped the script? I mean, I was so sure I knew who you were."

"And now?"

"I'm not. I mean if you're related to Poppa Dave..." She smiles and holds her hands up, playfully surrendering. "Kidding. I'm kidding. But on a real note, at Java Joy, you seemed so *different.*" She winces. "Sorry, but you were, the way you walked up all take-charge to save the day—"

"With all my cash?"

She giggles. "Yes. With all ten bucks." She's still smiling as she watches me. "I was having *the* worst day. All I wanted was a strong cup of coffee to ease the stress, after I'd talked with Rox earlier that morning. I'm sorry I projected all my frustration onto you."

"I get it."

"Later, I realized I wasn't mad at you..." She trails off then she shakes her head. "Rox and I share the same dad, different moms. I kind of felt replaced when Dad married her mom, Vanessa. New family, new priorities"—she shrugs—"but he always sent money."

A puzzle piece falls into place.

"Always a wedding save-the-date or a check, never his time." There's a bitterness in Harper's tones as she says it.

I trail my hand over to hers and intertwine our fingers. My heart wrenches with a familiar hollow ache.

"You're nothing like him," she says. "But that day, your sweet gesture felt like Dad throwing money at a problem." She squeezes my hand. "And now he's getting married again, then Rox tells me the store was in trouble—"

"Love & Games is in trouble?"

Harper's eyes widen, and a flush grows on her cheeks. She withdraws her hand from mine and drops her head into her hands. "Shit. Please pretend I didn't say anything."

Crawling over to Harper, I slide my hand around her waist and pull her into my side. "Every business has trouble at some point. I'm sure you're working on a plan, but if you need me, I'm happy to help."

Her body stiffens. "We don't need any help."

"I meant advice or recommendations…" I pause for a moment. "You can trust me."

She softens. "Sorry, reflex."

"It's okay."

"Rox knows Dad would be happy to shell out the money, but I'd rather put our heads together and roll up our sleeves." She shrugs. "It's crazy because I've been so mad. But it's no one's fault. Last June there was this huge storm that blew out our electrical at the shop. During repairs, the damage turned out to be extensive. *And* expensive. The insurance claims it's an 'act of God,' and the landlord says it falls under regular maintenance and repairs payable by the tenant. We don't have enough savings."

I rub her arms as she melts into me.

"I don't want to lose everything we've built, but I just *really* don't want my dad's money," Harper says.

"Tell me about him," I say.

She smiles to herself. "Dad is the funniest, smartest man. He's accomplished, hardworking. I miss him so much." Her shoulders tremble. "He's a basketball fan with a full tool belt who barbecues for no reason at all. I still don't know if he just sucks at Monopoly, or he let me win, but he's the baddest iron you'll ever meet."

"Ah, so that's what the iron was about." I chuckle, recalling her mention of the game marker during the first practice at Love & Games. "He sounds like a good guy. I think I'd like him."

"You definitely would. He's a charmer and schmoozer." Harper quiets for a few seconds, busying herself tracing her fingertip over her cuticle. "He's also a hopeless romantic with three alimony payments, and in love with the idea of love. Somehow that equates to him leaving when he should be buckling down to put in the work, you know?"

"Yeah." *Firsthand.* "So, he wants a relationship with both you and Rox?"

She's quiet for a beat like she's considering this point of view. But she doesn't answer my question. Instead, she drums her fingers on my chest and asks me, "How about you? What type of wild family drama did your parents come with?"

I twine our fingers, lifting hers to my mouth for a kiss. "Pop was my father figure."

Harper tips her face up. "I'm sorry. I didn't mean to—"

"It's fine. My story wraps up neatly with a bow. I never knew my father, but Pop was there at every track meet and Dads 'n' Donuts. When Mom couldn't make it to parent-teacher meetings, he was there."

"I love that so much."

"He was the best. We spent summers here collecting McDonald's game pieces and playing Monopoly on a rickety table, so old, one of its legs eventually broke—midgame! I can confirm duct tape will only take you so far. We were forced to replace it." A melancholy laugh bubbles inside me, remembering us trying to steady the table. The game with all its pieces and fake money and memories...they were way more important to us.

Her voice is soft when she responds like she's just registered the juxtaposition of our relationships with these two men who shaped the people we've become.

"So that's why you were so close to Pop. Why you moved here to fix up his house."

Inwardly, I wince.

My skin burns with guilt.

Shame and sorrow close my throat. I chew the inside of my cheek to keep from crying.

"Yeah," I say.

Harper is right—partially. Pop and I were as close to father and son as we could be without the title. But he was more than just a male figure in my life. He was my family, my best friend, my role model. All I ever wanted was to make him proud. And I wasn't there when he died.

I feel my breaths coming faster, my chest tightening.

Harper's comment is the perfect opening to finally tell her about Penelope. That I'm not just here to restore Pop's house to its former beauty. I'm also here to insulate myself away from a woman who didn't care for this old house nor the man who owned it. By her standards, Pop and San Diego weren't extravagant enough to visit. So, I missed those last summers with the man who I loved most.

When he died, I felt like I chose Penelope over Pop. So,

finding out she was moving on…it only reopened the wound of losing him.

I swallow back my tears.

Harper twists to look up at me. "Declan."

"I'm okay. I just miss him…" The tension in my shoulders tightens as I bite back the hurt. "He died two years ago, and I wasn't there."

I'm working myself up to telling Harper about Penelope when she slides the game board to the side and crawls into the space between my legs. Gently, she brushes her lips over mine, letting the heat and the heartache melt into the kiss.

"If you're trying to keep me from buying St. James Place, it's working," I say as I draw my knee up and lower her back against it.

"Oh, I'll remember exactly where we were. I was winning."

With my tongue, I pry her lips apart. I'm met with bittersweet, sensual licks as I taste her sweet moan. Fire blazes across my skin as she slips her fingers beneath my shirt. I kiss at the parted corner of her mouth, working my way to the sensitive flesh behind her ear.

Harper arches her back, lifting to the press of my fingers at the small of her back as I pull her closer still.

With us, every kiss feels new and different. This one is a slow dance. Moving shoulders and hips and curling toes. We're tangled up in a blur of hands and desperate breaths before she gets to her feet, tugging me with her, leading me to the couch.

"Do you work tomorrow?" I ask.

"I've got this Monday off. Let's just stay like this and not move," she says as I snuggle her into my outstretched frame. She closes her eyes and lets her body meld to mine, the veil of sleep weighing us down.

"You won't get an argument from me." I chuckle and tug the soft throw blanket from the back of the couch over us. With the remote, I flip through a few channels and settle on a Denzel movie for noise.

"I'm just going to rest my eyes for a few," Harper mumbles.

The soft brush of her breaths on my forearm ebbs into a slow rhythm, and as I bury my face in her hair, I know this thing with Harper isn't about games or sex or the fact she gets the appeal of Pop's drafty old house. I'm blindsided by the realization that I've been in this city with old friends and even older dreams, and only now with Harper in my arms does this city, this house feel like my home.

CHAPTER FIFTEEN

HARPER

GO

JUDGING BY THE waning darkness outside the window, it's the tiniest hours of the morning when I wake up starving. All I can think about is the pack of Red Vines sticking out beneath the magazine on the coffee table across from us.

"Come on," I whisper, stretching my fingers out. *Dammit.*

I heave a sigh and resolve to wait for Declan to shift a bit.

My movie, *The Cutting Edge*, is on television. Kate gracefully skates past Doug, the hockey player turned figure skater, as he gets up close and personal with the ice for the hundredth time, and I'm getting into the movie—well, as much as I can, when there's a rather large, beautiful man molded to my body.

We slept together. Just slept, but still. It was nice.

I'm reeling, thinking about how sleep might've gotten in the way of "letting go," when my stomach frog-croaks super loud.

Maybe not finishing my omelet wasn't the best choice.

The instant I move, Declan shifts, tightening his arm around me.

"I need to feed you." His voice is gruff as he tugs me flush against him.

"If you can reach those Red Vines, I might be able to make it," I say, arching my back. "By the way, you just missed the toe-pick scene, which—in my opinion—is one of the best parts of the whole movie."

Declan grumbles, pressing into my arch. "Did they get to the famous Pamchenko Twist yet?"

"Nope." I bite my tongue to stifle a laugh. "You know, the fact you remember the name tells me you're a closet rom-com fan. Which means—"

"Which means…" he parrots.

"We're going to have to watch this movie again when you've had more than four hours' sleep."

Shit.

A surge of panic washes over me, and I stiffen. *Presumptuous much?* I shouldn't be making plans beyond tonight, even if it is just a movie. "You know, if you want," I eke out in a futile attempt to recover.

He buries his face in the crook of my neck. "No, I want to. All the romance movies. Hockey players, billionaires with red rooms, rakes… If it's got a happily-ever-after, I want to watch with you." He chuckles good-naturedly, but I feel my heart expand as he squeezes me close. "We need popcorn, Red Vines, throw in some chocolate. Wait, should we learn the songs so we can sing during the montages?"

"You're not funny." I stifle a laugh. Except my shoulders

tremble, giving me away.

Declan must sense I'm barely holding on. He tickles me on my sides. I giggle uncontrollably, trying to wriggle free from his arms.

When I finally escape, he pads into the kitchen after me. As he bends into the refrigerator, it takes every ounce of my strength not to laugh when I say, "Nice backsplash." Which, the seafoam green subway tiles Declan installed, they're amazing.

In addition to other things…

He pops up his head over the refrigerator door, smiling as he follows my gaze trained on his backside.

"What? I'm complimenting your handiwork," I say.

Within minutes, he warms up our leftover brunch. We sit at the counter eating and talking about movies and books, then places where we eventually want to travel. In addition to board games, we learn we both love amusement parks, art galleries on occasion. For the most part, we prefer to stay in.

At some point, the conversation moves back to the floor, and we pick up our Monopoly game where we left off.

It's so fast, but everything feels right. Easy and effortless. Maybe too easy. How many times have I heard people say, *When you know, you know*? I don't, though. I wouldn't even know where to begin. Still, the flutter in my chest, my tingling flesh, and the long lingering stares Declan and I share… Somehow, he makes everything feel within reach.

I remind myself he's leaving soon. That one amazing weekend isn't a guarantee of more. *Because self-care.*

When neither of us rolls the dice, we stare wordlessly. I'm breathless, my heart skittering as Declan pushes the board to the side. He tugs me into a kiss.

At first, we take our time. Learning, exploring, feeling our way around each other's bodies. My hands are in his thick, dark waves, on his neck, on his back as he deepens the kiss. I let his clean, woodsy scent band around me, awakening all my senses.

Nothing feels like enough. The need to be closer, connected in every way, it's almost unbearable.

I tug at the hem of his shirt.

A sultry rumble of laughter vibrates through him as he sits back to yank it over his head, leaving me an unobstructed view. I reach out to glide my greedy hands over the fine, dark hairs converging into a fantastical arrow pointing south.

"Better?" He leans in to nip at my bottom lip, smiling like my wish is his command.

"Oh, my goodness, yes."

"Yeah?" He chuckles, sinking his fingers into my hair as his kisses travel to my neck.

Fueled by the fire blazing in Declan's eyes, I lower myself onto my back. It feels like there's a "sharp curve ahead" road sign, and we should proceed with caution. Somehow, as I lift the hem of my dress, tugging and anxious to get my panties over my hips, it's freeing. I don't want to slow down. I don't want to think. I just want to feel.

But Declan stops me.

His voice is desperate as he pleads, "Please, let me."

And so I do.

I watch as he swallows and the muscles at the sides of his jaw go taut. As he skims his strong fingers over the top of my waistband. As he, painstakingly slow, drags down the pale pink fabric until the cool air washes over my exposed skin.

A shiver curls down my spine.

He works them down to my ankles, allowing me to, one by one, free my legs.

Every inch of me throbs and tingles as I lie here, waiting, wishing he would hurry up and stop tormenting me. But by the slow, measured rhythm of his breaths, rowing his shoulders. The way he draws his eyes to my mouth, on edge. He's losing restraint, too.

"Are you sure you want to do this?" he asks.

"Yes, please," I say too quickly, nodding. I'm sure he must think I'm reconsidering or that I'm spooked by what's about to happen. I'm not apprehensive about sex with Declan. I'm not sure there are words adequate to express how much I want to do this with him. It's got little to do with the way my pulse races. Or the incessant throb and clench low and tight in my belly, threatening to send me over the edge just watching him watch me.

It's Declan.

It's this unnervingly beautiful man who, despite our rocky start and my misconceptions about him, is gentle and lighthearted with me. It feels easy to be myself, to laugh, play, be vulnerable. *Sexy.*

He surveys me as if weighing the truth in my words. Then he traces the pad of his thumb over the swell of my lower lip. Electricity sears through me as I take it into my mouth, running my tongue along its length.

With my free hand, I hook my finger through his belt loop and tug him closer. Every nerve ending in my body comes to attention as I dip my hand inside his jeans and find his thick, hard length.

He groans and closes his eyes against my touch. As I am, he seems to be memorizing, savoring the feel of us.

When I release his finger from my mouth, he opens his eyes and lowers his chin. He brushes his lips against mine, a low growl spilling out as he lingers for the tiniest moment.

"I want you so bad, Harper."

Fire licks through me as I say, "This might sound strange." My voice is shaking. "Are you thinking this is going to be a one-time thing?"

He gives a confused laugh. "Uh, I hope not?"

"Okay, because I was thinking we can save the sweet stuff for next time."

"You're not going to be upset later that we skipped...foreplay, and all that?" he asks tentatively.

"We met on New Year's Day. Today is the twenty-first. That's basically three weeks of foreplay." When he cranes his neck back to search my face, I quirk a smile. "What?"

"Nothing. It's just good to know the feeling's been mutual."

"After the kiss in the shop..." I laugh. "I totally wanted you. Ooh, and when the rain started coming down last night, you were like this insanely good-looking wet dream."

Declan freezes.

With a renewed urgency, he tugs my dress over my head, and tosses it, letting it fall in a puddle of fabric at my side. He makes quick work of unclasping my bra, before he gets to his feet, and pulls me up with him. His fingertips roam wildly on my back as I rush to unzip his jeans.

In one fell swoop, he scoops me off the ground, wrapping my legs around his waist. We're a blur of hands and mouths and lust as he falters, fumbling to feel his way down the hallway.

"Your legs are so smooth," he says, the rough scrape of his hands sending heat swirling down my spine.

"I shaved for you," I mouth into the kiss.

"Damn, I feel so lucky."

"You will be tonight," I say, and that does it.

When we reach the first bedroom on the left, he tightens his arm around my back as he bends down to the nightstand. He tears the foil wrapper, then sheaths himself before flitting a glance from me over to the bed, I imagine, giving me one last chance to slow things down.

"I don't want boring sex with you," I say. *If this is temporary, I want the fantasy.*

The corners of his eyes crinkle with amusement. "Is that so?" Declan teases as he backs me over to the far wall, flattening one hand. The other grips my hip to lift me up high enough to guide him to the meeting of my thighs.

As he glides inside me, a kaleidoscope of flickers and sparks flash behind my eyes. Almost like the world around us quiets, every sense magnifies. It's everything. I feel everything.

My breathing shallows to a whisper.

"This is..." I close my eyes, baring my throat to him as I loosen my grip on his shoulders, sliding my greedy hands into his hair. "You are..."

"Exciting, amazing. Hopefully not boring," Declan says.

A ragged laugh escapes me as our rhythm staggers. Teasingly, between slow and fast as he finds our sweet spot. Our bodies synchronize, and I'm so in tune with the fit of us, his breaths, his heartbeat. It's the most delicious feeling. All-consuming, beautiful.

"Let go with me." Declan's voice is gruff and tattered.

One last time, I remind myself this is just sex. That Declan's leaving. That once he's gone, he'll forget all about me.

Then I catalogue every sound, scent, the feel of his hair between my fingers as I gasp for breath. I squeeze my thighs tight around him, locking my ankles, memorizing the connection between us as he cages me between his arms and rolls his hips, deepening the feeling. Only to start the sweet torture all over again until we're breathless.

As I arch my back, letting the crown of my head rest against the wall, he lowers his mouth to my breasts. My skin blazes as he drags his tongue in teasing circles in delicious torment.

Then heat and shivering quakes curl down my spine.

As we come down, the rush of panic consumes me. I want to find my clothes and make a run for it because nothing about what we just shared can be categorized as *just* anything. Certainly not just sex.

BY MIDAFTERNOON WE finally leave the bed. Declan makes pancakes and we laze around on the couch, eating and making a game plan to tackle the paint situation. When we're good and stuffed, he lends me a T-shirt and a pair of drawstring sweatpants. Then we get to work.

"How are you doing over there, Tops? Almost ready to

rotate?" Declan asks as he drags his roller vertically up the far wall in the back bedroom.

"Just about..." I say, holding on to the ladder as I stretch to get the edges near the ceiling. "How's it looking?"

"I'm thinking Biscotti Beaches was the way to go." He chuckles, still teasing me about the paint color.

We started in Pop's room. Now we're knocking out the front bedroom. Next is the kitchen, then we'll keep going until we work our way to the front of the house. We've got an entire system. He primes, I paint, the music plays, cross-breezes drift through the open windows, this beautiful bungalow gets a second chance to shine.

Win-win.

Except, with every stroke of my paintbrush, I'm reminded how the little bungalow on my vision board wasn't just a magazine cutout. My plan was always to own a house. Two years ago, I moved out of Mark's and into Rox's spare bedroom intent on padding my savings with enough for a down payment plus a few months' mortgage payments. Then I'd find a cute little place, choose the furniture and appliances, a couple lamps, artwork. My personal touches in every corner.

The song on the radio ends and an ad for Mike's Mic Comedy Club blares through the speakers. Anthony Goode is back in town next weekend by popular demand.

Declan and I burst out laughing.

"Yeah, it's all fun and games until he roasts you in front an entire room full of people..." I say.

He laughs. "Seriously."

"Although, I've got to say..." I glance over at Declan. "I

feel like we got the last laugh."

He walks over, holding his brush away from his body to kiss me. He lingers for the tiniest moment. I would never try it with anyone else, but the mood feels so light and playful, and there's already bisque-colored droplets speckled over his cheeks....

"Hi," I mouth into a smiling kiss then swipe my paintbrush over his beautiful cheek.

Declan releases a small gasp, his eyebrows lifting as he drops his roller onto the plaster liner covering the floor. "Oh, you are going to get it for that." He's adorable and ruthless as he scoops me into his arms, wrapping my legs around his waist. Laughter rumbles over us as he rubs his cheek against mine.

Then, I see the mischief in his eyes.

"No, I was just playing around." I squeal as he backs me against the wall I just painted. The one that has yet to dry. I feel my entire backside glide onto the slick surface. "Oh, my goodness, Dec—"

He covers my mouth with his, letting his hands roam freely over my waist, hips, up my sides, finally dipping his fingers into my hair.

"We need to get you out of these clothes. You're covered in paint." Declan punctuates each word with a kiss. "I'm thinking a hot shower."

He carries me into the shower fully dressed. Cold water sprays over us as we peel off each other's clothes, kissing, laughing, shrieking until the temperature heats.

"I still can't believe you didn't see my paintbrush coming." I shake my head, smiling. "You took it like a champ, though."

"Oh, I'm not afraid to get dirty." Declan flashes me his trademark lopsided grin as he turns me around. "Here, let me. Looks like I got a little overzealous against the wall," he says as he picks a clump of paint from my hair, holding his hand out to show me the gooey evidence.

The moment feels intimate in a way I didn't expect. We're standing in this shower, naked, covered with paint, his hands moving carefully, tenderly through my hair as he guides me under the spray. It's sweet and attentive, but I don't want to get confused about what we're doing here.

An overwhelming need to fill the silence washes over me.

"My ex, Mark, the one you met at the comedy club. I once dropped a wooden spoon while I was cooking spaghetti. The sauce splatted onto his pants. He completely freaked out on me," I say with a shaky laugh.

Okay, so mentioning Mark to Declan feels rude, but desperate times, right? Except Declan doesn't assert his machismo on me. Or brush it off like many guys do when his fragile ego is threatened. He simply makes a logical assumption.

"So, you and Mark were pretty serious then if you lived together," he says.

"I don't know."

Declan doesn't fill the silence. It's almost like he can see me feeling my way around the subject, and I'm grateful for his patience.

"At the time, it was more about having a place to live." I laugh. "We'd seen each other in passing a handful of times at Chamber of Commerce meetings when Rox, Nadi, and I set up the business. When we finally sat next to each other, we talked, and fell into a friendship."

Declan's hands stop moving. "Is he still important to you?"

"No, he's a good guy, though. We were just better at being friends if you know what I mean. Things with us were familiar and comfortable, safe. Our fights were never about the raw, vulnerable stuff." Declan scrapes his fingers over my matted curls in long strokes. "Have you ever gone back to someone when you know the reasons you broke up in the first place are still applicable—if not more so—as they were back then?"

"Yeah. A little too well."

I lean into his touch. "Oof, I hear a story in there."

Declan grabs a bar of soap from the small, recessed shelf, lathering it over my shoulders as he tells me about his ex, Penelope.

"Ours was a classic case of staying too long at the party." There's restraint in his tone as he talks. "We'd been together since med school. She's also an ear, nose, and throat doctor."

A burning sensation swirls in my chest. "Wow, college sweethearts. That's big."

"Yeah. Next thing you know, you're living together, and all your friends are getting married and having babies, and you think that's the next step." He pauses as I turn, taking the soap from him to glide it over the hard slopes of his chest. "People change, though. We never stopped to address the changes in us, our goals, what we saw for our futures. It was assumed, I assumed"—his voice hardens as he corrects himself—"we were supposed to stay together. She didn't."

"I'm so sorry, Declan. I didn't realize."

When he looks at me, the hurt stains his cheeks. It's embedded in the tight set of his jaw, the hard cords of his neck. He isn't just here to renovate Pop's house. He's running, starting over.

I gulp down a breath to stay quiet.

He must sense the rising panic inside me because he shakes his head. "We should've ended things a long time ago." A smile tugs at the corners of his mouth. "This is probably going to sound corny as hell, but I'm here to rediscover the person I was before her."

"It sounds brave," I say, and it surprises me. When I think about Dad going from relationship to relationship, I was certain he didn't consider the hurt he was leaving behind. He never cheated, though. Maybe not staying was how he showed that he cared.

Declan traces the pad of his thumb over my lips. As he lowers his head to kiss me, I feel weightless. There's an unexpected easiness between us. We've been honest with each other on a level that makes us vulnerable, and it feels reassuring somehow.

"You're shivering," he mouths into the kiss.

"Yeah, should we maybe"—my teeth chatter as I cling to Declan, shivering—"get out of this water before we turn to prunes?"

He nods, then turns off the water. As he tugs a towel off the rack, wraps me in it, and kisses the tip of my nose, I'm more confused than ever. This was supposed be nothing more than a fun adult sleepover. Sex, painting, playing games, and watching movies. Somewhere in between kissing, laughing, and pulling paint clumps from my hair, I'm overwhelmed by how much I want this. The cute little house with Biscotti Beaches on the walls, and Declan and me rediscovering ourselves together.

CHAPTER SIXTEEN

DECLAN

BUILD EVENLY

I'VE SEEN HARPER every day this week. Morning coffee, late lunch, midday quickies. We alternate between promoting Love & Games online and completing more renovations before we end up back at Pop's. With the paint done, we've moved on to new sinks and light fixtures. She's eager to get to decorating, but it'll have to wait until tomorrow. The community's really come out for the Love & Games scavenger hunt.

When I step inside the store, Harper's got her phone pressed to her ear, and she's beaming as she waves me over to the register where she's the designated clue-giver for Monopoly Hunt Headquarters.

I'd been intimidated about the event, initially. Then she let me in on a little secret: It's just a regular scavenger hunt with clever Monopoly-themed clues, placed at a handful of participating local businesses meant to include the family game night sector of the community.

There must be at least a few dozen people in the store

alone. Adults, kids, news reporters. They're all here lending a hand to help save a small business—even if they don't know it.

My heartbeat kicks up a notch as I take quick strides, weaving through the sea of people to get to her. But it's her that takes my breath away. The shift behind my ribs becomes more pronounced whenever we meet again.

"Hi." She bites her lush lower lip and holds up a finger to me. "Okay, Mom. I've got to go..." She trails off, tapping her fingers to her thumb showing that her mother is rambling before she crosses her eyes and makes a silly face. "I will. I promise, now I've really got to go. Mm-hmm. Mm-hmm. Okay, love you, bye."

"Sounds intense," I say.

A flush dapples her cheeks, and I focus on the way her teeth sink into her bottom lip. "Everything with my mother is intense." Her expression softens, and she leans forward on the counter like she wants to lunge for me.

I shove my hands in my pockets not to pull her over the counter like a savage. *How is it possible I want her more every time I'm near her?*

"I missed you," I say, leaning in to give her a peck on the cheek.

A low moan spills from her as she closes her eyes. At least I know the torture is mutual.

"God, I wish we could go somewhere," she whispers, "for just like a couple minutes."

My breaths lodge in my throat. "Yeah. Um...if you keep talking like that, I'm definitely not going to make it to the next business for another clue."

Harper giggles. "Okay, I'm sorry, but I just keep thinking about last night when you—"

"Please stop talking unless you want this *not* to be a family establishment anymore." I scrub a hand over my face, a little more than half-serious.

"He's not wrong." Nadia stretches into the small space between Harper and me, laughing. "Think you guys can keep it PG while I run to Booked Up to drop off more clues?"

"Bye, Nadi." Harper closes her eyes, shaking her head and laughing. "Love you, too."

"Oh, I got your text," I say when Nadia leaves. "What's the favor you wanted to ask me?"

She fidgets with her nails then blinks up at me.

"Whatever it is, I'll just tell you, I'm inclined to say yes." I stretch my hand across the counter to take hers in mine. "But there's a catch…"

"Does it involve Park Place and Marvin Gardens?" She tilts her head to look at me over her brow. "Or are you thinking more along the lines of a repeat of paint day because I've got some ideas…" she says suggestively.

"Is it too late to go with your idea?" We both laugh. Clearly, I need to get more creative. "Uh, I was going to say I'll make dinner if you agree to watch *Battleship* with me tonight while we decorate…"

"Hmm… So, no ice skater/hockey player romance?" She pouts, feigning disappointment.

"We've watched *The Cutting Edge* twice already. I'm pretty sure I've got the Pamchenko Twist and all the toe picks down pat."

The smile tugging at the corners of her mouth as she leans in is well worth whatever favor she wants in exchange.

"All right, what do you need, so I can get out of here? I'm holding up the line." Before she replies, I lightly brush my lips over her salty sweet ones. She tastes like caramel popcorn. If I didn't know how much this scavenger hunt means to Harper's business, I'd steal her away now.

Harper's eyes are still closed when she says, "No pressure at all. I know you haven't decided to stay in San Diego." She opens her eyes, then blurts out, "If you don't end up staying, would you consider flying in to be my wedding date? My dad is getting married in June. Fourth time's the charm!" She flashes me a half smile, half cringe.

Everything in me stiffens.

There's a seriousness implied with being her date to her father's wedding. It's meeting her parents, taking the next step. Not that I don't know how I feel about Harper. What we've been doing these past few weeks is more than fun and games. But five months from now?

"I, uh—"

"It's totally fine if you'd rather not." Harper's eyes dart over to the door like she'd rather be anywhere but here, and it feels too familiar. My heart wrenches when she bows her head.

Falling for Harper isn't the hard part. I already feel like I'm halfway there. It's the staying in love that scares me. Making plans neither of us knows whether we'll be able to keep. We're connecting the dots before we even know what the big picture is. I want Harper with every inch of my being but there's too much uncertainty. Is this move to San Diego permanent? Will she want me around by then? *Will she leave like Penelope?*

The noise and movement of the crowd rips me from my thoughts. When I look back to Harper, I'm unnerved by the sadness in her expression. I hate that I'm the one who put it there.

"Harp, I'd love to be your wedding date," I say.

She gives me a small smile, traces of sadness etched between the lines. "I promise, it's fine if you don't want to."

"No, I want to," I say, squeezing her hand. "There's a medical conference in June. I'm just not sure what the date is, but yes. If you want me there, I'm up for anything, Harper Sloane."

"Does that include dinner invitations my sister accepted on our behalf next Friday at Francesco's?" She winces.

Behind me, a person clears his throat before I can get my bearings. I shift gears to scavenger hunt mode. "Sure thing, on that last question." I wink, then say "I'll trade you" as I hand Harper the giant Scottie dog token replica I got from the Thai restaurant down the street on the last clue.

Harper quickly catches on.

"Yes, sir. You're exactly right. There are eight color-groups on a Monopoly game board." She feigns exaggerated pensiveness. "Your next clue is 'Swing or slide pass Go without a trace. Skip Short Line and go straight to Park Place.'" Her green eyes widen as she mutters under her breath, "As in *Park* Place."

"You know, it just hit me. I think I have an idea where to go." I whisper that I'll see her tonight for dinner and *Battleship*.

"Okay, love you." She gasps, though I'm equally surprised. Her expression twists with shock as she freezes and blinks a few times. She's speechless.

As am I.

It feels like nothing more than a slip of the tongue. Just like she told her mother on the phone and Nadia before she left. It's habit. Something she says to people she cares about. Which, at the least, I know she cares about me. But how much? And what kind of caring? Like a close friend or a family member?

I don't want the casual out-of-habit tongue slip. I want to be so much more. I want the real, intimate, promise-of-a-future-together *I love you.*

We stare at each other for a few seconds. I'm still deciding whether to blurt out that I think I love her, too, or continue this confused customer bit when the impatient man shoulders in front of me, and the moment is lost.

AFTER THE NEIGHBORHOOD park, the last stop of the scavenger hunt is the tattoo shop. I'm two people from the front of the line, still reeling about the fact Harper loves me—*if* she loves me and her words weren't merely out of habit. I'm scrambling for ideas how to tell her I think I'm in love with her, too, when someone taps me from behind.

"Declan, right?" Mark, Harper's ex, flashes me a tentative smile.

"Hey." I return his smile with one that, I'm sure, comes off about as enthusiastic as I feel.

I've been running around town scavenging game clues, when I should be back in that store talking to Harper, making more plans for our future. As much as it scares the hell out of me to uproot my life in Las Vegas and start over in San Diego, I know it'll make all the difference if it's with Harper.

Right now, the last thing I feel like doing is comparing notes with her ex.

"I think we got off on the wrong foot," Mark says as I pivot slightly to face him. He's holding the same scavenger hunt clue that I'm waiting to exchange. "Harper and I share a lot of history. I just want to see her happy. If that's with you..." He throws his hands up.

Okay, Harper said he was a good guy. Maybe I read him wrong.

"Thanks, man. I appreciate it," I say.

When the line moves, we both shuffle a few feet forward.

"So, are you new to San Diego?" Mark asks.

Come on, man.

I pull in a lungful of air and blow it out slowly, running my hand through my hair. When I glance back at him, I'm waiting for the other shoe to drop as I say, "Yeah. I'm considering a permanent move from Vegas."

"Vegas, huh? Long-distance relationships are tough."

My neck stiffens. I remind myself to breathe when I feel myself growing hot with annoyance. "Listen, Mark, we're good." I nod, trying my best not to sound like a complete dick, but he's pushing it. "Thanks for your concern, but I think Harper and I will figure this out together."

"Oh, yeah. I didn't mean to—"

"You're fine." I force a smile, moving forward in the line as the decision Harper and I need to make pushes its way to the forefront of my mind.

A familiar pang of guilt flares in my gut.

In Vegas, I've got a home, friends, a medical practice, patients I've grown to care about. But Mom's the only irreplaceable tie, tethering me to that city. I hate that a life with Harper feels like a familiar choice. One I still regret. I chose Penelope over Pop. Will I regret choosing Harper over Mom?

"I'll see you around." Finally, the purple-haired woman in front of me picks up her clue, then says her good-byes to the young tattooist.

When he waves me over, I move to the counter.

"Hi. The answer is Community Chest Tattoo," I rush to say, ready to get out of here.

The man bends to grab a small treasure box from beneath the counter, though he hesitates before he hands it to me. "Everything okay? You look a little nervous."

"Yeah, I'm just exhausted. Thanks for asking."

He nods, surveying me a second longer then slides the chest over the counter.

Relief sets in when I think about delivering my full collection of items over to Harper, then heading home for the day. But when I turn around, the weight of Mark's gaze settles in my stomach.

"It was good seeing you, Declan. If you decide to stay, I'm always around."

The thing is there's nothing antagonistic about his words. If anything, it's an extension of friendship between two men who *might* live and work in the same community.

But my paranoia zeroes in on those last three words.

I'm always around.

Pop's house is almost done. Later today, Harper and I are picking up a few odds and ends to decorate, then that's it. I'm scheduled to leave in two weeks, and I'm still not sure if I should stay. *I've got to be there for Mom.*

He'll be here, though. No matter my decision, Mark will be ready to pick up the pieces of Harper's heart. Who knows if the reasons they broke up will still apply? But he'll be the good guy. The friend who's familiar and comfortable, safe.

I'll just be gone.

CHAPTER SEVENTEEN

HARPER

TURN TO PLAY

WHEN I GET off work, Declan picks me up from Love & Games. He gives me a quick kiss on the cheek, then we drive to Home Goods. We slip in and out of the brightly colored aisles tossing in accent pillows, new linens, and a pale green area rug to go with the rest of the knick-knacks we'll need to stage the rooms. As we check out and drive to Pop's house, I pretend not to notice the stretching silence between us.

I accidentally told Declan I loved him.

Albeit it appeared to catch him off guard. I barely believe I blurted it out for the first time in front of our entire community. I just figured he'd say something when we saw each other again.

Of course, my mind snags on everything that happened right before. Was it the tiny hesitation when I asked him to be my wedding date? Maybe dinner with Dad is too much too fast. Maybe he regrets starting anything with me when he's leaving in two weeks. Maybe he thinks I said I love him to get him to stay.

My heart feels like it's in my stomach when we get to Pop's. I feel like I'm just going through the motions as we pluck out old furniture pieces from the garage, adding them to the new items we picked up. We spend a couple hours hanging art, rearranging furniture, dressing the beds in fresh white linens. Each room, strategically styled with accent rugs, pillows, and throw blankets. We add plants, bookends, new lamps, and decorative knickknacks. We're exhausted by the time we finish, so I throw a bag of store-bought spinach ravioli in a skillet before we settle in bed with our plates and two glasses of merlot to watch *Battleship.*

THE SPORTS CHANNEL is blaring on the television when I awake, still feeling weighed down with uncertainty.

"Hey, you're awake," Declan says as he enters the room holding two steaming cups of coffee courtesy of the Keurig, we added to our Home Goods haul. He walks over to plant a quick kiss on my lips then sets one on the nightstand next to me. "We're out of creamer so I used milk. I hope that's okay."

I nod, forcing a smile. "Yeah, it's fine."

Then Declan slips into the bathroom. A few seconds later, the spray of water groans from the pipes, and the glass door clicks shut with a reverberating echo.

"You're sure you don't want to join me?" Declan says.

"No, I'm okay," I call out, swallowing back the tightness in my throat. My hands tremble as I throw back the blankets in a dizzying frenzy, rummaging around for the jeans and T-shirt I wore yesterday. "Shit, shit, shit."

I'm so mad at myself.

Tears singe the corners of my eyes as I struggle to get my leg into my pants. I fell in love with a man, played house, let myself get lost in a dream. Like this was all a game, risking my heart. All when I knew this thing with Declan had an expiration date. We haven't discussed anything. We don't have a label. We freely use words like *we*, *our*, *us*, but we've never said what those words mean.

"So stupid," I mumble to myself as I yank my shirt over my head then realize it's Declan's. The green Community Chest shirt he wore that first Monopoly practice at Love & Games.

I stiffen my body against the shakes, pinching my lower lip to stop the trembling.

When the shower turns off, I hurry to wipe my eyes with the hem on his shirt, turning to face the closet.

I've got to get out of here.

"Everything okay?" Declan asks a few seconds later.

In my periphery, I catch sight of him leaning casually in the doorframe of the bathroom. He's shirtless and barefoot in only a pair of loose gray sweatpants hanging dangerously low on his hips. Water droplets dapple his glistening skin. *Jesus.* With both hands gripped on the ends of the towel draped over his broad shoulders, he's distractingly beautiful, and I know without a doubt I've let my priorities get out of focus.

"I've got to run. I need to get to the store before the last Monopoly practice," I rush to say. "Rox wants to give us a rundown on the sales following the scavenger hunt. She might have some news on the loan status, too, so..."

Declan doesn't fill the silence.

I wish it didn't feel telling but it does. In every way, it shows me I've been looking at us from a one-sided view. I love him. I want him to stay. I want to live happily ever with him in this beautiful house that doesn't just feel like a home again. It feels more like us than Pop.

As mad as I am at myself, anger and resent toward Declan simmer inside me, too. Why isn't he telling me how he feels one way or the other? What we share isn't something you let a person down easy about? Certainly, it's not something you ignore.

"What are we doing?" I ask Declan, hating the way my voice wavers between hopeful and desperate. *We.* Again, that tiny word flutters straight to my heart. I'm beginning to see that might be the problem.

I've been following my heart and losing my head.

The crease between Declan's eyebrows trenches. "I'm asking if everything is okay, which I've got a hunch it's not."

I force myself to look at him. To watch as he recognizes the tears in my eyes, the hurt twisting my expression.

"You're shutting me out, and I don't know why," I say. "I don't deserve the silent treatment because you don't know how to end things with us. If what you feel for me isn't love, I can handle it."

"Fuck, Harp, that's not—"

"That's exactly what's happening, and I blame myself because I should've seen it coming. Pop's house is done. You did what you came to do. Now you're leaving."

Declan scrubs both hands over his face with a groan. The muscles at the corners of his jaw tighten. He's clearly annoyed we're even having this conversation, but I continue anyway.

"I know we've been spending a lot of time together these past few weeks. It was supposed to be fun playing Monopoly and renovating this house, but I screwed up. It's not your fault I fell in love with you." He gasps, but I stay the course and quickly ask the question before I lose my nerve. "I just need to know one thing. Was I a rebound? Were you biding your time with me until you return to Las Vegas and reconcile with your ex?"

I want to be wrong. God, do I want to be wrong, but the fear flaring in my gut, twisting down my spine, tells me I'm not.

Declan pushes off the wall and closes the distance between us in one hurried stride. In only the completely disarming way he knows how to do, Declan glides his hands over the curve of my cheek, cupping my face. There's desperation in the way he searches my eyes.

When he hesitates, I sense he's losing his restraint.

"Baby." His voice is tender, sweet. "What we're doing here is so far from a rebound."

My heart thuds against my chest. I close my eyes against the familiar sting searing at the corners.

"Of course I don't want to leave. I came here, running from my hurt, to fix up the house where all my childhood summers were spent with my grandfather. I thought I could hammer away my regrets. Play Monopoly in a tournament to honor him. Forget about the fact I wasn't here when Pop died because the woman who ended up betraying me didn't like it here." He stares at me unblinking for a moment. "I'm starting to remember what it felt like to live, play, build something bigger than myself. Because I met you."

"But you're leaving."

"I don't know yet." The muscles at the sides of his jaw twitch. "That day at the coffee house, I was supposed to meet with a Realtor Murph referred. She had an emergency. We never ended up meeting, so I haven't even started the process of listing the house. I haven't decided whether I should."

I nod, knowing how life has a way of shifting under my feet when I'm just trying to find balance.

Declan swipes away my tears. "I came here to start over, rediscover who I am." His voice lingers just above a whisper as he softly blows at my tears. An easy smile dances across his lips. "You make me so crazy. Half the time I think I'm losing my mind how much I think about you, what you're doing when we're not together. My mind's been on you." He kisses the tip of my nose. "So no, I'm not biding time to move back to Vegas. As much as it scares me, I'm falling in love with you, Harper Sloane."

I gasp, my heart squeezing.

He brushes his lips over mine, slipping his tongue between my lips. His hands are on my face, moving through my hair, over my neck. That squeeze makes its way down low and tight in my belly.

A sigh spills from my lips.

Then electric pulses shoot through me as he tugs me closer, walking us backward, lowering us to the bed. I hold on to his lean torso, wrapping my legs around his waist. Slowly, he glides both hands up my outer thighs before latching on to my ass and sliding me closer still.

"I can't be late. I really need to meet with the girls before this last practice."

Declan ignores every word coming out of my mouth as he drags my jeans off then yanks his sweats down. He's hard already.

"We're in love. We need to celebrate it." The texture of his voice is rough and throaty, the deep timbre…oh, my goodness, it electrifies me. I don't think I'll ever get enough of hearing it. *We're in love. Dear God…* "I'll be quick."

WE MAKE IT to Love & Games with three minutes to spare.

When he pulls up to the curb, we kiss like it'll be forever until we see each other again, even though he'll be here for practice in an hour. After the fourth or fifth *I love you*, I finally drag myself out of the car and stand on the curb.

I miss him before he's even turned the corner. I'm just about to go inside when the sound of burning rubber skidding on the asphalt jolts my attention back to the street.

I melt when I see he's rounded the block and come back.

Declan lowers the window, leaning over the passenger seat. He flashes me a middle-melting smile. "Is it a bad thing that I miss you already?" he asks.

It takes me less than a second to reach the curb and dive through the passenger window to kiss him. In an embarrassing display, half my body hangs out of the car. I've got both hands cupped to the curve of his jaw as I kiss him like he's leaving for war instead of a few quick errands.

"You are such an overachiever." I laugh.

"So, this was a good surprise?"

"You did well. Definitely earned yourself some points for later," I say.

He shakes his head then kisses me once more, leaving me boneless. My eyes are closed, my libido is throbbing, and my panties are wet as I back out the window.

"Remember that thing you did with your tongue that time?" he asks. When I nod, he waggles his eyebrows. "I'm expecting a repeat performance tonight."

He drives off, knowing exactly what he's done to me.

I've barely dragged my shamelessly horny self into the store when Rox and Nadi start clapping obnoxiously.

"Let's give her a hand, ladies and gentlemen. She finally found a man who knows how to mess up her hair," Rox says way too loud.

My eyes dart around the store, but thankfully it's early and there are only a few customers browsing the shelves in the back. I try to keep a straight face. The smile tugging at the corners of my mouth is a dead giveaway, though.

"Is this a love thing because *someone*"—Rox waggles her eyebrows—"hasn't come home for more than a change of clothes since she met him?"

Nadi cocks her head at me. "Is *someone* ready to overshare?"

"*Someone* is tired of talking about herself like she isn't in the room. I think we all know we're talking about me and *Declan*." I breathe his name like the damn sex God he is.

We all laugh as I walk behind the register then tuck my purse away before hoisting myself up to sit on the back counter. "To answer your question… Yes, we're in love."

"And?" Nadi asks, but Rox lifts her chin, and I know she's eager to hear my response.

"And that's it." Heat swarms over my face. "I don't know if he's staying in San Diego. I'm just going with it." I shrug.

Rox's shoulders relax. "Before I forget, while you were off falling in love, Dad called to make sure we were still on for dinner with him and Everly…" She trails off, eyeing me before she says, "I might've told him things were getting serious with Declan."

"Why?"

"Harp, you're practically living together. Whether you want to admit it, things are serious." Rox's eyes widen like spilling my business to Dad is cool.

I'm going to the wedding. We're doing dinner to meet Everly. "What happened to taking it one step at a time?" I ask. The last thing I need is my father asserting himself in my romantic relationships.

"You said it yourself, you're in love with Declan." Rox shrugs.

"Okay, whatever," I say, turning my attention to Rox's color-coded spreadsheets sitting by the register. "Let's just get started."

Like a pro, Rox starts her compliment sandwich by highlighting the great turnout at the scavenger hunt. She reads positive comments people left on our social pages. Then she tells us there's still no response on the loan, rushing to add we should hear something within in the next seven business days.

She's just drilling in on her *we need to start thinking about worst-case scenarios* point—a not-so-subtle code for taking Dad's money—when a woman walks up holding a stack of boards games in her hands.

"Excuse, me. Do you ladies have a moment?" the woman asks.

Her red hair is in a loose ponytail, she's wearing yoga pants, and her smile is strained around the edges. Which, I'm going to go out on a limb, and guess is related to the fun-sized version of her standing near the display rounder, looking over at us. Something about the tween's thick black eye liner and perma-annoyed expression on her face gives it away.

"Sure," the three of us murmur our willingness to help. I slide down from the counter, Rox straightens by the register, and Nadi reaches out to take the stack of games to free her hands.

"I'm sure you all get this all the time, but I just wanted to stop by and thank you all." *Not what I was expecting.*

Again, like a set of triplets, we hum our thanks, asking if she has any questions or needs any help with anything else.

She waves us off. "My daughter, Sarah…dark eyeliner, black T-shirt, probably looking this way but trying not to alert us." She huffs out a laugh, flicking her gaze skyward. "Teenager in training as you can see."

We nod, doing our best not to laugh aloud.

"She's a sweet girl, going through all the changes. Emotions, peer pressure, friends, boys, mad at the world, we've all been through it." Then she pauses. Her lips quiver as she smiles. "She loves this place, though. It's like the only place left where she still gets to be a kid. I wanted to thank you for giving my daughter this space. For being positive role models in our community. You may not realize it, but it's so important she has examples of women doing amazing things and following their dreams."

My heart squeezes. This is why we built this business. We needed jobs and income, and the idea of working together were top of the list of reasons to start a game store. But we also knew how important it was for women to own businesses, create income, and give back.

"Oh, my gosh, that's so sweet," Rox and Nadi say in unison. Though, I'm speechless.

For the second time today, I feel the tears threatening at my eyes. This time it's with gratitude.

Nadi rings up her games, reminding her to check out our social media to see how we fare in the Monopoly tournament. Then she's gone.

Right on cue, Rox turns to me. "When we're at dinner Friday, it might be a good time to ask Dad for the money."

Then she walks away.

CHAPTER EIGHTEEN

DECLAN

COMMUNITY CHEST

A SOFT SMILE quirks the corners of Harper's mouth before she catches my lips. For a beat, I lean into the warmth of the kiss, letting it unravel the tension I've been carrying for the last week. Then I pull back because the last thing I need when I meet Harper's father for the first time is a raging hard-on.

"Relax. He promised he'd be nice," Harper says.

The parking structure where we parked isn't far from Francesco's. The walk won't take more than five minutes, but I don't want to risk being late.

"We should get going," I say.

Harper doesn't move, though. She's still watching me as she intertwines our fingers at our sides. She's breathtaking tonight. Her glossy brown hair is loose, parted just off-center, and tucked behind her right ear. Her deep red lips perfectly match the elegant satin dress draped over her golden-brown curves. I'm lost in the starlit forest of her glittery eyes.

"There's nothing to worry about, babe," she says, and I remind myself there isn't much I wouldn't do for this amazing woman.

"I'm good."

She pauses, searching my face.

"Seriously, it's no big deal." The fact I just said I'm fine and she's still telling me not to worry makes me think I should.

As much as Harper says her dad's opinion doesn't matter, that he has no place to judge our relationship, I know how important it is not to miss moments like this with family. I'd never want to get in the way of that.

Tonight is about Harper's time with her dad and a chance to get to know his future wife. This isn't about me. I've got no plans to let it be.

I lock the car then turn to Harper. "Got everything you need?"

Harper pecks my lips, lingering the slightest bit as she flattens her body against mine.

"Harp, tonight is important. I really don't want to be late," I say again, but the woman is ruthless.

She presses her breasts against my chest. Even through the thin fabric, my skin blazes beneath her touch.

"We've got a few minutes..." She trails off, flashing me a teasing smile.

I bite my lip, determined not to think about the fact she isn't wearing a bra to avoid the straps. How hot it would be to bend her over the hood of my car in this dark, seedy-looking garage.

Like she knows where my mind has gone, Harper rises

up on her toes to whisper, “After dinner,” as she dips her hand into the waistband of my slacks.

Fire blazes through my veins, my cock straining against the loose fabric. I groan in frustration before whisking her in wide strides toward the restaurant.

“Please, behave,” I say.

She smiles. “Maybe you shouldn’t have looked at me like that then.”

I haven’t met her father, and already the end of this night cannot come fast enough.

When we finally make it to Francesco’s, the hostess quickly shows us to our table. Almost immediately, I feel the tension drain from my shoulders when I see we’re the first ones to arrive. We’re seated in the center of the dining room facing the door, which gives me a slight advantage to get a good read on her father before he sizes me up.

The way a man carries himself, how far back his shoulders sit, how high his chin is raised, his posture, and his shoes. They all tell a story.

The second Harrison Sloane enters the dining room, the quiet music and low chatter all seem to fade away. He’s used to commanding a room. Especially with a beautiful woman on his arm. He’s tall with rigid posture, and an air of wealth radiates from his regal bone structure. By his lightly dusted gray hair and sharp jaw, anyone could tell he’s older. Though, the way his tailored black suit and crisp white dress shirt hang on his lean frame, it’s apparent he’s agile, athletic. He cares about his health. Probably plays squash, runs easy half-marathons when he’s not swinging his nine iron at bogeys and eagles.

"Is that him?" I ask.

"I don't believe this. I knew it." Harper's still looking at her phone, but she glances up, tilting her head to see past the couple at the next table. "Mm-hmm. That's Dad."

Instinctively, I feel my posture correct itself to match her father's and get to my feet. But Harper goes back to whatever's got her attention on her phone, so I'm on my own.

When they reach the table, I extend my hand. "Nice to meet you, Mr. Sloane. I'm Declan Wilde." There's too much bass in my voice to be natural.

"Pleasure." Her dad shakes my hand and angles his body to make the introductions.

He only has a few inches on the tall, elegant woman at his side. She's got to be in her late forties or early fifties, but her spirit, soft smile, and delicate features are timeless. She's poised and unassuming. Her bone-straight, inky black hair is cut asymmetrically along the curve of her jaw. She's wearing a classic black dress with pearls. Still, I don't get the sense she's demure. A quiet fire burns in her eyes. She's a deliberate observer.

"This is my beautiful fiancée, Everly Chen," Sloane says.

"I'm so sorry we're late." Everly's smile beams. "I keep telling Harrison how rude it is to keep people waiting."

Harper looks up just as I shake her hand.

"Hey, Dad," she says sweetly, standing to give him a huge bear hug, which surprises me, given her aversion to accepting his help. When she pivots, opening her arms to Everly, I notice the slightest hesitation. Then she goes in for a genuine embrace. "Nice to finally meet you, Everly. Congratulations on the engagement. You guys seem really happy."

There's a tinge of sadness laced in her tone, but she smiles anyway. From Harper's stories, I can only imagine how hard it is to let someone new in when history has shown you can't be sure how long they'll be around.

A pang of guilt wrenches my stomach. I'm leaving in a week. I haven't given her an answer whether I'm staying. I keep thinking, what if I make the move, giving us the benefit of the doubt, and we don't make it? Will I regret it? Resent her?

That's the last thing I want.

"Thank you so much. We are. I just...I can't believe we're really doing this!" Everly says. She's bubbling and exuberant, every bit the blushing bride. "I'd already accepted being alone, you know? Settling was never an option."

"Absolutely. It's like, *Hey if it's not going to happen, then so be it.*"

Everly leans in conspiratorially. "You two make a nice-looking couple."

They laugh, and Harper takes her seat while Everly settles in the chair across from her, leaving me face-to-face with Harrison Sloane.

Far too uncomfortable under his piercing gaze, I flash him a tight smile and scoot my chair closer to Harper pretending to be engrossed in their conversation.

Thankfully, Sloane seems content to let the women acquaint themselves. I'm guessing he's got questions for me, though. His finger is pressed to his upper lip, his chin raised, fiery brown eyes narrowed to scrutinize my every move.

Instinctively, I mirror his rigid posture and raise my chin, too. My hands are clasped on the table, and I'm biding my time.

A few minutes later, the women's talk turns from *how did you meet* to everything weddings when the waitress arrives, saving me from the awkward silence. Sloane convinces us to skip appetizers, so she fills our water glasses and takes our entrée orders.

"Well, now. Where is Roxanne?" He leans back and shifts to look over his shoulder. "She should be here. It's not like her to be late."

Harper swipes her thumb across her phone screen and angles it toward her dad and Everly. "That's because she isn't coming. It's too *coupley*."

"Oh, that's too bad." Everly's sharp shoulders slump, and she presses her lips tight. Her hair falls in a curtain over her left shoulder as she leans close to Harper. "After all the fun stories Harrison's told me, I'm excited to get to know you both. Hopefully, she'll be able to make it to the bridal shower next month."

"It's just as well." Harrison pats her hand affectionately, but then he turns to his daughter. "Gives me more time to meet with your young man here."

"Yeah," Harper says. "And I'll get to know Everly."

He flits an endearing smile to his fiancée before continuing. "It's a good time for us to discuss some things, too."

A thick silence hovers over the table.

"Like what, Dad?" Harper doesn't look at him, but her legs bounce under the table as she picks at her cuticles.

"Well, for starters, Roxanne mentioned you're under pressure with the stability of the game store. She said you might be willing to accept financial—"

"Sure, what else did she say?" Harper's tone is curt.

"I figured we could talk about what happened with your mom—"

"See. I knew you'd find a way to turn financial help into talking about the past." Harper puffs out her cheeks then slowly releases the air. "Listen, this is Rox's idea. A precautionary measure. I don't want your money. I never have."

Mr. Sloane's expression wars between outrage and anger. "Now, just a minute. If you have something to say, then say it."

"Maybe we should go, babe," I say, but my words fall on deaf ears.

Harper peeks her tongue out between her lips, nodding. Whatever it is she's about to say has been weighing on her.

"Let me get this straight. Rox gave you a full rundown on my life. The business is going through a rocky time, and shocker, I'm in a *serious* relationship, so you thought, *Hey, it's the perfect time to save the day. If things are going well with this new guy, she'll understand my life decisions better?*" She shakes her head. "What Declan and I share isn't a marriage with children involved, Dad. Our situations are nowhere near the same."

The second the words leave her mouth, she's up off her chair, dashing through the tables toward the restrooms.

"I'd better go after her," Everly says.

Then she's gone, too. And I know this is the opportunity Sloane's been waiting for to get me alone.

"As you can see, things aren't ideal between my daughter and me." He sits up taller and his broad shoulders tense. For the first time, I get a glimpse of the man underneath the iron façade. "Make no mistake, I love both of my daughters. Harper might not agree with the choices I've made, but I'm still her father."

"Yes, sir. I understand."

My answer seems to satisfy him.

He relaxes his shoulders, and his expression softens, but he's stalling, considering how much he wants to say. "When Roxanne asked about money, she said you might help Harper see the benefit of accepting—"

"No, sir." I cut him off because I know exactly where this conversation is heading.

In the back of my mind, all I hear is Harper's voice when she first told me about hard times falling on Love & Games. *He thinks money makes up for his absence. So quick to throw money at the problem.*

"With all due respect, I'm here for Harper," I say. "She's important to me, and I won't betray her trust."

Sloane harrumphs. "Ah, yes. Her walls." He taps the fork tines, his eyes unfocused. "They've been locked around her heart for so long, I didn't think she remembered how to let anyone in. Then Roxanne tells me she's found a man. A new Monopoly partner, a kind doctor, who wears his heart on his sleeve…and she let him in." His lifts his chin to meet my gaze. "She let *you* in."

Disbelief bleeds into his tone like this realization doesn't compute. He's her father, and I'm a man she's known for less than two months.

"Sir—"

His throat bobs. His eyes dull, lifeless. "I just want to

know how you did it," he says.

Every response I come up with feels inadequate when this man, who at first sight comes off as solid and unbending, turns out to have a Harper-sized hole in his heart. What am I supposed to tell him? That I have no clue? That I'm in love with her and praying she doesn't change her mind about me?

I open my mouth to speak but then close it just as fast.

"Forgive me. I should be saying all of this to her." Mr. Sloane waves off the comment. "Do you know what it's like to search for something always just out of reach?"

Yes.

THE REST OF the weekend, I think about Harrison Sloane. The dejected look on his face, the sadness in his tone before Harper returned to the table and we left Francesco's. History has shown her letting people in doesn't guarantee they'll stick around. I don't want to be one of those people who she regrets letting in.

So, it's Monday morning. Once I drop Harper off at Love & Games, I've got a decision to make.

I honk the horn, then chuckle to myself as Harper yells from inside the house that she's coming.

"Come on, Harp. You're beautiful," I call back before my phone rings on Bluetooth.

One look at the screen, I feel my shoulders drag downward.

Mom.

I flit a glance at the house to the front door still open, where I'm expecting her to run out any minute. Rox called another emergency meeting, and Harper's driving herself crazy wondering how Rox will react about her walking out of Francesco's on their dad and Everly—on their backup plan to save the store.

Quickly, I press the button to accept the call.

"Hi, honey." Mom's voice reverberates through the cabin of my car. "I'm just checking in on you, seeing how everything is going with Pop's house, and..." *When you're coming home*, I add.

I give the car a little gas, revving the engine. The last thing I need is to start the moving conversation then Harper comes out.

"Hey, Mom. Listen, I'm just about to run out for a bit. Can I give you a call back in—"

"I'm in the hospital." Before I can get a word in edgewise, she quickly adds, "I'm okay. It's silly. I was trying to reach the flour on the top shelf, and I lost my balance, somehow. Landed on my wrist. Just a small sprain."

My jaw tightens as I listen. Every nerve ending in my body stands on edge as I zero in on the incessant tapping of my fingertips on the steering wheel. For, I don't know how long, the line goes quiet. All I hear is my own shallow breaths, my heartbeat syncing to the rhythm with my fingertips.

Harper's keys jingling as she locks up the house jolts me out of my daze.

"Mom, I—"

"Promise, honey, I'm fine. Go on and get back to whatever you were doing. I just wanted to tell you before anyone called." I hear the smile in her tone. "I didn't want you to worry. Now go on, okay?"

I scrub my hands over my face, my pulse slamming in my neck. Dread rises in my throat until I'm choking on anger. How can I even consider leaving Mom alone? *What if she…?* I shove aside all thoughts of the unthinkable.

Mr. Sloane's words pinball inside my head, lighting every synapse in my brain.

Always just out of reach.

The instant her father said those words to me, I felt the shift behind my ribs. Why keep searching when everything is within reach with Harper? I'd asked myself. What's so wrong with letting my heart take the lead when there's a chance to have a home, love, fun, games, happiness?

I'd never forgive myself, that's what.

"Okay, Mom," I say.

When she ends the call, I've got just enough time to send a text confirming a meeting this morning with Murph's Realtor before Harper hops into the passenger seat, shutting the door behind her.

Wispy strands of her warm brown waves fall around the soft curves of her face as she seems to sense my discomfort. "What?"

She let you *in.*

I look at his amazing woman who had to sneak into my heart when, against the odds, she willingly let me into hers.

"Nothing." I swallow, giving her a small head shake.

She doesn't buy it, though. She stares at me for a quiet moment, searching my eyes.

"You're going to be late," I say after a beat, veering into the lane.

Last week, when she asked me about leaving, I'd been reluctant to decide, afraid of the consequences. I'd been stuck in my head, thinking about how I'd let my relationship with Penelope dictate so many choices I still regret. Waiting, for a warning sign to flash bright red, telling me I wasn't, once again, letting my heart make decisions I should make with my head. I'd been searching for an answer that seemed just out of reach.

Now I have it.

I can't stay.

A ghost of a smile plays on Harper's lips a little while later when we pull in front of Love & Games. As she leans over to plant a soft kiss at the corner of my mouth, she lingers for a few seconds.

"I love you. Let's talk when I get home," she says.

Nodding, I slide my hand to the base of her neck, deepening the kiss against my wrenching heart. I hold on tight, savoring the moment, letting her tenderness be a balm to my raw nerves.

Then she exits the car and slips into the store.

When I get back to the house, I tidy up for a few minutes. I unload the dishwasher, wipe down counters, sweep, and relocate our unfinished Monopoly game to the living room.

We spent the last seventy-two hours playing Monopoly. There'd been music and the Super Bowl on television playing in the background, phone calls, texts. It's a single never-ending game that's included sleep and meal breaks, a little embezzling by my beautiful banker, and some minor move miscounting. Neither of us wanting the game to end.

Somehow, rolling dice, buying and selling tiny red and green properties as we circled the board of a make-believe world, felt easier than talking about the fate of Love & Games. Or how she left things unsettled with her father. Easier than talking about our future.

Soon my phone pings with a text from Alana, the Realtor, letting me know she's outside. I give her the go-ahead to park in the driveway, then meet her at the door.

"Thanks so much for allowing me to stop by today. I'm so sorry it's taken me this long to link up with you again," she says as she exits her car.

She can't be taller than five feet, though I get the sense she's one of those larger-than-life people, brimming with personality. She's got glossy dark hair, bright brown eyes, and a smile almost as big as her baby bump.

"Come on in." I hold the door while she climbs the porch steps.

"Thank you, I can't wait to see all the things you've done with the place. I *love* these old bungalows."

Once she's inside, I offer her a water bottle while I ask how she and the baby are doing. She tells me she's staying hydrated, and due in a month. She and her husband have been over the moon, preparing for family coming to town, her hospital bag, and the nursery.

As my mind drifts to Mom alone in the hospital, against the guilt spiraling up my spine, I remind myself it's a small sprain.

"Let me tell you." Alana curves her diamond-clad hand

to the bend of her stomach. "The thing I'm dreading most is my family visiting." She laughs, then takes a small sip from the water bottle. "I'm just glad they don't live here if you know what I mean? Holidays and vacations together are one thing, but we need limits… We've all got our own lives."

The tension in my shoulders lessens when I imagine Harper and me visiting Mom for holidays, taking vacations together. Maybe one day, Mom flying in to help with a new baby…

"Are you worried about your parents living away from you?" I ask.

"Well, yeah. There's always that tiny seed of worry lying beneath the surface. I love them so much, and God forbid anything happens, I'm a flight away—a few hours' drive away. The good news is there are telephones, ViddyChat, email, text." She laughs. "We don't have to be right underneath each other to love and care. We just can't forget about them, you know?"

"Yeah." I smile, feeling lighter.

After Alana finishes the bottle, I give her free rein to tour the house. She calls out about the original wood floors and crown molding. Despite my concerns, she insists on inspecting the wall in Pop's room where the black mold was, assuring me it's common with older houses.

When she meets me back in the living room, she's wide-eyed with excitement.

"It's beautiful, Declan. That kitchen backsplash, the staging… We've still got to look at the comps and do some paperwork but you're not going to have a problem selling. I've got a few clients looking in this area, too." She presses her hand to her chest. Then she digs into her tote bag, fishing out a packet of paperwork "You might not even need to list it once they get a look at it—"

"Alana, would you mind giving me until the end of the week?" I ask.

It's almost imperceptible but something in her expression warms. Then her gaze flits to the Monopoly board on the leather trunk as if only just now she registers the tiny top hat and Scottie dog approaching Go. She glances around the space for a beat, at the furniture, the artwork, all the tiny little touches.

My heart squeezes as I stare at our game. At this house we spent hours, days, weeks, pouring our love, making it into a home.

Our home.

When Alana returns her attention to me, the corners of her mouth curve with a soft smile. "I'm guessing you had some help with the place. Someone special? She did a beautiful job with the house," Alana says, setting a business card on the end table. Then she rummages around the bottom of her tote, coming up with her keys. As she rests her hand on my arm, she leaves me with one last tidbit. "Take your time. Make sure your heart is in it."

Her empathy fills me with a renewed sense of urgency to talk to Harper.

"Thanks, I will."

CHAPTER NINETEEN

HARPER

BANKRUPT

AFTER ROX, NADI, and I lock up the store, I jump in my car headed straight for Pop's house. At the first red light, I call Declan to let him know I'm on the way, but I get his voice mail.

"Baby, the emergency meeting is over. I'm headed to see you. The loan was denied, so Love & Games is…" I swipe at my eyes, refusing to let the tears fall. "Well, let's just say, unless I can come up with a windfall of cash, we've got to take my dad's money… Which, I don't know, it feels selfish, but I just feel like I'd rather close the doors. So…" I'm rambling and I don't even know if he's home, but when the light changes, I let the car steer itself to the only place I want to be. Where the only person who I want to see might be. "Anyway, I could use a hug and I don't know, maybe—"

"If you're satisfied with your message…" My phone's robotic voice mail attendant interrupts my message, and I end the call. If Declan gets it, he gets it. Either way, I'll hopefully see him soon.

"Please be home. Please be home," I chant a few minutes later as I hang a left onto Pop's quiet tree-lined street.

But when I pull up to the house, there's a champagne-colored sedan in the driveway with a license plate that reads SDRLTR.

San Diego Realtor.

For a second, I sit frozen in my car. I stare at the letters, waiting for them to change. To scramble and rearrange themselves to stand for something other than a glaring sign that Declan is leaving. That no matter how I feel or how much he claims to love me, I'm a temporary fixture in his life.

Realization settles in the pit of my stomach.

He's tried this house and me on for size, and I guess we don't fit. So, he's going back to Vegas.

"Why do you do this to yourself?" I tighten my grip around the steering wheel as I let my head fall back against the headrest, but sunlight glints off the car's metal license plate frame, taunting me.

Just in case I was going to try to fool myself, there's the truth in bold, gold block letters informing tailgaters everywhere how much it pays to consult a Realtor.

My neck and cheeks burn with humiliation. My vision blurs as I fumble to put the car in drive just as Declan appears at the front door with a petite Asian woman with long dark hair and a professional gray suit struggling to maintain its shape around her huge baby bump.

"Harp, where are you going?" Declan calls when he spots me. He must see my splotchy tear-strewn face and the jerky movements of the car as I back up and turn to get out of the space.

He takes off in a full sprint after me as I pull into the lane and slam my foot on the gas.

"Please, wait!" he yells, but I can't stop.

He follows me around the corner and almost catches me, too. But he runs out of steam, staggering to halt in the middle of the street. With his hands clasped behind his head, struggling for breath, he watches me drive away. For a few hundred feet, I watch him, too. Until his beautiful silhouette grows smaller and smaller, until he fades into the distance.

As I steer the car out of his neighborhood, my pulse races and my chest tightens. All I want is to turn this car around and arrive five minutes later. The Realtor would've been gone, and I'd feel his arms around me while I cried. He'd tell me everything with the store was all going to work itself out. That Love & Games would be around forever. That what he and I have built together in this short time, it's worth staying for.

I let the windows down and swallow air in huge gulps. I let it sweep over me, drying my tears.

My phone rings as it filters through on Bluetooth. Because I'm so desperate to talk to Declan even if I can't be with him, I press talk.

"I can't believe you're really leaving—" I start, but it isn't Declan's familiar bass-filled voice.

"Harp, it's Mark. I'm not going anywhere. Are you okay? I'm coming—"

I flit my gaze to the dashboard, confused and flustered. "No, it's okay. I'll be fine. You don't have to come."

"Listen, I know we're not together anymore, but I'm still

here for you. As a friend, I'd still like to be there for you. So, I'm leaving right now," he says before I can tell him not to.

I don't have the energy to call him back and argue one way or the other, so I drive home.

Mark beats me there.

When I get out the car, he rushes to my side, gathering me into his arms.

"I'm here," he says.

But as I wrap my arms around him, letting my tears dampen the fabric of his T-shirt, all I can think about is how much I wish he was Declan. I want Declan's clean, woodsy scent and the brush of his beard against my cheek as I tip my chin up to kiss him. I want his warmth and the way we fit together.

Mark and I go inside and settle on the couch.

I feel nothing and everything all at once.

"Is Rox here?" Mark asks as he moves with a familiar ease around the kitchen. He digs into cupboards and into the pantry grabbing mugs and sugar to make me tea.

"No, I don't think so. We left the game shop at the same time, but she might've stopped off at the grocery store."

A few minutes later, he sets two steaming cups in front of me on the coffee table then scoots in beside me on the couch cushion.

"Like old times, huh?" A look of uncertainty passes across his kind face as he flashes me a small smile.

"Yeah," I say, thinking about what a nice guy Mark is.

He's always been sweet and thoughtful. Honestly, I don't know why I could never see him as anything other than a friend. Even when we dated briefly, it always felt forced.

There wasn't anything passionate about what we shared. I never felt any sparks or tingles. I never went to sleep and woke up missing him, wishing I could spend every waking minute with him like I feel about Declan.

"I feel like I've got a hunch what this is all about, but do you want to talk about it?" he asks.

I force a shaky smile, blinking back fresh tears.

"He's leaving." My throat closes on me, and I shrug, unable to say more without crying harder.

Mark gives me a slow nod. "So, you love this guy."

A weight settles on my heart hearing Mark voice my feelings about Declan so definitively. It's not a question, but a conclusion. And I feel so bad. It's got to be difficult for Mark to sit here with me sobbing over another man when he's always made his feelings for me clear.

"Well, where's home for him? Is a distance relationship an option or would you consider moving?"

My scalp prickles with shame because I've considered packing up my entire life and starting over in a new city with people who I don't know. All to be with this man who makes me feel more alive, more loved than I've ever felt.

But it's not just about me.

"No. My home is here. My family and friends. The business we built together…" I trail off, guilt corroding my insides. I've been so selfish. What kind of coward watches her business go up in smoke then runs off in the name of love like my dreams never mattered? Like the family I've built is replaceable. If I don't stay, what makes me any different than Dad?

"Okay, then maybe you can convince him to change his

mind," Mark says sweetly.

I'm just about to lie and tell him I'll be fine. Skirt my way around the fact I don't want to have to convince the man I love to stay with me, when a knock sounds at the front door.

"Will you get that for me? It's probably Rox with her hands full." I sit up and stir my tea staring as the amber liquid whirls, creating ripples.

Mark pushes to his feet and walks over to the door. "Who is it?" he calls before glancing through the small window on the side of the door.

I wait for Rox's voice.

But Mark unlocks the door and cracks it just enough, so when I look up, I catch sight of Declan standing on the other side.

My mouth goes dry and my heart races with a manic energy. I'm so mad at him, and still my pulse throbs traitorously. I feel all my good judgment and logic about what I should do for my family and my business being cast aside, if it means there's hope for Declan and me.

We're at an impasse, though.

He stands unwilling to come in and my weak knees won't carry me farther than this couch. So, we stare at each other from the short distance with hurt and love and a whole host of other emotions in between sparkling in our wet eyes.

Mark clears his throat.

"I'm going to leave you all to it. I'm here if you need me." He flits a protective gaze at me before wedging past Declan.

And then it's just us.

Declan curls his lips between his teeth as he sucks in a lungful of air, then releases a harsh breath.

"Seriously, Harp?" He lets out a bitter laugh. "That guy is who you called to console you and"—his dark gaze flickers with annoyance as he spots the two mugs on the coffee table—"what, did he make you fucking tea because you're hurt?"

"You don't get to be angry with me," I say. "I'm not the one who was just with a Realtor about to move on with your life like what we've been doing is—"

"Is what? What exactly have we been doing, Harp? See because I thought we had something real here." Declan drags his fingers through his hair, clutching fistfuls of dark curls in his grasp. "And yet, the second you think you know what you saw, you go running back to your ex who's all too happy to accept you with open arms."

"We're just friends," I bite out. "He called when I was on the way here, and he heard me crying."

"Right. You were crying. After you, what, saw her car and decided you knew all you needed to know? Or was it when I ran after you on foot," he points out, "to tell you I decided not to sell the house."

"What?"

"Yeah. The Realtor who I'd made an appointment with a month ago stopped by to drop off comps and a business card just in case I change my mind." He lowers his voice, so I have to strain to hear him when he says, "She complimented the paint and the décor, and the whole time I was thinking about you. How Pop's house didn't feel like my home until I shared the space with you. *Fuck.*"

"Dec..."

"And here you couldn't wait even an hour before you found someone else to..." He lets the rest die on this tongue. He kneads the back of his neck, a grimace twisting the shadows and lines of his handsome face.

"You're staying?" I ask, standing, but he holds up a palm telling me stay where I am.

The distance between us shreds my insides. I miss him. Talking, bickering, bantering, all of it. I miss the easiness of what we had—what, not even five minutes ago, I was so willing to give away.

He pinches the bridge of his nose, and I can almost see the wheels turning in his head, figuring how to let me down easy.

"Look, I don't know what you want me to say." He blows out an exasperated sigh, and my stomach churns. "How am I supposed to trust you? I feel like you've been playing me." The vein at his temple throbs as he clenches his jaw. "Like this has all been a game for you."

A toxic fury mixes with dread, burning my throat. I feel so stupid. I didn't give him a chance to explain, and now I've ruined everything. And for what? A business that may or may not survive? My pride?

Shit.

My pulse thunders, and my breathing grows ragged. "I'm sorry. I shouldn't have jumped to conclusions, but I saw her license plate and I was so hurt thinking you were selling the house and going back to Vegas."

Declan's shoulders sag at his sides. He closes his eyes. "Listen, I can't do this right now. I need to be able to trust you, and right now I don't see how I can."

My neck and my cheeks burn with shame.

When he looks at me, his eyes are red and watery, and my heart can't handle it.

"But you came all the way here to tell me you were stay—"

"I was," he says sharply, his words cutting to the bone. "I don't know what I'm doing now..." He trails off, and I so badly want him to finish his sentence. Now that we're no longer together? Friends? *In love?*

Heat burns my cheeks, and I touch my face, feeling the wetness.

Declan sees them, too, and his whole demeanor softens.

"At the end of the day," Declan begins again, all business like he's fulfilled his end of this temporary arrangement, none of his heart, "I have so much respect for you, but this, us, this isn't Monopoly or a fun tournament to me. I can't play games with my life. Not anymore."

That last word is like a knife to my heart. *Anymore.* It's so final, and I know it's over, but it pisses me off. How can he give up like we're nothing? Like minutes ago, he didn't rush over here to tell me he was staying for us.

It's like we've been tiptoeing around a minefield of my doubts, and suddenly, they've all detonated.

"So, I'm not allowed to make mistakes. Got it." It's immature and ridiculous, and I know I don't have a leg to stand on, but that's where my head is. Maybe if I get a rise out of him, make him feel something, it'll help him remember.

I fidget with my hands, picking at my fingernails, waiting for his carefully placed mask to break.

"Don't you think somewhere in the back of your mind you still had doubts about us if you didn't cancel the Realtor appointment? Don't you think I had a right to be scared when I saw her car?"

Declan looks away, and I know my weak questions aren't enough. All his fire, all the anger, it seems to fizzle out.

"I'm sorry. I can't do this," he says.

A heavy sadness tears through my chest, wrenching my heart. I just want him to hear me. To say let's try once more. To not give up.

I squeeze my eyes closed and let the tears fall.

"Couldn't you give me one more chance?" I hold my breath.

Redness creeps into his cheeks, but he shakes his head. "Harper…" My name dies a tortured death on his tongue.

I lower my chin to my chest, desperate and deflated. "Pretty please, with sugar on top?" I force a smile through my tears.

But Declan scrubs both hands over his face and groans. He cares, but it hurts. Too much.

"My mother is in the hospital. She's okay," he hurries to add when I gasp. "But I was willing to leave her alone in Vegas with no family around, the same way I left Pop. I was willing to uproot my life," he says. "Start all over again for you. For us." He whispers the last part as he clasps his hands behind his head and stares at the ceiling. "Yet you were bothered by what you saw. We didn't talk or work through it together. You were ready to throw in the towel just like that."

"I know, and I'm sorry." My throat hitches. Even as I say

the words, I'm focused on the sharp, jagged snap of my heart breaking.

Declan levels me with a pained stare. "It was so easy for you to walk away. Your mind was made up."

And now, evidently, so is yours.

We're standing a few feet apart, but it feels like miles divide us.

My pulse thunders in my neck. I swipe my sleeve under my runny nose and sniffle. "It's okay, I guess… I understand. You've been hurt before, and you don't want to hear excuses. I had my chance." I'm rambling now, prolonging the inevitable. Every nerve ending in my body feels exposed. I'm raw or numb, or some combination of the two.

The room grows quiet as the silence stretches between us. For what feels like a lifetime we stare at each other. The moment irreversible somehow. We can't take any of it back. The line has been drawn, and we've been reduced to some watered-down version of two people who once loved each other.

The weight of it settles on my heart and plummets to the pit of my stomach.

Then, without another word, he turns and walks away.

Sobs rack my shoulders as I stare blankly at the door—the reality of what I've just lost too big to absorb.

CHAPTER TWENTY

DECLAN

GO DIRECTLY TO JAIL

AS SOON AS we receive our drinks, Murph twists on the barstool to face me.

"So, you're really leaving tomorrow?" he asks.

"Yup." I sigh.

We're at a no-name dive bar a few blocks from the university. It's a Friday so it's packed. Loud, grimy, with college basketball games on every television screen, and a trivia game going on in the back near a raised stage. Every few minutes, a player scores and the volume rises to a level that makes it impossible for me to hear myself think.

Honestly, I'm counting on it.

I'm tired of listening to what my heart has been telling my brain for the past week. *Have I made a mistake?*

When the noise dies down, I take a long pull from my glass then set it on the waxy wooden bar.

"Do you think I made a mistake with Harper?"

Murph blows out a breath then lowers his head. His ankles are hooked around the legs of the stool, but he bounces his knee restlessly. His tone is low and tentative when he finally asks, "Was it your decision to end it?"

I stare unfocused at the television-lined wall behind the bar. "She took one look at Alana's car in the driveway and assumed I was selling Pop's house."

"Well, weren't you? I mean, wasn't that always the plan, selling the house, getting the taxes off your hands?" Murph asks.

I grab the chilled beer bottle that's been sweating in front of me, then pour the rest of its contents into my glass. I tip it back for a long pull, letting the cool liquid soothe me. Then I say, "It was."

Murph nods like he's still gathering the facts. "And is your mom still in the hospital?"

"Nah, it was just a sprained wrist, but that's the part that gets me about Harper. After what happened with Pop, I was still willing to leave Mom in Vegas alone for Harper." Shame and embarrassment coil around me. "I was ready to uproot my house, my career, everything I've known, for her. And she couldn't even give me the benefit of the doubt."

"That's fucking brutal," he says.

I scrape my fingers through my hair. "Yeah. I guess we were already headed in that direction. No sense in going back down that road, right?"

Murph presses his fist to his mouth, watching me, surveying the damage.

"Welp. You said you wanted to have fun and rediscover yourself." Murph fans his arms out like we've reached the mountain top, and this shitty bar is the answer to all my troubles.

On the screen, the point guard from San Diego State shoots a field goal, and the crowd in the bar goes ballistic. People whistle, holler, and jump. Just off to the right of Murph and me, a waitress loses her footing, but I swoop into action, settling her and the drink tray before she falls.

"Thank you," she purrs.

She's petite, shapely, with a blonde ponytail, and cute. Young, but certainly a girl who knows how to have fun.

The corners of my mouth tug into a smile as I loosen my grip on her shoulders. "You're all good. Just…be careful. It's wild in here tonight."

Her smile is megawatt and inviting as she walks away.

"Holy shit, bro. She definitely wants to—"

"Don't say it."

We both laugh. Of the two of us, I'm not the one who's smooth and stealthy when it comes to getting in there with women.

"Like I was saying, you're in the right place. Enough beer." Murph waves down the bartender and orders shots for us. Three each, like he's lost his ever-loving mind. "I say we get shit-faced and get you a rebound before halftime. The bathrooms here are pretty clean."

"You're disgusting, you know that." I cock my head to my friend, who still feels like my old college buddy. This is what I need. Not to think. To be around a man who can separate all the shit from Shinola. Or in his case, random hookups to hack a heartbreak.

A deep, guttural laugh claws its way out of me, and it feels good. I've felt so heavy lately when I'm supposed to be having fun. Figuring out what the hell I want in this sorry excuse for a life.

When our shots arrive, Murph divvies them up and levels one at his mouth. "Don't think about it. Just throw 'em back."

Because I'm so tired of aching and feeling half-empty without Harper, I do.

Each one singes my throat as it trickles past the heavy hollow ache in my chest. I breathe it out like fire.

Murph grunts as he polishes off his last shot, pounding his chest barbarically with his fists. "That's what I'm talking about. You ready to have some fun?"

There's a lull in the college basketball crowd. In the back near the stage, the microphone crackles to life as the trivia moderator asks a question, "What American holiday is celebrated on February second, and is also a film?"

A man a few stools down from us yells out, "Super Bowl!"

Murph shakes his head, genuinely annoyed. "Fucking Neanderthals. It's *Groundhog Day*," he mutters loud enough for me to hear.

"The answer was *Groundhog Day*," the moderator says a few moments later.

I slap my hand on Murph's shoulder. "You got it right."

"Damn right I did." He sits up taller. "Trivial Pursuit is for me what Monopoly is for you. Plus, I'm sort of a genius." He plucks his collar ceremoniously.

Yeah, okay.

But the name of the game nearly sends me backpedaling to Harper. Almost like the glue in our relationship, everything revolved around Monopoly. Practice, the tournament, our conversations at Pop's. Now, I'm unsure if I should even come back for the tournament next month.

The noise picks up, but we can still make out the questions.

"What is the name of the official national anthem of the United States of America?"

The same loud guy at the bar stumbles as he gets to his feet and yells, "'America the Beautiful'! Fuck, yeah! I'm killing it!" It comes out on a slurring roar, and I'm...unimpressed.

The vein at Murph's temple protrudes. "This is exactly what's wrong with this country. Some people are pissed about kneeling for the damn flag, but don't even know our anthem's name is 'The Star-Spangled Banner,'" he roars back.

Thankfully, the guy is too drunk to register when he's being corrected in front of a full house, but I recognize Murph's alcohol-fueled rage for what it is because it's like looking in a mirror. I take note of his posture. His tall, rigid frame. The pained stare and emotion-choked voice. The feverish, overbright eyes. He's desperate and clearly in denial.

"Don't tell me you're subscribed to complicated women issues, too."

He shoots me a death glare.

I hold my palms up. "Whoa! Touchy." Murphy Theodore Sikes doesn't do women problems, so my interest immediately piques. I give it a couple of seconds. But only a couple.

"What's her name?"

Murph doesn't even glance up at me, so I know this

ought to be good.

"Let's just say, this brand of complicated runs in the family."

Because I'm still reeling from the breakup, my initial reaction is to assume it's Harper. My body locks up with rage, and my blood nearly boils over, but then I take a deep breath. Murph and I came to an understanding a long time ago that we'd never break the bro code.

Then it dawns on me. "Rox?"

He appears to struggle to find the right words, but a slow smile spreads on his face. "She doesn't even know."

"So then tell her."

"Yeah, because that worked out so well for you." He immediately closes his eyes, sensing it's way too soon. "Sorry. Look, it's not that simple. The three of them are tight. Like family tight, and I know me." He heaves an exasperated sigh. "We're friends. Plus, she's not someone I'm willing to test the relationship waters with."

I almost fall off the barstool. "Who are you? Murphy, is that you? Using the *R* word so casually," I tease, but he doesn't see the humor.

He sits up and blows out another breath. He scans the bottles on the wall like he's contemplating ordering another drink. Then he shuts his eyes again.

When he opens them, Murphy is gone, and Murph is back. "I'm good. I just need…" *A warm body beside you to help you forget?*

Yeah, I know.

Another group of people squeeze into the already packed bar and wedge themselves beside us to order drinks. I'm not watching the games, and after those shots, I'm relegating myself to water for the rest of the night. I toss another glance back toward the stage where I notice the cute waitress setting a round of wineglasses in front of a booth full of women.

My heart isn't in it, and I decide maybe that's for the best. Maybe I should listen to my best friend and *un*complicate my life.

I turn to Murph. "Why don't we step out of the way and let these guys get drinks? Let's go play."

"This is your problem." He shakes his head. "You're worried about rediscovering yourself when you should be rediscovering your dick. I'm telling you that hot waitress with the perky tits was giving you fuck-me eyes."

His eyes drift curiously from my steepled fingers to the smirk on my face.

"Before you say another word…" I lift my eyebrows and cock my head toward the back of the bar. I've already noted the bar's server entrance located just off the hall to the "clean" restrooms.

The second he follows my line of vision, recognition lights up his eyes. "Let's go have some fun."

My thoughts exactly.

Before long, we settle into a two-seater across from the women in the booth, who Murph quickly acquaints himself with, learning their names and drink preferences. All part of his charm, I guess. They seem to eat it up, giggling and marveling as he exploits his trivia prowess. One by one, he answers the questions correctly, making it look easy while lining up his warm body of the night.

But my focus is on the waitress across the room.

She's nothing like Harper. To tell the truth, that's what fuels me. I don't want to replace Harper. I'm hoping someone different will help me understand why upholding a standard feels like shit.

On all sides of the cramped, dim space, the blare of the television and the echo of the microphone pinballs off the walls. The moderator asks a question about a European castle, and I know the answer, but now isn't exactly the ideal time for trivia.

Not when I still have my own unanswered questions.

Like why I feel like I'm being unfaithful to Harper just looking at another woman when we ended our relationship?

"Don't think about it." Murph gives me a reassuring slap on the shoulder.

The waitress searches my eyes, smiling.

Air lodges in my throat, and I don't know why I'm being such an asshat about this. I've dated other women. But that was before Harper. Before, I knew what it was like to be more than one of two warm bodies moving. With us, it was so much deeper. Our minds and souls joined in the fun. I could lose myself in Harper…

Is that such a bad thing? Being lost when she's the only one who knows how to find me?

I war with myself about walking over to the waitress. I should be able to do this. I should be able to stand, walk over to her, and try my hand at moving on. But I can't bring myself to do it. Not when my chest aches the way it does. Not when the noise, the drinks, the prospect of any future without Harper does nothing to numb my pain.

The microphone crackles with a piercing shriek.

"How many color-groups are there on a Monopoly board?" the trivia moderator asks.

I should be thinking about the fact that a beautiful woman is looking at me like she wants nothing more than to be with me tonight. I should, but all I can think about is the number eight. There are eight color-groups on a Monopoly game board.

A laugh bubbles inside me.

I once told Murph I hope to find someone who loves classic board games and amusement parks just as much as a good book, movie, or gallery. The funny thing is this game helped me find the woman who still holds my heart.

Almost as if she senses I'm not the *warm body for a night* type, the waitress tosses me a smile then turns back to the bar.

I knew that first day at Love & Games, again at the comedy show, and even more so when I walked away—a deep-seated tug to be with Harper. Our closeness felt tangible somehow. Each time we were together, I was more amazed how I could be comfortable and completely at ease with her. I'm more me around her than I have been in I don't know how long.

At this moment, I can't remember a time when I felt more settled with who I am. But if I'm going to make this right, I've got to get all my cards in a row.

CHAPTER TWENTY-ONE

HARPER

DO NOT PASS GO

"HOW LONG DO I have to be here?" I pout.

Nadi is too busy pushing up her boobs and checking her reflection in the glare of the window display to acknowledge me. Not that she has since she dragged me out of Love & Games ten minutes early, leaving Rox to close by herself.

It's a cold Tuesday in March. I could be home by now, curled up in bed, sinking into a good read about people who get their happily-ever-after. Instead, I'm hungry, tired, and freezing outside a local bookstore.

All in a day's work of being both a best friend and wing woman to Nadi, I suppose.

Although, I'm still questioning the logic.

As a brokenhearted raincloud, am I *really* the best person to give her support when she's approaching a potential new friend with benefits? Not likely. But my little social butterfly of a BFF seems to want me around. Built-in escape plan and all. You know just in case things suddenly go south with the hot, nerdy bookstore owner, Micah Hamilton, who she's been brazenly flirting with since the scavenger hunt.

Like I haven't noticed the bookstore around the corner, Booked Up, on Instagram commenting on every Love & Games post.

"Probably not *that* long," Nadi says. "Are you still going to the bridal shower for your dad's fiancée on the twenty-ninth?"

Nice subject change.

She knows I don't have an answer. That's ten days away. Beyond the tournament the following Saturday, I've been too busy putting one foot in front of the other to notice the calendar.

"How long is *not that long*?" I ask.

Nadi puckers her lips and pinches her cheeks until they're the same matching rosy pink. Before we left, she changed out of her high-waisted, bell-bottom jeans and long-sleeve crop tee and into a balloon-sleeve pink sequined dress that screams anything but *I just scarfed down four slices of pizza and unpacked dozens of board games.*

I groan because Nadi's *not that long* is like a quick game of Monopoly. It just doesn't happen.

After working all day, I want to barricade myself at home like I've been doing the last six weeks. *And hopefully think of something other than the fact Declan still hasn't changed his mind about us.*

We're *friends*. Whatever that even means. But I don't want the benefits without all the rest. I don't know about him, but *I* can't be anything less than completely in love with Declan.

My heart wrenches, and I bite my lower lip to keep the sadness at bay.

"Yeah, I'm going to the bridal shower." Pivoting toward the street, I let my head fall back on my shoulders and blow a breath skyward, the empty ache in my chest leaving me numb. *Shit.*

"Hey..."

At the worry laced in Nadi's tone, I spin around, aiming to look breezy. "Yeah?"

She squints, scrutinizing every inch of my face. "You okay?"

I nod way too many times to be natural, chewing the inside of my cheek. My eyes burn, and the faint taste of copper fills my mouth from where I've bitten down too hard. I shrug, and thankfully, Nadi doesn't push the matter any further.

Her meticulously arched brow rises. "I already told that man I'd hunt him down and ruin him. I will do *very* bad things to him."

We both laugh. I try to perk up for Nadi's sake.

"Now, what are we talking, five, ten, thirty minutes, an hour?" I ask after a moment.

"It's a bookstore, not an amusement park," she scoffs as if that alleviates my worries. Any place there are red-blooded men *is* an amusement park for Nadi. "Plus, this is a drop-in. He doesn't even know I'm coming." She beams, pivoting toward the entrance.

The good news is the second we enter, I'm no longer cold.

Booked Up is tiny. Like closet sized. But somehow, I

don't feel claustrophobic. Floor-to-ceiling open shelves make it cozy. Warm ambient light, rich dark woods, and a couple of crushed velvet settees blended between small round display tables. It's casual but refined in a grown-up, adaptable sort of way. And with a fireplace anchoring the space, there's charm to spare.

I trail behind Nadi, tracing my fingers over curated displays of brightly colored books and racks of tchotchkes when I notice a sign that reads GAME ON in the far back corner. Immediately, I'm curious about the bookstore's game selection. The bookstore's only a couple blocks away, and in North Park, that's a little too close for comfort as far as competition goes.

"Hey, Nadi."

When I look up, she's already two inches from Micah, giggling as she leans in and tucks her short blonde hair behind her ear. He's tall, lean muscles, warm brown skin, low fade. Aptly, book boyfriend material.

"So much for needing a wing woman," I mutter to myself as I weave my way toward the table with the sign.

Upon closer inspection, the display isn't board games at all. In an unexpected twist, it's books. *In a bookstore...*

"Get it together, Harp." I shake my head, laughing, and decide to browse anyway. I flit a glance over to Nadi and her book boo, whose collar she's now running the tip of her finger over. *Obviously, my services are no longer needed.*

I go back to scanning the books, fanning through pages of a romance novel. At first, I don't get why they're grouped together. There are various genres, different color themes, and authors. None of them related to games. But as I read the titles, it hits me. They're all books with the word *game* in the title.

A surge of renewed energy zips through me, buzzing and tingling beneath my skin. "That's an idea..."

Over the past month, my drive for Love & Games has been unfocused since Rox and Nadi voted to take Dad's handout.

We've cut the deficit by fifty percent, but it felt like a copout to let Dad close the gap for us. After the loan got denied, the crowd-source account brought in only a few thousand bucks, and tournament registrations hasn't drummed up the sales we projected, his money was the only option left. I didn't deliver a solution, so I checked out.

It was unfair of me to push back on our only solution because of my pride. It's about time I change that.

I grab a handful of the books, and though Nadi is going to kill me, I take wide, excited strides over to her and Micah.

Because she's all up on him, I clear my throat when I reach them.

He jolts away from her.

"Hey. Micah." He stretches his hand and gives me a hardy shake. "You must be Harper. Nadia told me a lot about you."

"Likewise." With a small smile, I lift a bright, teal-colored book with yellow script and an illustrated couple. "Found this on your GAME ON table. The funny thing is I thought you might've stocked board games."

Nadi's eyes snap to mine, and I know my idea has telepathically zipped over to her.

"Nope. Just books here...in Booked Up." He quips with

a sarcastic smile, and already I love that we have the same sense of humor. He'll have to if he's going to last more than a month with Nadi.

"Pretty sure I also saw bookmarks, socks, keychains, journals—" I'm on a roll when Nadi cuts me off.

"Plus, a host of smaller retail items," she says. "But have you given any thought to something a bit bigger for say, groups of two to six people to engage together? Like, maybe board games."

Micah crosses his arms over his chest and smiles, clearly onto our conspiratorial attempt to barter an agreement. By the open-mouthed silence, I sense he's ready to shut this whole conversation down.

"Before you say anything," I rush to say. "Do you have any books on classic board games? Monopoly, Clue, Trivial Pursuit, family fun, etcetera?" I raise a challenging eyebrow in question, but I know there's got to be at least one book here to further my argument.

He shakes his head and chuckles.

"You're good. I do have some titles. I think there's one on the history of Monopoly." He presses his lips together, his eyes glowing with amusement. "What exactly are you proposing?"

Nadi opens her mouth, but I jump in before she can get a word in edgewise.

"Cross-promotion. On a trial basis. You stock a few of our games. We stock an equal number of relevant books."

Taking her cue, Nadi adds, "We cross-post. Tag each other's businesses. Do a collaborative push on store events to increase our sales and foot traffic." She tucks her lower lip between her teeth seductively. "In turn, both our businesses thrive and we get to keep our doors open. So, we do more lunch dates. Dinner dates." It's so unfair using feminine charms, but she bites the tip of her finger when she says, "After-dinner dates."

Micah swallows, his resolve to deny Nadi anything visibly waning. The poor guy will definitely need to do something about the lovesick puppy look on his face before he takes the next customer.

He shrugs. "What the hell? Let's do it."

I have to physically restrain myself from breaking out into a happy dance.

"Perfect," I say casually.

Nadi tosses me a wide-eyed glance before turning to him and melting. They're totally going to hook up. And now that I think about it, I don't want to be here when they do.

"Okay, then. I nominate you to run it by Rox." I raise my eyebrows at Nadi before turning to Micah. "If everyone is good, let's do some gathering and brainstorming tomorrow. Figure out what games and books we think will do the best in each other's stores, then reconnect with a game plan."

We all agree, and I pivot toward the door, set to leave them to their canoodling when Nadi touches my arm. She tilts her head and squints like she's carefully considering the question on the tip of her tongue.

"Does this mean you're not giving up on us, on Love & Games?" Nadi asks. "I know your dad's money is in the business account, but we don't have to stop working toward long-term solutions."

At the serious turn of the conversation, Micah slips away

toward the register, giving us privacy to talk.

I release a sigh.

Collaborative cross-promotion is a small, innovative step in the right direction, but it's not going to do all the work needed. "If Dad's money is in our business account, I think we need to consider hiring a consultant to help us avoid similar situations in the future..."

She nods because we've had this conversation so many times since we learned about the hole we're still digging our way out of. His money buys us time, that's it.

"Rox and I are totally okay with drawing up a promissory note," Nadi says. "This is a business loan we intend to repay."

I nod, knowing the three of us are going to have to sit down and hash this out in detail.

Nadi lets her chin rest on her chest. "We've got to get back to all the reasons we started this business. Back to being us. Do you think we can do it?"

The question crawls under my skin, clutching my damned pride.

As much as I hate that Rox and Nadi ran to Dad, I'm ashamed I was so quick to say no. I've been too worried about broadcasting our failure to the world—what it says about the three of us as business owners. As women. Would it mean we don't have what it takes to fight? That we're not cut out for it?

"Honestly?" I search my best friend's sympathetic gaze. There's no judgment. She's genuinely trying to understand my perspective. "I've never doubted us when we put our heads together. I was wrong to make you and Rox feel bad for agreeing to take Dad's money."

Nadi softens. She sets her hands on my shoulders, squaring me to her. "Listen, I'm not trying to make you feel bad or take sides. I love you, and I love this business we've built together. Selfishly, I don't want it to end." She presses her forehead to mine. "All I'm saying is, maybe reframe it. Look at it from a different vantage point."

"I'm trying." Trying to look past a lifetime of learning that money isn't the answer.

But in this case, isn't it?

No matter where it comes from, isn't a gift about the thought and not the size or the amount? It's supposed to show appreciation and how much you value a person's role in your life. Isn't that the idea?

Haven't I been doing the same thing I accused Dad of, thinking about myself and what it means to me, rather than what it means to Rox, Nadi, and me?

"I know you're trying. The fact you even pitched that idea to Micah is proof. *He's so fucking hot,*" she mouths with a little growl, and we both laugh. "Just think about all the solutions out there, resources and support we haven't tapped into. This is just a new chapter for us. You said it before, we deserve to be here. Our community—the women and little girls in it—deserve to see us running meaningful small businesses."

Tears well up in the corners of my eyes.

God, I resent the fact that Dad sent checks and wedding invitations, but never spent his *time* with me. But it's that same resentment and unbudging pride that's ruining my life. It's robbed me of a relationship with my father, pitted me against my sister and best friend, and stripped me of the love of my life. I won't let it take the business we've built, too.

I nod, biting back another bout of tears.

"I'll do whatever the three of us decide is best, but I need you to know we wouldn't be the first business to accept help from a family member. We certainly won't be the last. And that doesn't mean we failed." Nadi tugs me closer and bands her arms around me. "Right now, I know the money is in the account, but we don't need to touch it yet. Let's just leave it as a last resort. We'll keep exhausting other options."

A hiccup bleeds into my cry, and we erupt into giggles.

"Sorry."

"I'm going to need you to get yourself together." Nadi squeezes me once more then swipes the pads of her thumbs under my eyes. "Looking like a raccoon. We have a reputation to uphold, and I'm trying to get some tonight." She bites her lower lip.

Shaking my head, I jam my hand into my purse for my keys, eager to leave so I can stop embarrassing the both of us.

When my breathing evens, I hug Nadi again. "I'm not giving up on us. The way I see it, we still have two weeks before the Monopoly tournament. We can totally do this." Nadi gives me a *that's the spirit* fist pump. "After we total the numbers, and see where we're at… And if this works with Micah, we might close the gap."

"That's what she said," Nadi jokes.

On that note, I'm about to leave when my phone starts ringing. I just know it's Rox checking on me again. We live and work together, so she's been worried about me, but I've kept our interactions to the bare minimum—house and business must-haves only.

When I slip my phone out, it isn't my sister.

It's Declan.

My gaze snaps to Nadi, all the humor gone.

The familiar weight settles on my heart. My lungs constrict making it hard to breathe. I feel like a ton of bricks weighs me down, and I'm crumbling inside. I prayed he'd call. Now I don't know how to talk to him. Not without crying. Not without wishing things were different.

The phone keeps ringing, persistent and unyielding, daring me to answer.

I can't play this game.

My vision blurs, but I just stare at Declan's name remembering every kiss, every touch, and every whisper we shared.

Before I can make a move, Nadi swipes the screen and sends him to voice mail. All in a day's work of being both a best friend and wing woman, I realize.

"He knows where to find you if he wants to make amends," she says, echoing my thoughts. "There's only face-to-face when your emotions are involved."

I swallow back the tiny seed of hope I had that Declan called to tell me he'd made a mistake. That he wants to try again because we're worth another chance. A second time around.

It hurts like hell, but I need to let him go.

CHAPTER TWENTY-TWO

DECLAN

DO NOT COLLECT TWO HUNDRED DOLLARS

MOM TURNS DOWN the radio. "Dec, do you have any more tape?" she calls from the kitchen where she's packing the breakables, careful not to agitate her wrist after the sprain healed.

I never followed through on listing Pop's house. So, I'm back home in Vegas, boxing up everything I own for the move to San Diego.

"Hold on one sec… I'm just about done. You can have this roll," I say as I glide the tape over the seam of a small box of books.

After I stack the box with the others along the living room wall, I walk over to the kitchen to pass her the roll, opting to take a quick breather. Over the past few weeks, I've been packing a room at a time. Once the kitchen is done, I'm set for the movers to arrive tomorrow.

"Ready for a slice?" I ask Mom, tearing off a pepperoni and sticking it in my mouth as I walk over to the fridge to grab us both cold bottles of water. Then I lean against the counter, scanning the bare walls and empty cupboards.

I'm really doing this.

For me this time.

"No, I'm not really hungry, honey. But tell me, how was the going-away party at the office?" Mom gently presses her fingers along the box seam, removing the air bubbles. She doesn't look up at me, but I hear the sadness in her tone.

I stare down at my feet.

"It was fun. A little bittersweet, too. I'll miss my staff, my patients, the comfort of my routine. They're excited for me, though, taking this adventure." I chuckle to myself. "Apparently, it's been a running joke that I never go anywhere, have fun, or try anything new," I say over a mouthful, thinking about the huge leap of faith I'm taking. New city, new home, new office, new relationship. *Hopefully.* "I guess go big or go home, right?"

Mom's voice is soft, soothing as she lifts her chin to survey me. "Have you talked to her?"

A wave of humiliation floods over me as I bow my head. "No. I've reached out a few times. Texts, voice mails." A desperate laugh claws past my throat. "Even an email once, but no. She doesn't want anything more to do with me."

At this, Mom backs over to the kitchen sink, leaning against it as she folds her arms across her chest to observe me.

"So, that's it. You're going to be in the same city, living and working in the same community, and you're letting her go, just like that." She shakes her head, and if I'm being honest with myself, it pisses me off.

"What else would you have me do, Mom?" I bite out a mirthless laugh, resenting the implication that I haven't done enough. She's acting like I didn't open up to Harper. Or plan to move to San Diego to be with her when Harper proved how much she didn't trust me. And still, I've sucked up my pride, reaching out to her. I'd say, all my unanswered attempts... She's made her feelings crystal clear.

"Go see her," she says simply, like it's the easiest thing in the world to show up on Harper's doorstep. Or at her place of business when she doesn't want to see me.

Mom picks up a slice of pizza, chewing as she listens.

"Oh, so she can shut me down in person, I see." I nod, sarcasm dripping from my tone. "So, be a stalker. Uh-huh. Should I also get on my knees, crawl, beg and scream for her to take me back?"

"Yes!" Mom's voice is a thunderous explosion. "Yes, baby. If you love her, you need to show up. Period. It's easy to ignore a call or text. Even an email can be relegated to spam." She smiles through her determination to get this through my thick head. Then she lowers her voice somewhere close to a whisper. "But, honey, if she can stand right in front of you and tell you to walk away, *then* you listen. That's how you know if this love is real. If being away from each other is tearing her apart the same way it's doing to you. You can't hide that kind of hurt."

My mouth goes dry and my hands tremble. Every inch of me tingles with anticipation as I hold on to this small shred of hope.

I nod because my head is swimming with questions. When should I show up? Where? What do I say when I get there? What if it works? *What if she tells me to walk away?*

As if privy to my spiraling thoughts, Mom erases the distance between us, pulling me into a hug the way she's always done—a balm to my pain.

"Don't worry about the when, where, and what. All that'll matter to her is the why." She rubs her hand over my hair before she cups her small hands to my cheeks to meet my gaze. "You love her. You've been miserable without her. You'll do whatever it takes to make things right. Beyond those reasons, honey, nothing else matters."

I close my eyes as she tugs my head down to kiss my forehead.

With a small tilt of her head, Mom blows a soft breath over my eyes.

"You smell like pepperoni." I chuckle through my rising panic.

"Now that that's out of the way," she says, satisfied she's accomplished her goal of getting me to be proactive. "I sense you need a plan of action. You said she has a thing about people not sticking around, so we need to prove to her you're there to stay. How much time do you have before you start up at Murph's office?"

My heart is still racing, my body on edge, but I'm grateful to have Mom on my team.

"Let's see, my start date isn't until mid-April, so I'll have a few weeks free."

"You still on the fence about participating in the Monopoly tournament? Might be a good place to start. The game brought you together." She shrugs.

I tip my head to either side, unsure a public venue is the right way to go. In the back of my mind, I was thinking something more intimate, quiet.

"What about this?" I say, unlocking my phone, reading the list Murph armed me with of San Diego sites. "Beautiful beaches, art and history museums, the USS Midway is right there on the water. I hear it's beautiful at sunset."

"Or a baseball game." Mom raises her eyebrows hopefully. "The zoo could be a great place, too. Especially if the animals are—"

I hold my hand up against her words. The last thing I need while confessing my undying love is to be an eyewitness to a mating ritual.

"You've given me a lot to think about during the drive down, so let's just leave it at that. I'll think of something to make it special."

We both laugh as I shift gears back to my mental checklist of things I need to get done before I leave. I scan the rest of the kitchen, which Mom has whittled down to a handful of drawers left to finish packing. Most of the furniture I'm leaving behind. Other than the bed, the stuff I'm taking is stacked in the living room.

"Okay, again, Mom, I just want to make sure you have my emergency and direct numbers at the office, plus Murph's number…" I trail off as I share the contacts on my phone, then check hers to make sure they AirDropped. "Also, if you need a getaway. Anytime." I slice my hands through the air. "Let me make sure you have Pop's address—"

She swats me on my shoulder.

"That's enough. Since we're checking off to-do lists, I want to get this off my chest. I know you're worried about me, but contrary to what you apparently think, I have a life, a job, friends, a church. Plus…you've inspired me to join the

Las Vegas Monopoly club."

"Mom, that's awesome," I say. "Maybe I'll take you on when I visit in May for Mother's Day."

"Well..." She flashes me a sassy, fist-planted-on-the-hip stare. "Maybe you ought to bring your A-game, Scottie."

The nickname reaches in my chest, gripping my heart.

Mom must register the sadness I'm sure is etched across my face.

"Honey, I know how much Pop meant to you, how much it hurt that you didn't get to be there to say goodbye to him." She takes my hand in hers, squeezing. "I also know that's why you're worried about moving to San Diego. You think this is Pop all over again, and you're abandoning me, but you're not."

I chew the inside of my cheek to keep my rising emotion in check. "It's okay, Mom."

"No, you need to hear this because I want you to go without regrets or worries. Pop died peacefully in his sleep. I'd been over the night before playing Monopoly with him. Gave him a royal butt-whipping, too." She squeezes my hand again when I force a smile. "He knew you loved him, Dec. Penelope couldn't take that away. Pop would be as happy for you as I am to know you're living your life."

I stare up at the ceiling, fighting the tears welling up behind my eyelids.

Deep down, I know I've been searching for a way to make it all right, bargaining. Somehow, by playing Pop's and my game, repairing the house he shared with the love of his life, I'd somehow clean the slate. Absolve myself of guilt for not being there to say goodbye.

I draw in a breath through my nose, a sudden lightness lifting me.

Hearing Mom tell me he wouldn't blame me. That she doesn't either, it's freeing. I just want to stand here and let the relief sink in.

"Thanks, Mom."

My phone vibrates against my thigh. I jam my hand in my pocket and fish it out, hoping it's Harper. *Praying.* As soon as I see the screen, my shoulders settle back into a slump.

Two missed calls from Murph, one text from Rox. Nothing from the woman I need to hear from.

"Is it her?" Mom asks. I flash the screen at her. Immediately, she hikes an eyebrow up at me. "A text from the sister. The plot thickens."

"It's probably just a reminder about the tournament or something," I say as I swipe to read Rox's text:

"Join ViddyChat Meeting
Wednesday, March 20 @ 7 PM
Meeting ID: 122 3564 8729
Passcode: 14324
For your eyes only!"

Mom cranes her neck out to read over my shoulder. "Ooh, that's tonight. Looks like a chance to show up if you ask me."

I tap out a quick response. *"I'll be there."*

I CLICK ON the ViddyChat link five minutes early, anxious to learn what's so important a phone call or text wouldn't suffice. Only, the host, Rox Sloane, hasn't joined the meeting yet. So, it's just me, another cold slice of pizza, and the black screen at my bare countertop.

Restless, I hit the tiny microphone icon, select mute, and blow out a breath.

Ever since Rox texted the invite, I've been trying to work out what this could be about, teetering between freaking out and utter curiosity.

Part of me is genuinely intrigued. I'm dying to know why Harper hasn't answered any of my calls, yet her sister is clear to video chat. Does Rox just want to see the look in my eyes while she berates me on behalf of her sister? Is she Harper's mouthpiece because Harper can't bear to look at me?

Another part of me—the part that gives me pause—wonders if Harper's even aware.

I hook my ankles around the legs of my chair and lean back, clasping my hands behind my head. "Please don't let me regret this…" I mumble to myself.

Leveling the chair again, I drum my fingers over the cool countertop before tapping on every icon on the ViddyChat interface. Briefly, I consider a tropical beach virtual background with clear turquoise water and palms stretching into the blue horizon. But when a ding sounds, announcing another participant, I quickly set the idea aside to prepare for my face-to-face with Rox.

Micah Hamilton—Booked Up has joined the call.

The notification flashes across the top left corner.

I have no clue who Micah is, and his microphone is muted. I swipe my phone screen to the text from Rox to double-check the meeting ID and passcode. Maybe I made an input error and joined someone else's meeting by mistake. Or maybe Micah did.

I'm just about to ask him to turn his microphone back on when more notifications shoot off like wildfire.

Harrison&Everly has joined the call.

Vanessa Sloane has joined the call.

Rita Sloane has joined the call.

Jade Sloane has joined the call.

My heart lodges in my throat, and I'm holding my breath as they keep coming—as I search for Harper's name. If her father and his fiancée have joined, what's this about? Who are Vanessa and Rita Sloane, and how are they related to Harper and Rox? Sisters? Cousins? And who is Jade?

One by one, their pictures populate in a grid next to Micah and me. But then more dings sound and more notifications zip across the top of the screen.

Skates has joined the call.

Nadia Sikes has joined the call.

Murphy Sikes has joined the call.

I think about the two calls I missed earlier from Murph when Mom was helping me pack.

What is going on?

Rox Sloane has joined the call.

Finally, the dinging stops. All *eleven* of us stare at our screens like some warped *Brady Bunch* lineup. I know Skates, Rox, Nadia, and Murph, who looks extremely pleased with himself that—as it turns out—this call *isn't* only for my eyes. Micah appears to be about as baffled to be on here as I am. Like he's two seconds from feigning technological difficulties to escape. But the way Harrison's and Everly's attention darts from each other to the screen connects a big piece of the puzzle for me.

Fourth time's the charm wedding, Harper had said, when she asked me to be her wedding date—*which probably isn't going to happen now.*

Shoving the thought aside, I survey the rest of the group. On close inspection, Rita, Vanessa, and Jade each have a distinctive look to them. Rita—sitting in front of the tropical beach background—has steely, assessing green eyes, warm olive skin, and Harper's chestnut waves. Vanessa, who I'm assuming is Rox's mom, has green-gold eyes and face-framing highlights. Then there's Jade who looks to be a mix of Black and Asian with her cool complexion and dark hair.

I rake my fingers through my hair, studying the spectrum of expressions from oblivious to blindsided, even pissed to be part of this ambush.

"Rox—" I say, but then the computer crackles to life.

A bold yellow border highlights Rox's tiny cell. Almost immediately, I gather not only has she lured us onto this call without giving us a heads-up what it's about, but she's muted us.

All ten of us.

You've got to be kidding me.

"We've got ourselves a full house tonight," Rox says. "I'm glad to see you all could make it. Thanks so much for joining."

In short order, she informs us we have approximately forty-five minutes before Harper gets back from the grocery store—if she needs to, she can buy us five more minutes by sending Harper on a wild goose chase for a no-name product.

Then, I get it.

Rox's plan isn't to have a conversation with us, it's to talk *to* us—uninterrupted.

"In the interest of time, I'll provide introductions as I go. If you're on this call it's because you're connected to Harper, Nadia, me, or Love & Games in some way, and we need your help."

Ah, so it's the business.

"Some of you may know that we've fallen on financial difficulties after last June's big storm. While we have a backup plan—thanks, Dad—we're focused on long-term solutions. Including, but not limited to, increasing our social exposure leading up to the annual Monopoly tournament, and any residual sales that come from this push." She pauses, appearing to gather her thoughts or check off a bullet point. "We have ten days. We're still down fifteen thousand, give or take a few hundred including donations and preliminary tournament sales." She's all business as she flips a page of her notebook. "The trajectory is trending up with the social media push, thanks to Nadia. The games/books swap with

Booked Up is doing well, too. So, thank you to Micah."

But then she lifts her gaze and stares at us pointedly. The shift in her demeanor visibly goes from diligent business owner to ruler-wielding principal.

We're all in trouble.

"None of it is enough. Not to close the gap in such a short period, and we can't lose this opportunity."

Skates, though I'm not even sure why he's here, raises his hand. Micah blows out a breath. Then all the older Sloane women and Harrison shake their heads. But my eyes snap to Nadia's and Murph's matching stress faces on the bottom row.

I'm dying to know the plan here.

I find the small hand at the bottom of the screen and raise it, hoping participation in this call is permitted.

Rox must see it because she stops talking for a few seconds, tilting her head slightly. She could be looking at any of us, but I sense the glare narrowing her stony gaze is meant for me.

"Take me off mute," I mouth as I chuckle.

"Class, it seems we have a question from the man of the hour."

Man of the hour?

"Hopefully, we'll have time for all questions when I'm done. For now, I need to get to the solution I've come up with—one that involves all of you." She makes a point of shifting her gaze to look at each one of us. "Now, we have a BusinessFunder account to crowd-source funds, but we haven't maximized its potential. This is where Declan comes in…" She trails off, rubbing her hands together like her wicked plan is coming together.

I knead my temple and smile, staring at the screen.

Do I want to know where this is going?

"For those of you who don't know Declan, long story short, he and Harper are in love and too stubborn to do anything about it." Rox clears her throat like she's about to let us in on the scoop. "The problem. Long-distance relationships rarely work. He went back to Vegas, she stayed here, they lived unhappily ever after. However, if my sources are correct, Declan recently made the decision to return to San Diego permanently. Solution. Yay." She gives us a little clap.

I sigh as she—hopefully—begins to make this all make sense.

"Don't worry, I'm getting to the grand plan." She flattens her hands against the air. "He needs to do something *big* to get her back." She shrugs. "What a coincidence because we need something *big* to save Love & Games."

Because she's having way too much fun at my expense, and I know she's hell-bent on making us wait for the Q&A portion of this torture, I knock on the screen. And keep knocking until she unmutes my microphone.

Rox heaves a sigh that I've interrupted her fun.

"Do I get a say in any of this?" I ask.

Reluctantly, Rox unmutes me.

"I'm willing to embarrass myself with whatever crazy plan you've come up with to save the game shop if it means I get to see Harper." I steeple my fingers, lightly tapping my fingertips together. "Now, what's the plan?"

Rox shifts in her chair, straightening her posture. She gives us a huge smile. Then, she flips her wrist, recognizing we're almost out of time before Harper returns from the grocery store.

"Here's what we're going to do..."

In two minutes flat, Rox outlines the plan.

She will man the Love & Games booth at the tournament. Skates oversees gaslighting the Monopoly community and rivalry between Harper and Walt. Nadia and Micah will boost the BusinessFunder on social media on both the Love & Games and Booked Up store accounts. Murph is on video duty. The Sloanes—Harrison plus his ex-wives and fiancée—will keep Harper busy.

Which leaves me.

Next week while Harper, Nadia, and Rox are at Everly's bridal shower, I'll meet Murph and Harrison at Love & Games to make a video of me publicly groveling. More specific, on the video, I'll ask Harper to meet me in front of the building where the Monopoly tournament will be held at the Love & Games booth half an hour early... Only, if she loves me and takes me back.

The kicker: The social media gurus in our dozen minus one are going to blast the post on every social media platform with links to the BusinessFunder and the game store. Apparently, love sells, and we're hoping some of it will also sell some games.

So, yeah, this ought to be fun.

CHAPTER TWENTY-THREE

HARPER

ROLL DOUBLES

MOM, ROX, AND I arrive at the restaurant where Everly's bridal shower is being held ten minutes past the hour, which, in Everly time, converts to about an hour. So, when we make our way through the French doors to the patio where the Chen party is seated, she halts all conversation and stands to welcome us.

"There they are." She beams from the head of a long, pink, cloth-covered table. "You made it."

We murmur our thanks for the invitation, but I don't miss the implied *late* at the end of the sentence. I take a deep breath, doing my best to stifle an exasperated sigh.

"Wardrobe malfunction," Mom says by way of explanation for our tardiness. She forces a giggle, and the women hum their understanding.

We flash the group a smile. There are three empty chairs, but we don't dare move an inch. After arriving *un*fashionably late, neither of us would put it past Everly to issue another demerit for seating ourselves without invitation.

Patiently, I take in the table with the overflowing vases of peonies, gold-trimmed ceramic teapots, and full place settings complete with stemware for a four-course meal. Thick, cream-colored cardstock agendas are set at every chair next to… *Are those name cards?*

I shoot Everly a tentative smile.

"Nonsense. I'm so glad you all were able to attend. Please join us." Everly gestures a manicured hand toward the empty chairs. "As you can see, it's assigned seating, but I thought you might feel more comfortable together."

As soon as we're settled with Rox at my right and Mom at my left, Everly introduces us to the other women seated around the table. To Mom's and Rox's credit, the navy shift dress with the gold jewelry and strappy neutral heels they selected for me is on par with the understated elegance of the group. This is only Everly's second impression of me, and while we had a great connection at Francesco's, I want to solidify our common ground.

Everly Chen is the picture of refinement. Her inky black hair is parted off-center and elegantly swept up into a side chignon. She's wearing pearls and light makeup. As if there was a memo, she and her friends are dressed in lace and satin sheath dresses in varying metallic tones. Everly's rose-gold lace dress somehow manages to make her look ritzy and sophisticated without being too proper or washing out her cool complexion.

She introduces her mother, Meili Chen, on her left. Next to her are Everly's two young coworkers sporting all the prim and proper ladies-who-lunch vibes. Their names escape me. Maybe Kelly and Kirsten? The women to Everly's right seem more like my cup of tea, though. Based on the matching sexy red-and-black gift boxes on the table in front of them, I get the impression they're the breezy, down-to-earth party girls. They couldn't care less if Everly opted for a bridal shower in place of a bachelorette party. They're the type to play raunchy, alcohol-fueled penis games as a proper send-off into marriage. Whether or not her mother with her polite smile, quiet grace, and traces of tradition and disapproval seeping through her gently clasped hands is sitting next to her.

I'm guessing leather zip-front panties aren't part of the family tradition.

My gaze drifts over the rest of the bridal-shower-appropriate pastel and metallic gift bags and wrapped boxes, and I bite back a grin.

Bold, parentheses-shaped lines frame Everly's tight mouth. She seems nervous her friends will embarrass her as she swallows and peeks over at her mom.

"Why don't you start, Mom? We'll work our way around the table to save the best for last?" she suggests, her gaze darting to the red-and-black gift boxes before she smooths her dress and takes a seat.

Soon, the soothing background elevator music is in full swing. The waiter arrives carrying a tiered tower of cucumber sandwiches in one hand and gold-dusted pink macarons in the other. We're eating, sipping tea, laughing, and sharing stories as Everly opens presents.

For all of five minutes, I'm not thinking about how much I miss Declan. I don't feel that sinking feeling in my stomach dragging me down. Then guilt flares in my gut that I can be happy for any amount of time without him.

Rox squeezes my hand under the table and flashes me a smile, reminding me to be present.

Thankfully, Everly doesn't just make eye contact and talk, she uses names, so I'm able to follow along with the conversation.

The party girls turn out to be as fun as I'd thought.

The blonde second on Everly's right with the gold dress bites into a crudité and holds up her hand.

"Wait," she says dramatically, a little tipsy off champagne. "I'm serious. I knew Harrison was it for Everly when she took one look at him and said, 'I don't know how, but I'm taking that man home tonight.'" She bursts out laughing and nearly chokes on the finger food. "I thought, 'Hey, he's not wearing a ring, he looks healthy, he's rich…'" She coughs out a chuckle, trying to clear her throat.

At the woman's left, another woman in a silver dress, apparently registers the company at the table because she bumps her friend's slender shoulder, and her eyes go wide and round in warning.

"Shit. Sorry, girls." She presses her fingers to her mouth and looks sheepishly over at Rox and me. "We're all grown here, right?"

Everly holds up a hand. "That's not exactly how it happened. Sorry, Mom." She shakes her head and apologizes for her friend's profanity and crassness before a ghost of a smile plays on her lips. "Might have been the third date…"

The women all shift in their chairs, eager for an Everly story.

"Hope this isn't awkward, Rita." Everly pulls her bottom lip between her teeth.

Mom waves her off. "Not at all. That ship sailed decades ago. Harrison is family and my friend."

Seemingly satisfied with her response, Everly continues. "We were downtown on a Saturday night. Harrison and I had decided to walk off our dinner."

I scoot my chair in and clasp my hands on the table.

"He'd stopped at the window of Love & Games, the store Harper and Rox own," she explains to her mother and friends. "There was pride in his eyes as he looked at the display of board games. I noticed he'd zeroed in on a Monopoly board, so I asked if he'd played a lot with the girls." She twists the sparkly ring on her finger. "'Harper and I used to play,' he'd said."

There are echoes of empathy in her voice as she goes on to tell the table about the stricken look on his face as he'd confessed to his estrangement from me. How it hurt him to give me space to come around after he left my mom and married, first Vanessa, then Jade. He said he hated the distance that had grown between us as a result and regretted we weren't close anymore.

"A man who grows from pain and loves hard despite it..." Everly trails off and catches my stare before tossing me a soft smile. "I'd already taken to him pretty quickly, but that was the moment I fell in love with him."

Every other woman at the table, including Meili, swoons.

In my case, the sinking feeling in the pit of my stomach floods back and pulls me under again.

Dad and I are alike. I'd meant to give Declan time to sort through his feelings. I didn't want to be a complication or a factor in Declan's choice to stay the same way Dad didn't push me. These past weeks, I hoped Declan would come around on his own. *But what if he doesn't? What if the distance only grows until we're so far apart we can't find our way back?*

With my hand pressed to my locket, I toss Everly an appreciative smile. We are two different people from two different worlds, but in our hearts, we're the same. Like me, I know she's doing this for Dad, and I can't thank her enough.

I've got to tell Declan.

I'm set to excuse myself with some made-up emergency, but Rox taps me on the shoulder. When I look around, the women are all staring, their attention glued to their phones.

"What?" I ask, feeling self-conscious. "What happened?"

"Go on, sweetheart, take a look," Everly says.

Everyone stares at me with these heart-wrenching expressions like they're torn on my behalf.

A small laugh slips past my lips. "You guys," I say, taking Rox's phone, but my heart skitters, and every emotion I've been fighting over since Declan left lodges in my throat.

It's him.

Declan.

It takes me a second to realize what I'm looking at because the video is muted. It's a stream on Instagram. Not only have I been tagged alongside my closest friends and family, but it has also been liked, shared, and reposted. Thousands of times, even though it was posted only minutes ago.

My heart wrenches. The achingly familiar sight of him after being apart so long magnifies how much I've missed him.

He's in his usual dark-washed jeans and my favorite denim button-down with the sleeves rolled to his elbows exposing the warm tan skin of his forearms. His silky dark waves are tousled, and his warm brown eyes are so serious it hurts my heart to see him grappling with whatever it is he's saying.

I still haven't gathered the nerve to unmute, so I survey his surroundings for clues first.

That's when I notice where he is.

There's a giant cutout of Mr. Moneybags with stacks of board game boxes and the dark blue Boardwalk property card poster in the background—all things we carry at Love & Games. Behind him, the pine shelves and pops of red and pale green peek from the sides of the screen. *He's inside the store.* But why? When?

I try and fail to make out his words through my tears and the frantic beating of my heart.

"Is this right now?" I ask Rox. Then I lift my gaze and search the rest of the faces at the table, registering the lack of surprise in their expressions. *They knew.*

Looking past Rox to Mom, I ask, "Did you know, too?"

She nods slowly and shrugs. "He loves you, baby."

Nodding, too, I swallow and do my best to focus as I unmute the video.

"Some of you may know me as a local doctor in town at Murphy Sikes Ear, Nose & Throat, or from practices from the Monopoly tournament held at a game store on University called Love & Games."

He's here. He joined Murph's practice.

Just off to his side in the corner, Dad peeks into the

camera before a hand waves him away.

A laugh bubbles up inside me to see my father and the man I love so much together—going to so much trouble *for me*.

I'm listening, hanging on his every word as he talks about Monopoly and the store bringing us together, but I'm more focused on watching him. The way he keeps rubbing his hands over his jeans and swallowing, he's nervous. Almost like he's afraid, which makes me pay attention.

"Baby, I love you so much," he says into the camera as he takes a step closer. "I know this is not exactly the most conventional way of doing this, but I thought since I met you here, fell in love here, and became part of this community here, it was the best way to get your attention."

He takes a deep breath and slowly exhales.

"So, I, Dr. Declan Scott 'Scottie Dog' Wilde"—he chuckles—"will be at the Monopoly tournament, this Saturday, March 30, at the convention center where there will be thousands of people along with so many others we know and love. I will stand in front of the Love & Games booth near the information stand, thirty minutes before the tournament."

Laughter bleeds into my tears because this has Rox and her romance movies written all over it. I love her to pieces for it.

I reach over and squeeze her hand, letting warmth swell in my heart.

"If Harper 'Tops' Sloane accepts my apology and loves me, too, I ask her to come kiss me. Love me. Be with me. And in case this isn't clear, I don't want to be friends with you." He swallows, biting back a grin. "Let's go beyond Park Place and Boardwalk together. Advance to Go with me. Everyone, come see if she wants this Hasbromance."

I am full-on blubbering, laugh-crying. He's so freaking adorable, and utterly humiliated, but he doesn't seem to care. Neither do I because I can't imagine my life without him. I've never been so happy to hear someone say they don't want to be my friend.

CHAPTER TWENTY-FOUR

DECLAN

GET OUT OF JAIL FREE

ON THE SATURDAY of the tournament, I have no clue if Harper will show up. If this gesture is too grand, too over-the-top for her. But I'm here. In front of the Love & Games booth with my heart on my sleeve, and my future hanging by a flimsy thread.

"Take a couple of deep breaths." Rox slaps a hand on my shoulder, squeezing reassuringly. "She'll be here."

I nod, hoping my nerves will settle. I could just as easily do intimate and quiet. Just the two of us, one-on-one clearing the air. A few whispers about how we got here and how to find our way back as we hold each other close with no one else around to hear… We're not larger-than-life people, but I'm willing to try anything to at least get her attention. Hopefully, all those old nineties romantic comedies we watched pay off.

Movement around me snatches my focus, and I lift my gaze.

With another deep breath, I take in a lungful of air and

slowly release it.

A crowd has formed.

On a quick guess, at least thirty and growing fast as more people trickle into the group and news vans park along the curb. They're all wired and buzzing with excitement to see a romantic gesture play out—or not.

"Not too much longer, guys." Rox rounds the table armed with twenty-five-percent-off flyers as she approaches them. "Check out the tournament and stop by Love & Games anytime this week to redeem your coupons. You're definitely going to want souvenirs after today." She flashes them a wide, conspiratorial smile like there'll be autographs and a photo op.

The woman is a sales and marketing genius.

I just hope she's right about Harper and me.

"Declan!" A male voice from the crowd calls my name, and the phones go up like weapons drawn, ready to get the elusive viral content the world wants so bad. A few girls swoon, and my heartbeat ratchets up.

I scratch my scalp and toss them a small smile before I flip my wrist. My pulse quickens as I search the passing cars. Still no sign of Harper yet. The Monopoly tournament starts in thirty-five minutes, and one way or another I'm going to be a headline on everyone's feed.

Or worse, a meme.

Because I'm playing in the tournament today, broken-hearted or not, I fish out my phone. I scan the three or four backup strategies Harper and I went over to quickly amass cash and properties, remembering how she'd gotten frantic about auctions, trading mortgaged properties, and the elimination of side deals. The thought sends me spiraling into memories of us. I want to win for her, but my mind keeps straying to a different end game.

My nerves fray all over again thinking about seeing her after almost two months apart.

Will it be awkward between us? Will she forgive me? What if she plays along for the cameras to help her store and this is all business? Will she just walk away clean when it's over?

A vibration trembles against my hand and a notification drops from the top of the screen. A text from Murph.

"I'm just passing the box office. I think I saw her walking straight to you."

The roar of cheers thunders as I lift my head, searching frantically.

Butterflies race in my stomach the instant I spot her near the crowded information booth. Her gaze pins me in place, and I'm breathless. The ground feels like it's sinking beneath me. All my thoughts are scattered. I'm too nervous to think straight, so I focus on her.

Her hair is pulled back in a ponytail. There's just enough time for me to see she's wearing fitted jeans, tennis shoes, and a red T-shirt with the Love & Games logo and the word TOPS centered below it. She breaks out into a full sprint. There's a mile-wide smile on her face.

My heart cartwheels in my chest. Warmth radiates through my body.

I don't know whether to move out of the way or steady myself for the catch but hope flutters inside me. Harper doesn't give me time to choose. She lunges into my arms and starts peppering kisses on my cheeks, eyes, chin, and finally, my lips.

"Oof. You came." I band my arms around her waist and pull her body flush against me, the kiss intensifying. A slow smile builds as I nip her lush lips. "I missed you."

Around us, the sea of people on the busy sidewalk breaks out into applause and howling whoops. The reporters drone into their mics, making sure the cameras are getting this.

Harper throws her arms up in a victory V.

The crowd eats it up.

All the tension in my neck and shoulders release, and it's unexpected, but tears well up behind my eyelids. I don't care what others think because I'm in love with this woman.

"Hey," she says softly, pulling back.

With a shake of my head, I bite back the words, but my eyes are locked on her. I swallow, letting relief wash through me. "You're early."

She gives me a shaky laugh. "We've waited long enough. You didn't think I was going to let you go that easy, did you, Scottie? I'm so in love with you, Declan Wilde."

I close my eyes and inhale. I feel light and giddy. An overwhelming happiness blooms in my chest. If only I could just sink into this moment and never let it end.

"Say it one more time. I want to make sure this is real."

Harper pulls her bottom lip between her teeth and gives me a sweet smile as I lower my hands for a better grip. She pants, shifting against the grip of my hands.

"Dr. Declan 'Scottie Dog' Wilde, I love you. I love you. I'm in love with you," she says between kisses. "I'm so sorry I didn't give you a chance to explain. I was so stupid. I was just so scared this was all temporary for you—that you wouldn't stay. I convinced myself I was giving you the time you needed—"

"I know. I should've talked to you. It started with the game, but you and me, we're so much more. I don't want to be *just* anything with you. I want to be everything with you." Her soft green eyes are wide and glowing. "I don't need time to figure out you're the love of my life, Harper."

She lets out a huge breath, and then tears are streaming down her face. "These are happy tears," she clarifies in case I couldn't figure it out on my own.

I dutifully kiss her shiny cheeks, reveling in her touch.

"Hey, Tops," a familiar nasal male voice calls from behind her. She twists in my arms. We both focus on his tall, lanky frame and shock of inky black hair. He's in his trademark rusty brown shirt with the giant wheelbarrow and a *W* inside a Superman emblem. *Freaking Walt.*

"Yeah?"

"Glad you finally came to play this year," Wheelbarrow says, challenge lacing his tone.

Harper lifts her chin. "Damn right. We'll see you in there."

"I hate that guy," we say in unison as he enters the building.

Harper turns to me. She swallows and flashes me a pointed stare before saying triumphantly, "Tag team. We're doing the Sloane Twist."

"It's fine. This isn't *The Cutting Edge*. We're not Kate and Doug." I laugh and squeeze her against me. "You said it yourself, the rules are different."

"Do you want to win?" she asks with all the seriousness of a fierce, blockbuster movie heroine.

I nod, loving how the romantic comedies have rubbed off on us both.

"Then we're putting it in." She wipes her cheek on her shoulder. "Also, I got you a matching shirt for the intimidation factor. When we walk in there looking hardcore Walt won't know what hit him."

"THIRTY MORE MINUTES," the tournament host's low baritone bellows over the hall. He's a tall, burly guy with side-parted gray hair who looks like he'd be better suited to weight-lifting than emceeing a Monopoly competition.

A few raucous cheers fill the air from the disqualified players around the room waiting for a winner to be announced, but the noise dies down quickly.

We need to concentrate.

Harper and I are two-thirds of the way through round three. We've banded together for a common goal: dethrone Walt. We've beaten the Hasbaristas in round one and the Community Chesterfields in round two. Of the twenty or so tables that were full of competitors this morning, this is it. Now it's us, Love & Games vs the Jailbirds—none other than my former tablemates, reigning champ Walter "Wheelbarrow" Huang and Eugene "Whistleblower" Horace.

We're seated at a round table in the center of a large ballroom. Stark lighting shines down on our game board, and it's quiet but tense. Meanwhile, I'm trying to concentrate on

Monopoly and not the rest of our ViddyChat crew gathering in the corner of the room.

I roll, praying our plan doesn't backfire.

Six.

"Yes!" Harper gives me an enthusiastic shoulder bump as she smiles excitedly. That's good for me. The better her mood, the better her reaction. *Hopefully.*

I nod and collect my windfall. "Nice. This ought to help some."

From Virginia Avenue, my Scottie dog bypasses our opponents' entire orange color-group and lands on Free Parking. Since total cash and assets determine the winner at the end of the game, we take the lead—or a larger lead because the middle of the board is full of hundreds from everyone landing on Income Tax and Jail Money.

Harper doesn't gloat aloud, but she nods to her nemesis triumphantly. Walt's face twists into a death stare in response.

I can practically see him calculating their deficit. Just like Harper suspected, they immediately raced around the board to scoop up Boardwalk and the electric companies. While they nabbed single properties, we kept to our plan—four color-groups, all the railroads, and Park Place later (to block the Jailbirds). We have three houses on every property, and we're rolling in the dough.

"There's still twenty-five minutes left," Eugene hisses, and yanks the dice from the board. "I wouldn't celebrate just yet." He nudges his thin-rimmed glasses up the bridge of his broad nose. His thimble is lined up to land on B&O Railroad or any of our yellow color-group, any of which will break them, especially since Walt just shelled out two thousand beautiful rainbow dollars when he landed on Pennsylvania Avenue.

Time is almost up.

Harper flits a glance to my fingers drumming on the table. I press them flat to steady my nervous energy.

"So...what do you want to do with the thousand bucks if we win, Declan?" Harper stares off wistfully, and a ghost of a smile plays on her lips.

The Jailbirds have been gloating the whole day, claiming there wasn't any *real* competition this year, so I don't blame her for rubbing it in a bit.

Eugene blows on the dice and lets them tumble across the middle of the board. All four of our heads follow as they land.

Money.

"Ventnor Avenue." Harper's positively radiant as she announces our property. "With three houses. Double the rent since we have the color-group. I believe that'll be sixteen hundred, please."

The crowd buzzes, getting antsier as the clock winds down.

A flush spreads over Eugene's skin as he slaps each bill on the table. Based on his tantrum, it'll be a few seconds before he completes his count. When the winner is announced, it's going to get loud and crazy, so I turn to Harper now.

"Actually, this is kind of off-topic, but the other day, I was thinking about the store—"

"What about it?" She glances over at me before returning her attention to Eugene.

"Looks like the arrangement with Booked Up is working out well. There are a few other local businesses and community members who enjoyed the scavenger hunt and events and might be interested in helping out..." I say, easing into my point. "Also, there might be other ways to raise money besides your father."

Her brows dip in a quizzical look. The weight of her sparkly green eyes lands on me. "Yeah..."

With a quick peek over at her, I continue, "I'm hoping you might consider letting me be a part of that group." I pull my lower lip between my teeth, giving my heartbeat a chance to even out.

Heat blazes in her eyes before she surveys me from underneath her long lashes. "You want to donate to Love & Games?" She laughs sweetly, confusion braiding her eyebrows.

Again, my fingers are restless, so I pick up a railroad card and examine it. "I wouldn't mind helping that way, but no. Do you—"

"It's my turn." Great Wheelbarrow Walt reaches between us to retrieve the dice. He rolls and lands safely in jail. It's a move he seems satisfied with, and he blows out a sigh of relief and runs his fingers through his shiny black hair.

"Do I what?" Harper asks, distracted.

She turns away from the game and squares her shoulders to me, searching my face.

My pulse picks up, my heart jackhammering against my chest. "I've got a proposition for you. If you accept, maybe we can use the prize money toward something else."

Eugene leans toward Walt, and they start whispering.

Probably doing an interim tally, but then they seem to notice no one has rolled.

Walt rocks back on the hind legs of his chair and glances at his watch. "Really, you guys are having a personal conversation now? There's still time left on the clock."

I shoot him a hard stare.

We've got about ten more minutes of play time. He's, no doubt, banking on her moving from Community Chest and landing on Boardwalk.

"You can't just drain the clock," Eugene whines. "It's your turn, Tops. Roll."

Harper is still engaged in the game, but our conversation has piqued her curiosity. As she rolls, she doesn't even look to see the total on the dice. She narrows her eyes and keeps watching me.

Walt curses under his breath.

"Lucky," Eugene scoffs.

"Declan, what is it?" Harper asks. Her smile is huge as she moves seven spaces to Go and collects her two hundred dollars. Her eyes dart from my face to my pockets before she leans back and peeks under the table. "Is this, like, a weird apology promise thing?"

We both laugh because she's not making sense.

"You're cute when you're way off base," I say.

Behind her, the red digital clock winding down snags my attention. The mic crackles to life, and the host starts shuffling over to our table. "We're almost out of time. Please, make you final moves," he says.

It's my turn, but all I can think about is making this move with Harper—making her happy. I take a deep breath and swallow before jamming my hand in my pocket and fishing out the last BusinessFunder printout.

Her eyes snap to mine.

"Do you want to save Love & Games with me, Harper? Rox said with all the sales and the events, you closed a big part of the gap. She linked the crowd-sourcing account to my viral video, and—last we checked—this is the total. We're about nine hundred and thirty-seven dollars short." Before she can put all the puzzle pieces in place, I finish. "If you're okay with it, I don't mind using the prize money to cover the rest." The words come rushing out of me as the buzzer goes off.

The host's voice booms. "That's time! As soon as we get the final totals, we'll name our winner," he announces.

On cue, the entire conspiracy crew shuffles over to us to seal the deal. In front of Rox and Harrison, Nadia and the four Sloane wives hold up a gigantic BusinessFunder check payable to Love & Games. At their sides, Murph, Skates, and Micah give their best spirit fingers.

The room erupts with applause, and there's lots of movement.

Except for Harper.

She's stares at me with what I hope are happy tears in her beautiful green eyes.

I slink down to the floor on my knees in front of her, taking her hands in mine. "We all love you so much. *I* love you so much. You're it for me. I just want to make you happy. I want you to keep challenging me. Let's never stop playing games and loving each other." My heart pounds against my chest, and I can't seem to catch my breath. I'm rambling. "If there's a yes in there anywhere, maybe you'll come home with me—"

"To Pop's house?"

I shake my head. "Our house. I want us to live in the house where we fell in love," I say. "And maybe you'll consider marrying me one day—"

"Yes." Her voice is a whisper.

My mind races a million miles a minute, but her answer sends me skidding to a halt. "To which part?"

A warm, musical laugh billows through her tears. "All of it. As long as it's with you."

Before she changes her mind, I get to my feet, sweeping her up into my arms. Her lips crash down on mine.

At some point, I come down from my high long enough for the moderators to finish totaling the assets for both teams. Based on the Jailbirds' mortgaged properties, it's not even close. Along with another life-size check, we're crowned the winner and given a big, shiny, lacquered gold trophy fittingly shaped like a top hat. We take lots of pictures with the big paper checks.

Surprisingly, Wheelbarrow Walt even comes over. "Congratulations. You earned it," he says.

We really did.

CHAPTER TWENTY-FIVE

HARPER

GAME OVER

I HATE WEDDINGS. I mean, I love them, and I want to have my own one day, preferably soon with Declan, but I do hate the part where I always end up crying.

It starts out fine with all the merriment and to-do about looking great and making sure everything goes according to the never-ending itinerary. We get to the church. There's oohing and ahhing over the dress. After the will they/won't they part of the ceremony, it's on to the froufrou reception with a cocktail hour and the introductions of the entire wedding party. By that time, I'm numb enough to make it to the speeches before the waterworks.

Declan and I are seated at a table just off to the right of the wedding party. It's practically the farthest table from the entrance, but even from back here, as soon as Dad and Everly are introduced as Mr. and Mrs. Sloane, I feel that slight tickle at the back of my throat.

My shoulders tense a bit, and Declan squeezes my hand. "Are you all right?"

I shake my head to wave it off, but then the familiar prick at my eyes starts.

"Weddings." I force a smile. "They make me emotional."

He scoots his chair closer and releases our hands to drape his arm around my shoulders before planting a kiss in my hair. "I love you."

I flick my gaze upward because every time Declan says it, my insides go all mushy. Coupled with the whole happily-ever-after effect of weddings, it nearly breaks the dam.

"I love you, too."

He leans in and slowly brushes his lips over mine.

It seems unreal that five months ago I was still trying to figure out what I wanted. It's almost as if as soon as I stepped up to the challenge, Declan showed up, and everything started falling into place.

"Aren't they beautiful, ladies and gentlemen?" the deejay asks over the mic.

On the dance floor, Dad flips back the tails of his tailored tuxedo with all the drama of a matador before holding his hand out to Everly. She's got the biggest smile on her face, and she's wearing a breathtaking lace and tulle ball gown adorned with beautifully draped appliqués and her trademark pearls. She's the picture of bliss. Her chapel train trails elegantly behind her as she takes his hand and circles him.

When she stands in front of him again, they begin to sway to the first tinkling notes of Ed Sheeran's "Thinking Out Loud," dancing a cute and classic two-step while staring into each other's eyes.

"They're so adorable," Rox says just low enough for me

to hear. "The way he rests his hand at her waist... He's so gentle with her."

"I know," I say, tuning into the song and their dreamy gazes. "I don't think I've seen Dad this happy in a while."

It's the line about hands and not being able to play strings anymore that finally does it. It's not only because Dad is getting older, but it's always his hands I remember when I think of him. Tears stream down my face at the memory of Dad fishing his hands into the breast pocket of a different tuxedo and whipping them behind his back before producing our lockets.

We're still Daddy's Girls.

Rox is still a number-crunching badass who knows exactly what she wants. I'm still feelings and signs. But we've got our family. No technicalities allowed.

To think I might have missed this day.

As my crying morphs into hiccupping sobs, Rox flashes me an annoyed expression. "Get it together, please. This is a happy occasion." She laughs.

Now I'm laugh-crying, which I'm sure is about as attractive as my smeared makeup. "They picked the most depressing song."

"What are you talking about? It's beautiful."

"And morbid," I quip.

Even Mom laughs with us.

After the speeches, we eat plenty of expensive food and toast to love and never giving up. Then, Dad finds me on the dance floor with Declan, and cuts in.

Through the entire song we laugh about the latest Monopoly beating I gave him last month. Declan and I filled our little bungalow to the brim with family and friends. Somehow, we all ended up huddled around the Monopoly board in the dining room, turning our housewarming into family game night. When it was down to Dad and me, we played for a good two hours. Just the two of us until Everly walked over, in a last-ditch effort to steal him away.

She'd rubbed his shoulders and leaned close to his ear. "Sweetheart, why don't you come sit and watch the movie with me?" she'd said.

But it was Dad's response as he squinted, pretending to concentrate on the board that made my heart swell.

"Not even a chance," Dad had said. "It's not every day I get the chance to play my favorite game with my Harper." Then he peeked up at me as my eyes watered. "Now, don't go getting teary-eyed on me, so you'll have an excuse when I beat you."

I'd laughed through my tears. Somehow, I'd almost forgotten how much fun we used to have, teasing each other, making up random rules.

Being like this with Dad again, close, playing our favorite game, laughing, hugging, dancing. It feels like no time has passed.

At our side, Everly dances with Declan as she leans in to tell me Dad's been practicing for our rematch, which only amps up my waterworks.

We switch back, and Declan pulls me flush against his warm, hard chest, his clean, heady scent wrapping around me. As I peer up at him, he swipes the pad of his thumb beneath my eyes before he presses tender kisses to my lips.

The beat picks up, and a bunch of people beeline for the

dance floor. Soon, the ties and heels come off. There's tipsy, uncoordinated dancing to the latest shuffle slide. There's even a "Soul Train" line, during which Declan and I break out our fully choreographed moves, which were a lot easier in sweats than my satin emerald-green dress. We still earn whoops and hollers from the other guests, though.

The second Dad and Everly cut the first piece of the giant cake, Declan and I stuff our faces. We eat as much delicious buttercream as we can, chuckling while we give each other messy sugar kisses.

"Good God, you guys are literally the worst." Rox shakes her head at us. "Get a room."

Declan stands, twirls me around, then dips me back. "I'm taking this one home with me tonight."

"Ooh, good one, Champ," Rox says, using the nickname she gave Declan after we won the Monopoly tournament and shot Love & Games into the viral stratosphere. Playfully rolling her eyes, she grumbles, "You guys are too perfect for each other."

He bites his lower lip and tugs me upright.

Our lips are a whisper apart, my breaths growing shallow.

"Seriously. There are children present," Rox says, but then she sighs. It comes out as a breathy swoon, and I'm right here with her.

I'm in this constant state of bewilderment, excited and emotional all the time when I think about Declan and me. Like, how is this even my life? I've watched countless dating shows and romance movies, buried my nose in books with happily-ever-afters, and never once did I think I'd get my own. I never thought I could be this happy.

Yet, between board games, sexy painting while we fixed up an entire house, and getting roasted by a comedian, I'm in love with a man who is everything I've ever dreamed. He's beautiful with an amazing heart, and because of him I have amazing relationships with my family and friends. My business is doing better than ever, and all I can think about is spending forever with him.

I want all of it for my sister. I want the silliness, the tingles, the orgasmically good sex for my sister.

"Rox, for once, I want you to put away all the books on relationships and body language," I say as she stubbornly folds her arms across her chest. "Find someone who challenges you then play the hell out of the game." Because there are impressionable ears around, I skip the steamy bits. "Then, when you can't take it anymore, let go."

"She's right," Declan admits, throwing his hands up as if to say *who knew?* I swat his chest playfully as he continues. "In all seriousness, though, Rox, there are no definitive answers with love. One day you're heartbroken and fleeing your hometown, and the next you're a Monopoly champion waking up to a crazy Monopoly-loving coffee lady every day. But she's everything I ever wanted and more. Go figure."

Declan nips at my lips.

"I love you so much," I say, leaning into the kiss.

One of Everly's nephews takes Rox's hand, spinning her into his arms as they dance away.

Then it's just Declan and me.

"What was that?" he mouths into the kiss.

"Just looking out for my little sister. Paying it forward if you will." I laugh.

"You laugh, but I owe my life's happiness to a cup of coffee and that Monopoly flyer." Declan smiles, pulling back to search my eyes. His expression warms until it's filled with yearning and sweetness. "I'm so in love with you, Harper Sloane."

"And I'm in love with you, Declan Wilde."

He kisses me again and I close my eyes, melting into him because it was all worth it—every adventure, every game, every second of the journey. And I couldn't have chosen a better partner.

The End

Don't miss the next book in the Love & Games series, *Trivialized Pursuit*!

Join Tule Publishing's newsletter for more great reads and weekly deals!

Acknowledgements

The thing is, when I set out to write *Monopolove* I thought about how much I love spending time and doing fun things with the people I care about. I'm a board game junkie (I know, shocker). I used to throw these elaborate game nights where the fun was both intense and loud with laughter and the competitive spirit charged in the air. But then, life, work, jam-packed schedules, global pandemics... They sort of got in the way. So, I did what so many authors do. I re-imagined a world I wanted to see with characters surrounded by family, friends, board games, and full hearts.

Thank you for spending your time with the Love & Games family. Hopefully, since you're reading the acknowledgements, you loved Harper and Declan's story, and will read and re-read it time and time again.

I'm going to start by thanking my husband. Daniel, I know I'm this computer zombie who rarely sleeps, always has my fingers attached to the keyboard, and rolls into bed at the tiny hours of the morning, so thank you for supporting my dream, making the best omelets on your days off, and helping with the kids. I love you so much and I'm thankful for you every day.

To my girls, it fills my heart with so much love to know that you're proud of me. That you tell your friends—and teachers, *yikes*—that your mom is an author. I hope seeing me follow my dreams emboldens you to dream big.

Mommy and Daddy, thank you for making me a selective introvert, nerdy book lover. I love you so much and thank you for always cheering me on.

To my editor, Roxanne Snopek, thank you for mixing in the "dig deeper" questions with the cheery comments and laughs. Your work helped me put my best book forward.

Jane Porter, Nikki Babri, Meghan Farrell, and Cyndi Parent, thanks for welcoming me to the Tule family and making my publishing dreams come true. Special shout-out to Denise, Kelly, Fortune, Lisa, Stacey, Heather, Janine, and Rebecca.

To my Wordmakers family, Tasha, Lisa, D. Ann, Randi, Kris, Ali, KK, Meka, Coralie, and anyone who sat in a Zoom room helping me work through edits and shape this project into a book I'm so proud of, thank you. You are the best group of writing ass writers a person could ask for.

Margo Hendricks, my BWP, thank you for always cheering me on and lifting me up. For reading various versions of this book, thanks to Elizabeth Spaur and Jen. Lauren H. Mae, our brainstorming sessions really got me on track. Joanne Machin, I'm so thankful for your help crafting pitches and queries. Bailey from Twitter, I made sure to include the bit about collecting McDonald's game pieces lol!

Finally, thank you to my romance community, authors, readers, book content creators, my cover reveal team, and my early beta readers—Andrea Gonzalez, Linnea Elaine, Brittany McMunn. I'm so grateful for you all. You make this job fun!

If you enjoyed *Monopolove,*
you'll love the next books in the...

Love & Games series

Book 1: *Monopolove*

Book 2: *Trivialized Pursuit*
Coming in July 2023

Book 3: *Clued in Christmas*
Coming in October 2023

Monopolove Book Club Questions

1. At Java Joy, Harper is at the end of her rope and her café app malfunctions, but Declan comes through with a good deed and pays for her coffee. What did you think about Harper's response, projecting her hang-ups on him and insisting to repay him?
2. Harper and Declan's relationships with their parents have influenced their views on love. When it comes to relationships, what role do you think family dynamics play?
3. Would you ever enter a board game tournament?
4. If you had to trade places with any character in the book, who would you choose & why?
5. Which character could you see yourself dating?
6. If you oversaw casting the movie version of this book, who would you cast as each character?
7. Harper and Declan's first and second impressions of each other were less than favorable. Have you ever given a person a third chance to make a first impression?
8. Share an instance when you witnessed kindness being shown to another person then you paid it forward.
9. How would you have reacted to Anthony Goode's stand-up routine if you were in Harper and Declan's shoes?
10. What Monopo-lingo word could you see yourself using?

A) Hasbrothers B) Hasbromance C) Hasbroke D) Monopolove E) All of the above.

11. If you could write one more chapter after the ending, what would you want it to include?
12. If Rox were to get her own book, who would you want her to end up with?

About the Author

Mia Heintzelman is a polka-dot-wearing, horror movie lover, who always has a book and a to-do list in her purse. When she isn't busy writing fictional happily-ever-afters, she is likely reading, or playing board games and eating sweets with her husband and two children. She writes fun, unforgettable, more than just laughs romcoms about strong women and men with enough heart to fall for them.

Thank you for reading

Monopolove

If you enjoyed this book, you can find more from all our great authors at TulePublishing.com, or from your favorite online retailer.

Printed in the USA
CPSIA information can be obtained
at www.ICGtesting.com
LVHW101655080823
754684LV00004B/56